Changes

Allen Wyler

Changes
©2013 Allen Wyler
All Rights Reserved

ISBN 978-0-9859942-5-9

Visit Allen online:

www.allenwyler.com

STAIRWAY⹀PRESS

AN ARMCHAIR ADVENTURER BOOK
STAIRWAY PRESS
SEATTLE

www.stairwaypress.com
1500A East College Way #554
Mount Vernon, WA 98273

The Armchair Adventurer

Cover design by Guy Corp, www.grafixCORP.com

DEDICATION

To all the doggies we have known and loved...

1

CASCADE MOUNTAINS, 12:31 PM

Fucking shoulder.

Chris Holden stopped climbing and planted his right boot firmly uphill. He leaned forward to take a long deep breath. Damned shoulder started in on him maybe ten minutes ago, a boring ache deep within the muscle. Shifting the rucksack strap didn't help it either.

He pulled a sweat-dampened bandana from his back pocket to mop his forehead again and glanced at Reed Allison, ten or so feet down trail.

Reed nodded. "No problem."

Reed was panting and sweating too, which made Chris feel better. Slightly. Because if Reed was having problems too, maybe it wasn't just being fifty-five and out of same shape that was the issue.

I should work out more regularly.

But he never seemed to find time.

Chris massaged his shoulder. "Ever wonder what it'd be like to be able to go back to, say, age twenty, knowing what you know now?"

Reed shook his head. "For the love of God, stop it."

"No, seriously. Tell me. What would you do differently?"

Chris stuffed the bandana back in his pocket and sucked another deep breath.

Reed raised a just-a-minute hand, slipped off his backpack and dropped it uphill so he wouldn't have to bend so far to pick it up when it came time to shoulder it back on. He fished a plastic water bottle from the side pocket and for a moment rested his elbow on his uphill knee, zeroing his oxygen debt before finally uncapping the bottle. He took a long drink before offering it to Chris. "Here, want some?"

Chris shook his head while struggling for another deep breath. "Better drink my own. Christ, anything to lessen the weight of this damned pack." He shrugged off the rucksack, let it thump solidly onto the rocky trail. It was sun-faded, an olive-drab Kelty, one of his son's prized possessions purchased from REI, when, fifteen years ago? He gently touched a worn spot of black netting stained white with dried sweat. Joel's sweat. Crusted into the fabric as crystals. The only physical remnant of his son's body. And even those small molecules were vanishing as crystals flaked from the pack. He had no ashes, no locket of hair, nothing but Joel's *things* stored in a corner of his basement: touchstones to the memory of his only child.

For Chris, Joel's spirit lived on this mountain. No one knew exactly where Joel had vanished, but Chris could feel—with the certainty of a parent—his presence on this trail.

Chris pulled a clear plastic water bottle from his pack, chugged two mouthfuls of tepid water.

Jesus it's hot. Feels like ninety degrees, although he knew it couldn't be more than sixty. If that. Even the water seemed too warm. Wetting his mouth helped. He worked his left shoulder back and forth, trying to comfort the pain, his gaze wandering over the pine forest stretching off to jagged white peaks and an azure, cloudless sky. Below them, nestled between several boulders, lay a rippling blue crescent of breathtaking beauty.

His pragmatism didn't allow him to personally buy into "the God concept," yet such awe-inspiring nature evoked a primitive gratefulness—to someone or something—for the ability to experience such beauty.

He said to Reed, "You didn't answer my question."

Reed removed his glasses, tipped back his head and poured water on his face. "Why should I? You get the same damned answer every time you ask it." He slipped his glasses back on, capped the bottle to re-stow in his pack.

Chris began to be concerned. His breaths continued to labor as his hunger for air increased. Not only that, the pressure in his left breast was relentlessly building. He sat down facing the lake and leaned back on his elbows and tried to suck in a deeper breath. Man, he'd let himself get out of shape. When was the last time he exercised for fun?

Reed muttered, "Good idea," and sat down too.

A quarter mile to the right, a broad swath of snow—one of the few surviving patches this late in August—funneled from a peak to the north end of the lake.

"You suppose that's where he is?" Chris asked with a nod toward the snow.

Reed picked a rock off the trail and tossed it downhill.

"Could be," he said.

Always the same questions. Always the same answers. Never any resolution.

Chris studied the snow, wondering, *Is Joel there? If we hike over, would we find him this time?* It'd been a warm, early summer, melting more snow than usual...

"I know this gets tiresome, Reed. Thanks for putting up with me." Every year he subjected Reed to this. A true friend was someone who puts up with your...your what? Emotional foibles?

Reed lobbed another stone. "I don't do it out of friendship. I do it because I like it." He glanced up at Chris, did a double take. "Hey, you okay?"

"Out of shape is all."

Reed was studying him now, clearly worried. "You sure? You're pale as hell."

Chris swallowed and sucked another deep breath. *Damned altitude.* "I know we've discussed this before, but I can't help thinking of all the mistakes I made. I keep wondering how different life might be if I just had another chance to do things over. You know, go to sleep and wake up a twenty-year-old knowing everything I do now. There'd be so many things I'd do so differently." How he raised Joel would be one.

Reed shook his head and tossed another pebble downhill. "For chrissakes, we've been over this again and again. You're not responsible for what happened to Joel. Joel is. And as far as anything else in your life, given the same circumstances and situations, you'd probably make the same decisions. And okay, so let's say for some unexplained act against nature you were magically transported to age twenty with all your present wisdom. Things might not work out the way you think."

Well, that's a different answer.

"No? Why not?"

"Because the way we live our lives isn't based on wisdom alone. You have this tendency to trivialize the influence personality plays in the choices we make. Okay, let's say you wake up tomorrow, age twenty. In spite of what you might *know,* your personality wouldn't change. You'd be held hostage to it. You're the only one I know who believes we make our own destiny."

Interesting point. One he hadn't considered. "So you're saying we'd repeat the same mistakes? That nothing would change? We don't learn from our lives? That's depressing."

"It's realistic. At least for the major issues, like whether we go to college or join the Army or get married. Okay, so let's talk about you in particular. There are things in your life—major things—I don't see changing. Certainly not the way you approach life. The way you procrastinated about Jan, for example. You waited too long. Why? Because you kept second-guessing yourself. Why? Because you're *you*. You aren't decisive when it comes to major life decisions. How would that be any different?"

A flash—a reflection off something maybe—caught his attention. Cupping both eyes with his hands, he squinted at the snow patch with the sun glaring off the lake. He pointed. "Hey, what's that?" he said.

Reed followed Chris's finger. A few seconds later, he said,

"Looks like hikers."

In spite of the sun, a chill burrowed between Chris's shoulders as if he was seeing a ghost. He looked harder. And now, changing the angle slightly, he could make out two hikers part-way onto the snow patch, the contrast of their parkas making them easier to discriminate.

A foreboding began eroding Chris's chest. Air! He needed air. He gasped, but his lungs seemed to work even less well than a moment ago.

Then it dawned on him. "Aw shit!" He, of all people, a cardiologist for chrissake should recognize the signs. He knew too well the entire spectrum of heart attack symptoms: from nothing at all to the classic crushing chest pain. His aching left shoulder wasn't the byproduct of age and being out of shape. This was The Big One.

He glanced around. Rocks, dirt, trees. Nothing but damned wilderness. Miles from the nearest interstate. No defibrillator, no oxygen, no EKG. No one but Reed, a lawyer, who would be worthless for dealing with it.

Shit! I'm toast.

A jolt of fear hit, surging adrenaline into his arteries, which in turn jacked-up his blood pressure and made his heart pump harder. Feeling this, and knowing it wasn't good triggered another surge of adrenaline, making things worse.

Shit, I'm killing myself. Calm down.

Bullshit, I can't, not knowing this. I'm going to die.

PORTLAND, OREGON, 12:33 PM

Something felt wrong. Really wrong. His gut knew it even if his brain didn't.

What?

Joel glanced up from the chopping board. The kitchen seemed exactly the same as thirty seconds ago: smelled of garlic, greasy steam, baking bread. He heard clattering utensils, rap from the box, a humming dishwasher. Everything exactly the same, except for...

The feeling vanished like a wisp of smoke, leaving only a vague impression of unnerving familiarity. Not exactly déjà vu. He knew how that felt. This just wasn't the same. Not quite a premonition either. He knew about those too, having experienced them often enough these last five years. No, this puppy had a real definite edge...like realizing something awful was about to happen, yet not having a clue what that might be. A chill slithered down his spine, tightening his anus.

Jesus!

"Yo, Holden, y'okay?"

He glanced over at the other line cook. "Yeah, fine. Why?"

The cook continued kneading a wad of dough, never breaking rhythm. "Cause all a sudden you got this funky weird, spacey look, man. You went pale as a ghost."

Low blood sugar, that it? He reached for the nearby Diet Coke and considered the stash of blow in his locker. Hadn't snorted any today, so that wasn't it either.

"Naw, I'm fine. Thanks."

Just glad it's over.

Potato-leek soup was what he was working on. This evening's featured soup. One of his favorites. Apparently the chef liked it too because he'd given Joel the thumbs up to use his own recipe. And *that*, everybody knew, was a real coup.

He never documented his prized recipes. Didn't have to. They simply made such blatant sense that writing them down seemed unnecessary. Didn't measure quantities either, as some cooks did. How do you measure what looks right and what tastes perfect? You don't. You simply mix ingredients knowing full well that no two batches ever turn out exactly the same. That's why he laughed when some fool said, "Oh, it's not as good as usual." Of course not. Nothing ever is. Usual—taken literally—meant average. Only a dork would want to produce average-tasting food.

Twelve years ago he made the potato-leek soup recipe for the first time. Twelve years old and already amped with dreams of someday becoming a master chef. Don't ask why or how he knew this would be his life's work. That dream had been budding in the soul of his brain for as long as he could remember. Just as it had for that crazy little rat in *Ratatouille*.

"You ready?" he calls from the kitchen.

"Whenever you are."

He ladles full two china soup bowls, sets them carefully on matching plates, wipes a thick drip from the edge of one, garnishes each with finely chopped green onions, then inspects the bowls with a nod of satisfaction. A great presentation will always make a delicious entree taste better.

"Delicious," Chris says.

"Maybe a bit dull," says Janice, the Step-Mom From Hell.

Joel is so nervous he can't eat. Instead, just sits and waits for the reviews.

"But," Dad continues, pointing at him with the spoon, "you really need to start thinking about doing something more serious with your life. This chef business just isn't...reasonable."

Janice nods agreement before primly dabbing the corner of her pouty collagen-injected lips with the linen napkin.

"Like?"

Dad carefully sets his spoon on the plate, presses his palms together, plants both elbows on the table, drilling him with his trademark serious expression. "Son, by the time I was your age I knew I wanted to be a doctor. Okay, I admit I was young, but the point is, if you're going to amount to anything and develop any kind of financial security, you need to start planning and working now, even if it seems premature. You can't just say 'I'm going to be a great chef.' That's crazy bananas. I know you know what the statistics are, what the failure rate is for a new restaurant. Especially in a city as competitive as this. Being a cook isn't something you can count on to support you through retirement. You need to plan on a career that provides something that people really need. Medicine, for example. Set your sights and work hard."

He's heard this spiel before—like a bad commercial—over and over.
"But I want to cook. I want to be a chef. Why can't you understand that?"

Dad sighs. "Son, you can always cook. Every damned day if you want
to. We all do. That's not something that…"

"Contributes," Janice finishes the sentence for him. As if she's Ms.
Worldly Knowledge, having completed all of one quarter of junior college as
an "art major." How contributory is that?

Joel hates her.

Joel snapped back from the memory, glanced around the kitchen once again before refocusing on the potato-leek soup. *Jesus, what made me think of that episode? Ah yes, the soup. That was the first time he'd made it.* He paused, thinking, *one of these days I'll call Dad.*

But not for a while yet. Not until I've really made a name for myself. Then I'll call and really rub his nose in my success.

He was only a sous chef. But hey, being an assistant chef at Chez Pierre wasn't too shabby, not by any measure. Especially for only a twenty-four-year-old kid. But his Dad wouldn't get it…he probably wouldn't even know what a sous chef was. And what would he say when he finally did call him? "Hi, it's me, Joel. Your son. I'm not really dead." How would that play?

He laughed at the thought and resumed chopping. That day would come.

CASCADE MOUNTAINS, 12:43 PM

Aw, Christ, hurts like a sonofabitch.

The deep gnawing ache made it difficult to move, to even breathe. Chris repeatedly tried to reassure himself, to talk himself into relaxing, to breathe in and out slowly. He knew that getting upset and panicky would only worsen the coronary insufficiency. As it was, each spasm of pain was flirting with death. Any one of them might cause his heart to stop, and then…

He knew too damned much. That was the problem. The fact

that the pain wasn't subsiding—and in fact worsening—scared the hell out of him. How could you possibly relax when you knew your heart might not beat again? All it took was for one of his coronary arteries spasming tight enough to squeeze off the blood to a major portion of heart muscle and bingo, Dead Duck.

Reed Allison's hand was on his shoulder now, gently pushing him back against the hill. He really didn't have the strength to resist so instead focused on a sky bluer than anything he'd seen before. And it was the sight of this incredible beauty that finally allowed him to relax and accept the pain for what it really represented: his death.

If he thought about it, there couldn't be a more beautiful spot to die than here with his son.

He glanced at Reed, who was now thumbing in numbers on his cell.

A cell phone? Here? Are you kidding?

He let his eyes drift back to the sky and sighed with heavy resignation. You had to die someday. That was an unavoidable part of life. But at age fifty-five? Didn't seem right—like he was being cheated.

Why here in the Cascade Mountains?

Suddenly, he saw the karmic symmetry, a comic irony of dying near the spot where his son had been killed. For some strange reason he found the thought comical and began to snigger. Which, in turn, increased the pain. He thought, *it only hurts when I laugh.* And this weird thought struck him as uproariously hilarious, morphing the snigger into an all-out laugh.

Then he was floating above himself, looking down at his body. How sad. He started to cry. It's too sad. Yet he also felt satisfaction at the life he'd lived. Sure, he'd made a few mistakes along the way, but the sum had been positive. He could leave this world having helped others, and this thought gave him a bit of comfort.

Then he heard Reed saying, "...in the Rachel Lake region."

No kidding? He actually got through? Amazing.

9

Come to think of it, we're not that far from Snoqualmie Pass's three ski areas. And a string of cell towers all along I-90.

He glanced back at the snow patch which might still contain some of the same ice crystals that smothered his son. He thought of one of their good days together before Joel started getting into trouble...

Joel sits at the table waiting for the verdict. Actually, the soup is damned good, Chris thinks. Better than anything he could slap together. Potato-leek soup. Not something everyone tries to cook from scratch. No question, his son has talent. For a moment he's very proud of him. Now, if he would just stop the drugs...

"Delicious," Chris says.

"Maybe a bit dull," Janice adds.

Chris looks at her and wonders, does she even remotely suspect the private investigator who followed her and Richard Keen to the 6th Avenue Best Western? Doubtful. Otherwise she would've been more careful.

Even though he despises her for the infidelity, he won't deal with it at the moment. Too much is going on in his cardiology practice to afford the distraction of a messy divorce. Besides, Reed advised him to continue building their case before filing the papers. The tighter the case, the more likely they were to prevent a contentious fight once the hatchet finally drops. Making the sordid outcome a tad like blackmail. Although Reed's strategy makes him feel a bit sleazy, Jan did bring this on herself.

He looks at Joel. Why cooking? The kid isn't gay, so that can't be it. What is it then? Try as hard as he might, he can't understand it.

"Come on, Chris. Stick with me!" Reed shouts, jarring Chris back to the present drama.

Fight! Hang on. You don't want to die here. Not now. This isn't your time.

But every movement, every word seemed slower—a bit more hazy—as he waffled on the edge of consciousness.

"Come on, Chris, I need your help here."

"Huh?" he mumbled.

Reed pointed downhill, his other hand tugging the front of Chris's shirt, pulling him up. "See that open area there? Coast Guard's sending a chopper to fly you out. But right now I need your help. We have to get you down to flatter land. Can you do it?"

Clammy with sweat in spite of the chilly air, the only thing Chris wanted to do was strip off his shirt and let the breeze blow against his skin. But Reed, still tugging at him, made sense. And he trusted Reed more than anyone in his life.

Screw the pain. Work though it. You may die in the process, but at least you tried to do something for yourself. Fight!

Chris struggled to his feet, stumbled, regained balance, and took three steps downhill before toppling over.

Reed pulled him up onto his feet again and draped Chris's arm over his shoulder.

"Take a step. Now another."

Aw shit, the pain is worse than ever...unbearable. "No. I can't."

PORTLAND, OREGON

Oh, man, there it was again: that weird, spacey feeling. But this time there was something else, too: a tightness in the left side of his chest, right underneath the pec. He started to massage it.

Man, this is too weird.

Then, as suddenly as it began, the pain vanished, replaced by a sure-as-shit realization.

Dad's in trouble.

CASCADE MOUNTAINS, WASHINGTON

Chris became vaguely aware of *whomp whomp whomp* a moment before the sound registered: a helicopter.

Chris tried to open his eyes but could only manage a tight squint in bright sunlight.

11

Oh, God, must've nodded off. Amazing, I'm still alive.

Eyes barely open, he glanced around. The lake remained to his right but where were the two hikers? Then he saw them, over by the snow patch, standing straight, watching the chopper circle in.

"Good, you're still with me," Reed said, kneeling close to his head. "Hear the chopper? That's for you. We're going to fly you to a hospital and fix you up. Everything will be fine. Just hang on."

God, what beauty. Spectacular.

Chris stared at the cobalt lake, the vibrant green of the pines, the brilliant azure sky. In fifty-five years he'd never seen anything so beautiful and mystical. It brought contentment. If this was where he'd die, so be it. He couldn't think of a better place than here, next to his son.

2

CHEZ PIERRE, PORTLAND, OREGON

"Joel!"

Amorphous light flickered at the periphery of consciousness...

"Joel!"

Another voice yelled, "I'll call 9-1-1."

"Joel! Can you hear me?" The first voice seemed closer now.

He blinked and cracked his eyes, only to be partially blinded by harsh fluorescent light. He inhaled warm humid air laced with garlic, warm bread, greasy suds, and heard the hum of a dishwasher. All the smells and sounds seemed so familiar yet totally foreign. Consciousness slowly resolved into focus, bringing a weird orientation. He was sitting on a greasy concrete floor, he realized, with his back propped against a stainless steel counter leg, his right hand clutching his chest. But the pain of a moment ago was gone. Gone also was the crisp pine-scented air and rhythmic sound of the helicopter rotors.

Confused, he glanced around, saw that instead of lying on a rocky trail sloping into Rachel Lake, he was on the floor of a commercial kitchen.

"Joel?"

His eyes were wide open now, looking straight into the face of a black guy who squatted on his haunches staring at him with obvious concern. *Yeah, okay, Luther Rabb, the maitre d'.*

Wait a minute! How the hell do I know him? I've never seen him before.

But then again, he *did* know Luther…just wasn't sure how. Which made this…this…whatever the hell it was, confusing.

Hold on, wait a minute. We work here.

Daniel too, the chef on Luther's left. What's more, he knew all Daniel's little idiosyncrasies, like stashing clean dishrags above his station so he'd have a fresh supply late into the evening. How most nights they all sat around and drank the bar's Knob Creek for an hour or so after shutting down. And that Daniel bought blow from him.

The better question was: what the hell's going on? The last he remembered, the helicopter was approaching.

Why am I so…confused? Why am I sitting on a greasy kitchen floor?

"Joel! You all right?"

Joel? Whoa, that's my son's name. He's dead.

He looked at Luther. "I'm…" *I'm Chris.* He knew that as well as he…

Really? You sure about that?

Luther put his hand on his shoulder. "Stay put, dude. The paramedics will be here any second now. I called 'em."

"No, I…" He struggled up onto his feet. But the dizziness grew worse, forcing him to reflexively grab the counter. He muttered, "Whoa, maybe I need to sit back down. Just not on the damned floor."

Luther and Daniel helped him to a chair, and he plunked down heavily, leaning forward, face in hands, elbows on thighs, trying to get his shit together in all this confusion…

Next thing he knew, Taylor was squatting next to him, looking very concerned.

Huh? Do I know you? Have we met before?

Are you nuts? We live together.

But how could that be? She didn't look familiar.

Sure she does.

14

Jesus, talk about confusing. There was no explanation...

Next thing he knew, two paramedics were taking his blood pressure and slapping EKG pads on his chest. Physically, he felt fine, though didn't say so, his mind still having huge problems sorting things out. A minute ago he was hiking with Reed Allison, then boom, he was in Portland surrounded by people he'd never seen before yet knew intimately.

One paramedic asked, "Can you tell me your name?"

Took a second before he could come up with the answer. And *that* was scary too, not knowing right away. *What the hell, did he stroke out a minute ago? Was that it?*

"Chris Holden," he answered.

"What day is it?"

Okay, that's easy. "Tuesday."

"Where are you?"

Ah, establishing a baseline level of orientation. A routine set of questions he'd ask when evaluating patients.

Amazingly, he knew the answer to that too: "In Portland. At Chez Pierre. I work here. I'm an assistant chef. I—"

What? Bullshit, I'm a doctor, a cardiologist. I live in Seattle.

Don't say another word. Not until you figure out what's happening.

The first paramedic told the second one, "Vitals are fine, EKG normal."

"No, he's *not* okay," Taylor said. She seemed very concerned. He wanted to tell her not to be, that he was fine, just a little temporary uncertainty. But until he figured things out, he decided it'd be best to not say another word. People ended up in locked wards by admitting too much...

The other medic looked at her. "What's wrong?"

Taylor shook her head. "He's confused. His name's Joel. His father—who lives in Seattle—is Chris."

No, that's wrong, I'm Chris.

He stopped to think about that. *Whoa...I'm...?* And wasn't so sure anymore.

15

No...I'm Joel.

How can that be? That's impossible.

"Here, lie down on this," the first medic said, pointing to a stretcher.

Yeah, might not be a bad idea.

He turned from the gurney and caught his reflection in the mirror by the door. And froze. Did a double take.

Couldn't believe what he was seeing.

His son Joel, buried five years ago in an avalanche, was staring back at him.

Then it started coming back to him.

3

CASCADE MOUNTAINS, FIVE YEARS EARLIER

Twenty feet ahead, Matt stops, turns to him, says, "Dude, this is work."

"You got that right." Sweating like a stoker on the Titanic, Joel sucks a deep lungful of crisp air. Ice crystals sparkle to his right, where snow-laden pines cast high contrast shadows on a brilliant white blanket. To his left is a precipitous drop with a view out across a frozen alpine lake and stunning blue sky. Not a cloud in sight. The scene contains splendor far greater than anything ever captured in a nature photograph. Moments like this are the only reason for busting ass on a pair of snowshoes. Snowshoeing! The ultimate stupid sport. And the ultimate break from having to make a decision. One that can cost his life.

"How about we stop for lunch just over that rise?" Matt yells back.

"What?"

The rumble spans two long seconds of disbelief as the brain isn't able to comprehend the ominous vibrations against the soles of his feet or the deep rumble in his ears. Two seconds of confusion punctuated by terror.

This is the second day of record-breaking heat after weeks of heavy snows, producing conditions they both knew to avoid but at the same time found too glorious to resist. But Joel especially needs a break from the stress of reaching a decision.

Joel glances uphill and sees a wall of snow hurling toward them. He screams, "Avalanche!"

Matt freezes in horror, eyes locked on the billowing white mass cascading down on him.

"MATT!"

Matt can't seem to move. And then, when he does, his legs seem mired in quicksand.

"MATT! RUN!"

In the next millisecond the survival odds register on Joel's subconscious: zero for Matt, fifty-fifty for him. He yanks the personal GPS from his parka and throws it hard at Matt, hoping only to mark the general location. He turns and tries to run—not fast enough either—from the thundering two hundred tons of snow hurtling down on them. A massive blur roars straight through the path they were hiking—swallowing Matt and drowning out any other sound. He catches a glimpse of red swept off the ledge toward the lake, swallowed in a mass of snow. More snow roars past like a long freight train.

Suddenly, the blur stops and dissolves into a quickly dying funnel of shifting snow. The avalanche missed him by only a foot.

Dead eerie silence.

Seconds pass and then a secondary brief rumble of more snow settling into the shifted terrain.

Panting, he bends over, grasps his knees. His heart pounds with incredible joy and gratitude for his being safe instead of suffocating in a dark freezing tomb. One fucking foot!

It registers: Matt is gone, swallowed by the avalanche. He, on the other hand, is alive.

He peers into the valley, sees no sign of Matt, not even a hint of red from the bright parka. Joel takes a tentative step in that direction, but snow shifts against his legs, rolling into the slide zone, warning him to stay away. He tries again. More snow crashes down. He backs up, terrified at being swept into the snow bank and buried too. And if he isn't buried, the fight to climb back up will sap his strength and make it impossible to go for help. Leaving him no choice but to leave and go for help.

He turns to start the trek back, hoping the GPS unit may, with luck, help them find Matt's body. But even that's unlikely.

Joel stands at the trail head staring at the rusted grill of his Volvo, weighing the situation. No question, Matt's dead. The moment a person is buried in an avalanche, they have maybe thirty seconds to claw their way out before suffocating unless they're wearing a survival pack and can use it, and someone is ready to dig him out. Then you might last a bit longer. Matt couldn't afford one of those packs. So, he's toast. And even if you knew where to look, any retrieval attempt would risk triggering another avalanche. And even if he did lead a search party to the slide site, what were the chances they'd ever find Matt under all that snow? Pretty damned slim. The GPS unit might not even be remotely close to the body. In hindsight, it was foolish to throw it. But he had to do something.

He sits on his haunches to think.

One thing's for sure: Matt is dead, with little chance of ever being found.

Joel starts shaking—both arms, both legs, his trunk—as the full impact of what just happened sinks in. Death took Matt, not him. Why? What did he do to deserve being saved?

Several minutes pass before the shaking begins to subside and stop. He wipes tears from his cheeks and blinks. Why in hell did he want to come here today? They knew, damned well knew the conditions and area. Snowshoeing here is stupidity at its worst. Jesus, if I could just turn back time several hours, this never would've happened. But he'd desperately needed to get away to clear his head and figure a way out of the terrible squeeze Delgado has him in.

Why was Matt buried? Why not me? Dad always says we make our own destiny, that each individual's life is 90% determined by our decisions, the remaining 10% by luck, fate, or divine intervention (depending on your beliefs). *I'd had Matt lead during that stretch, so, was I responsible for his death?*

On the other hand, if I were now dead, all my troubles would be solved.

Instead, Matt's dead and I'm still due to testify in front of a grand jury Monday.

Unless...

Is that really possible?

4

FRIDAY, 3:11 PM, BURIEN, WASHINGTON, TWO DAYS EARLIER

Fuck! A flashing blue light in the rearview mirror. Not good. Joel checks his speed. Right on the money. A burnt-out tail light, outdated license tag? Naw, can't be. I always check those things. So why the pull-over?

He looks at the image in mirror. Hmmm...an unmarked car.

Joel pulls into a deserted parking lot fronting a strip mall, rolls down his window. There's not much activity in the mall, just a bankrupt tanning salon, a Sprint store, a Papa Murphy's pizza place, a place that used to rent videos.

Two Hispanic dudes step out of the cop car, the fat one wearing a Hawaiian shirt and the not-so-fat one in an oversized LA Lakers tank top. Both wearing cut-offs. They split up, approaching the car from both sides.

The fat one on the driver side flashes an ID, says, "DEA Special Agent Delgado. Step out of the car, please."

"Yes, sir." Joel starts to step out, his mind racing. Any product on board? Not that he remembers. But the attaché case on the passenger seat is right there in the open for God and the universe to see. No way will they not look at that. He hears the passenger door open.

"Hands against the vehicle."

Joel faces the open driver-side window, hands on the roof, watches as the LA Lakers dude rifles the glove box.

"Anything I need to know about in your pockets? Needles? Blades?"

"No, sir."

Delgado sweeps both hands over him. Cars speed past on the street, no one paying much attention. He's sweating.

Something hard slams his testicles from below, followed by the slow relentless ascent of visceral pain burrowing straight through his gut, chest, and into the base of his brain.

"Oh, sorry, hand slipped," mutters Delgado.

Sweating, teeth clenched, fighting the urge to vomit, Joel tries to not show pain.

"Yo, Armando, look." Delgado's partner holds up the open black attaché full of rubber-banded packs of $100 bills.

Delgado asks Joel, "Pay day, Holden? Didn't know you're a working man these days. Legitimately that is. You got a pay stub to go along with this? But shit, this looks like pretty good wages. Must be union. Doing lots of overtime? How much you think's there, Pepe?"

"Least ten grand."

Delgado asks Joel, "Where'd you get it?"

Joel knows better than to say a word, but his skin prickles from fear. The money is Ortega's, due later today. He's only the courier.

Pepe carries the attaché around the car for Delgado to inspect.

"Let me guess," Delgado says, picking up a wad of bills. "This doesn't belong to you."

Joel doesn't answer. What can he say? Besides, right now he's scrambling for a way to replace the money. Because if he doesn't...fuck! No loans from Dad. That's for sure as a twenty-four-hour day. Reed Allison? Maybe.

"Hey, Pepe. Our homey's sweating." He turns to Joel. "You sweating, bro?"

Can't think of anyone with that kind of cash lying around.

"Make you a deal, bro," Delgado says, holding up the attaché case. "You show up Monday, give a sworn testimony to the grand jury, you walk away with this money."

Joel asks, "Today?"

Delgado lets out a sarcastic laugh. "You not listening, bro? Monday."

Joel shakes his head. "No, listen, I take it today?"

Delgado looks at Pepe and says, "Gee whiz, whaddya think, Pepe?" sounding like some lame white kid from a 50's sitcom. "That fair and square? He gets the money and walks?"

Rhetorical question, Joel knows.

Delgado says to Joel, "The fuck you think, bro? When you give us all you know we give you all the cash. Tell it to a grand fucking jury, under oath."

Joel shakes his head. "I don't deliver that money by 5:00 pm, I won't be alive to say shit on Monday." Which is the God's honest truth.

Silence.

Pepe gives a little sideways nod with a half shrug. "Kid might have a point, Armando."

Delgado says, "Holden, we been on you for six months now. We don't get Ortega, you'll do the time. Think about it. We'll be keeping an eye on you. You don't show up Monday, you'll...well, you really don't want to go that route, know what I'm saying? But guess what? It's your lucky day. You get the money. We have a deal?"

CASCADE MOUNTAINS, TRAIL HEAD

Delgado's men had been watching him like fucking predators since then. All the more reason to come up here to get away for a least a few hours. Maybe he'd just been handed a perfect solution, a perfect out to a very bad situation. Why not just walk away?

Yeah?

Yeah. Simple. Just walk away. Start new.

Hmmm...could work.

Joel bushwhacks a hundred feet from the car into dense foliage and hides the snowshoes under a heavy growth of salal. Stands back to inspect his work.

No one will find them for fifty years. Maybe not even then.

He scouts the trail head, sees the government car with Delgado's men in it, and cuts a wide detour onto the old logging road, figuring the two miles to the highway is an easy hike.

Yeah, this might just work.

By this evening, when he and Matt haven't returned to their car, those cops will begin to wonder. By then it'll be too late to start searching. They'll have to wait until tomorrow. Then a sheriff's deputy or forest service agent will come looking for them and follow their tracks. A helicopter might see the avalanche and maybe pick up the GPS signal...

Everyone will assume he and Matt are dead.

Problem solved.

He continues walking, weighing the possibilities.

Simply disappear. Just walk away.

It would be tough starting over with only the clothes on his back and fifty bucks in his wallet, but it's a damned sight better than any other of his other options. Besides, he doesn't own anything worth much. Everything material is replaceable.

Can he really start a new life right now? Where would he start, and how? He doesn't have a clue, but can't see any other choice. He's smart. He can figure it out.

Damned well better figure it out because I really don't have any other options.

What about Dad?

What about him?

He'll think his only child is dead.

Yeah, unavoidable.

Ironically, this points out a major point of friction between them: Dad always preaching, "Do the right thing, no matter what." But what about self-preservation, doesn't that trump righteousness? Damned right it does. Besides, Dad got over Mom's death. He'll get over mine. No problem.

A fresh start. I can turn my life around and profit from what I've learned. Yeah, this is the start of a new life.

By late afternoon Joel stands, thumb out, thinking: Portland, Oregon. The Western Culinary Institute is there. One of the best cooking schools on the West Coast. Yeah, this could be his opportunity to do the one thing he's dreamed of.

A car pulls to the shoulder of the road and he jogs to it, opens the door.

"Where you headed?" the driver asks as Joel slides into the front seat.

He starts to say, Portland, but thinks better of it. Odds are no one will ever ask this guy, but news of their tragic deaths might appear in the paper—along with pictures.

Would this guy recognize me? Better not take a chance.

"Los Angeles."

With those two words, he realizes just how radically his life is about to change. It feels good.

Testifying against a dude bad enough to kill me or really fuck me up no longer hangs over my head. I'm free.

He's giddy with relief.

"I can take you as far as Mercer Island. Will that help?"

"Hey, thanks a lot. That's a real help." He turns to look out the window. The less the guy sees his face, the better.

25

5

OREGON HEALTH SCIENCES EMERGENCY ROOM

He sat on the emergency room gurney studying the back of his hands again. Young smooth skin. Not the same turkey skin he'd grown so used to seeing while scrubbing outside the cardiac cath lab. He held up his left palm. The scar that had been there for the last forty-five years—the one from his first attempt at cleaning a fish—was gone. Jabbed the knife straight in. Luckily he didn't severe a tendon or nerve. A painful indelible lesson on the dangers of sharp blades. The things you learn growing up. He wiggled his fingers. They moved and felt like his. Just didn't look like them, was all. Very very strange.

He pushed off the gurney onto the floor in front of the mirror above the sink. And that was another thing; his body felt so different. Stronger, more rested, more energetic. No nagging ache in the right hip.

What the hell happened? One minute he was hiking, the next he was on the kitchen floor in Chez Pierre.

With Joel's mind and body.

Well, that wasn't quite right. Best he could tell, this was Joel's body but Chris's mind. Yet that wasn't exactly right either because he had Joel's memories too. Which he found incredibly interesting, this sudden ability to see both sides of shared experiences, good and bad. The potato-leek soup dinner, for example. Felt sort of like looking out from the inside of a mirror or like living in a dream. Leaving him disoriented and confused, yet at the same time fascinated.

Except, this wasn't any dream. This was very real. And very creepy.

What the hell happened? Was he totally psychotic? Was what he was experiencing—or thought he was experiencing—a major psychotic delusion? He pinched himself once again, and yes, felt pain. Huh!

One time, years ago in college, he dropped acid. Man, what a trip. But this was nothing like that. Then, the colors, sounds, and images were, well, psychedelic. You *knew* you were seeing a distortion. Now nothing seemed distorted or unreal. This felt absolutely normal. And this wasn't like any of the coke Joel had done, either. Not even close.

When he first regained consciousness—when everyone was standing around gawking at him—things were too confusing to even try to sort out. So he just answered the paramedic's questions and let Taylor tell them he was confused, that he was Joel and not Chris. So they loaded him into an aid car and brought him here to the emergency room where he overheard someone mention this was a teaching hospital for the med school.

When the ER doctor finally got to him, she started in with questions. Who are you? Where are you? What's the date? The basic Mental Status Exam he'd administered countless times in his own practice. He answered the easy ones such as who's the President of the United States, but when it came to his name and the city he was in, he messed up. So the ER doc ordered a neurology consult, MRI scan, the whole enchilada. All of which turned out normal. Now he was waiting to be discharged. The neurologist told him to go ahead and get back into his clothes but to wait for the ER doctor's instruction before leaving. So here he was, dressed and waiting to go home.

Allen Wyler

Strangely enough, he knew where home was: a one bedroom apartment he shared with Taylor. They were a couple, not roommates.

He sorted through his wallet again. Jesus, what a mind blower. Everything—Oregon State driver's license, credit cards, Social Security card—were Joel's. What made it even weirder was being able to remember applying for them. It turned out to be much simpler than he'd expected. The day he arrived in Portland—the day after walking off the mountain—he ordered a copy of his birth certificate from the King County Department of Records and then filed a request for a replacement Social Security card. No problem. Nothing could have been easier.

Curious to see to how the authorities handled his disappearance, he followed the *Seattle Times* on line. Three days after the avalanche a two-paragraph story mentioned "a missing hiker." The story named Matt but made no mention of Joel Holden, which he found disturbing. Why wasn't he named? Did it have something to do with Delgado? Delgado was the only reason he could think of.

He checked the mirror again. Yeah, Joel was staring back at him. He ducked side to side, trying to fake out the image, but it didn't falter. He pinched his cheek. Nope, it really was him in the mirror.

Jesus, how could this be?

His life as Chris had been dictated by rational linear thinking. A left-brain existence. After all, practicing medicine required it. He believed in only those things that could be measured objectively and proven scientifically. If you couldn't measure a phenomenon, it didn't exist. Simple as that. A philosophy that explained his agnostic approach to religion. He didn't believe in occult or paranormal activity either, chalking up such anecdotal experiences as innocent flaws of perception or, in some cases, simply craziness.

How could he explain this…whatever…that was happening to him?

28

He couldn't. But it was real, so there had to be an explanation.

Well, there was always the possibility he'd gone batshit crazy and this weird transformation he was experiencing was nothing more than a delusion. But that didn't seem right either in spite of being more plausible than any other explanation he could think of.

Maybe it happened like this: during the heart attack on the mountain he had a stroke that damaged his brain and, as a result, his "mind" was in this "state." But he couldn't seriously accept this either. This was too…real?

Taylor opened the treatment room door and cautiously peered in.

"The doctor's gone, so you can come on in," he said.

She slipped in and shut the door, wrapped her arms around him, and hugged. Without letting go, she said, "I was so scared. I thought you'd, like, had a stroke or something. But the doctor thinks maybe it was just a fainting spell."

Yeah, right. No, this was way more than a faint.

He gently removed her arms from him. "Could you give me a minute by myself, sweetie?"

Sweetie? Yeah, that's what Joel calls her.

She started to put her arms around him again but stopped, her eyes running back and forth over his face. "You okay? Want me to call the nurse back?"

He squeezed her hand reassuringly. "I'm sorry. Look, this may sound weird, but I need to be alone for a few moments…get my head straight. This has been so upsetting."

His words appeared to sting, so he squeezed her hand reassuringly. "I'm sorry. I know it sounds harsh. I just need a few more minutes by myself. Please."

How weird, he thought. He knew he loved her in spite of never having laid eyes on her until tonight. Well, Joel had. And he felt Joel's love for her, a love like he'd never felt for Janice.

She forced an understanding smile. Which was something she did when stressed. He knew this also.

"Sure. I understand. I can't even imagine what you must be feeling…"

You have no idea.

"Just a couple minutes," he assured her.

She nodded and left the room, unable to mask her disappointment.

He inspected his body more closely. Joel's face had put on a few years since he saw him last…the night they argued, the night before the avalanche.

Jesus! How could Joel have gotten into such a goddamned mess?

"No, son. You agreed to testify; if that's the deal you cut, you need to stand by your word. You have a tendency to always take the easy way out. You need to learn how to face adversity," he says, trying to suppress the anger from his voice.

Joel wonders: how can Dad be such a hard-ass when it's my neck on the chopping block. "But you don't understand. I testify, they'll fuck me over. Bad."

"Who? The drug dealer you're protecting? A drug dealer, for chrissake!"

"He's a friend."

"Friends don't fuck over friends," Chris says.

"It does if it means doing hard time. You would too if you had half a clue."

"What I don't understand is how you ever let this happen in the first place, dealing drugs."

He understood it now. Completely. Still didn't mean he condoned Joel's actions. It only meant that he now understood what happened and that Joel had been selling to kids in school as far back as junior high. Jesus, he must've been the world's lousiest parent to not know about it. Aw, man…how could he have raised his son to be a drug dealer?

"Who gave you permission to get up?"

Startled, he spun around. The Pakistani ER doc stood in the doorway, a knee-length white coat over blue scrubs, a Littman stethoscope clamped around her elegant neck, looking pissed. He knew the self-important attitude. Had seen it in colleagues. May have even been guilty of it himself on occasion.

"The nurse said to get dressed. I assumed that included being able to stand to put on my pants." He couldn't resist the touch of sarcasm.

She frowned. "You're free to go. We could find nothing wrong." She turned toward the door.

"Hold on a moment, let me ask you a question."

She glanced back over her shoulder. "Yes?"

"Please close the door. It's private."

After closing the door, she stood straight, both hands in her white coat pockets, looking directly at him, exuding cold professionalism and the lack of personal contact inherent from dealing with patients who are only transients in her practice. "Yes?"

How do I ask it without sounding crazy?

"Before the paramedics came, I had this really strong premonition. Premonition doesn't really describe it…it was stronger than that. It was like I was experiencing someone else's experience. I *knew* my dad was having a massive heart attack. And that's when I began having chest pain too, but I *knew* it was happening to him…"

He trailed off knowing his words weren't making sense and it wasn't exactly what he wanted to ask. But then again, how do you ask about something so subjective you don't understand it yourself?

She frowned. "What's your question?"

He realized what he wanted was a litmus test, a way to determine if he was nuts. But to tell her his psyche had been mysteriously teleported from the Cascade Mountains into his son's body wasn't going to play very well.

"So," he said, "is it possible for me to feel exactly what my father did? Assuming, of course, he *did* have a MI. I mean, to feel it in real time?"

She said, "Premonitions do occur. So do what are termed empathetic reactions. These make us feel sensations similar to what someone else may be experiencing. After all, there are claims that identical twins have, at times, felt exactly what their twin felt even when they're geographically separated. That happens not too infrequently, by the way, increasing the likelihood they really happen. But such things can't be measured scientifically, so there's no rational explanation as to how or why they happen. If you're asking about mental telepathy, well, that's not something I believe in, so I'd have to say I doubt it."

He needed more. Some way to explain what was happening to *him*.

"But is it possible for someone to be able to experience someone else's memories? Mental, I mean." But even the words made no sense as he listened to himself say them.

She frowned. "What do you mean? To actually be in possession of another's memories?"

"Okay, look, obviously I'm not you. But what if I could remember a few of your memories, say like something that happened to you in medical school?"

"I'm not following you. You mean that you know the facts I learned?"

"No. Not the facts." He paused, searching for a reasonable example to get his point across. "How about this: I'm sure every med student reacts differently to seeing a cadaver for the first time. What if I had your memory of that?"

She shook her head. "I still don't understand your question. It's impossible to have someone else's memories. On the other hand, it is possible, because of your own past experiences, to *think* you might know how I *felt*, but in reality, you don't. You can't. You're not me. So you can't possibly have my memories."

What did he expect? Yet he had to try again. "But what if I did?"

"*Believe* anything you want. That doesn't make it reality." She looked at him anew, asked, "Do you believe you have someone else's memories?"

Exactly. Joel's. Or at least that's how it fell here in Joel's body. But he knew better than to admit it to her. Not with that look she shot him.

She quickly added, "If you wish, I can arrange for a psychiatrist to see you. On an outpatient basis, of course."

Of course. "May I leave now?"

But she'd given him an idea.

6

JOEL HOLDEN'S APARTMENT

He followed Taylor up another flight of stairs, amazed at how different his body felt—the spring in his step, no sweating or grasps for breath the way Chris would after four flights. Certainly not the shortness of breath he'd experienced just before the heart attack. His flexibility, his joints, his muscle mass all felt wonderfully energetic, strong, *young*. No wonder some men opted for testosterone or growth hormone injections in spite of the risks. Man, if this was how it made you feel...

The strange thing was, he was familiar with every one of these stairs, having trudged up them for a year. Ever since he and Taylor moved in together. He knew which door was theirs even before Taylor stopped to fish her oversized key ring from her purse. And this wasn't just déjà vu, either.

Stepping into the apartment, he surveyed the small living room. How weird. He was seeing it for the first time, yet knew the contents and locations exactly. Even weirder was being able to remember how he'd acquired each item. The iPod from The Apple Store, the X-Box he'd saved for, the futon in the bedroom they slept on. Everything down to the rolls of toilet paper from Costco.

And Taylor? That was another totally weird thing. The moment he saw her, he remembered a ton of little things about her. Like how they'd met at Chez Pierre: She was working the bar the day he started as a line cook after graduating from WCI. He knew about the little mole on her right butt, the fullness of her right breast compared to the left, the way she loved to make jokes with sarcastic absurdities. Knew she was one inch shorter than his six feet and she was one year older, having grown up in Bend, Oregon. She worried too much about the thickness of her thighs, practiced yoga, loved tofu and Gray Goose martinis with a twist of lime instead of lemon. Most of all, she shared his dream of one day owning a four-star restaurant. Although he hated the term, she was the closest thing to being a soulmate he could imagine.

Taylor closed the door behind them, stripped off her coat. "You okay?"

He nodded. "Just tired, I guess." But this was definitely more than a little strange being with his son's girlfriend. Okay, sure, he was Joel now, but still...his situation was just beginning to fully sink in. Had Chris died on the mountain? Was this reincarnation? He paused to think about that. Was he no longer Chris?

Embryonic tears began welling across his lower lids. He squeezed his lids together and pinched the bridge of his nose to wipe them away. And felt an immense loss. Where was his old body?

"Joel?"

He turned away from her and cleared his throat, shook his head, cleared his throat again. "Just tired," he managed to croak.

She rested her hand on his shoulder. "Baby, what's wrong?"

He shook his head as the heavy sadness encased him. Chris couldn't be gone, his body cold and lifeless. If he were, where was his mind? He shouldn't be able to think. His neurons should be either necrotic or vaporized in a crematorium. Yet he still could think. Or at least he *thought* he could.

Or...

Was he in coma in a hospital, having been safely helicoptered off the mountain?

She stood studying him. "Want me to get you something?"

"I'll be okay," he said, walking to the fridge for a bottle of Talking Rain he'd put there yesterday. He didn't want her to see his tear-streaked cheeks. "Go ahead, take your shower. I'm just going to sit here for a minute."

Whoa, how strange. She always showers the moment she comes home from work. I know this.

With the familiar sound of water tattooing the modular plastic shower stall, he picked up the kitchen phone and dialed the Seattle condo. *If I'm alive, I should answer. But, if I'm dead or in the hospital…*

The line rang through to: "This is Dr. Chris Holden. I'm not in right now, but if you leave a message, I'll return your call at my earliest convenience."

A chill blew through him, followed by an ache in his left breast. Not as intense as the beginning of the attack, but with the same deep, gnawing character. He flashed on the shortness of breath and the panicky knowledge that his chances of making it off the mountain alive had dropped into the ten-percent range. He heard the *whomp-whomp-whomp* of the chopper…

I should be in bed now because I'm not on call tonight. Unless…

He disconnected without leaving a message. What could he possibly say? Besides, if he really was here in Portland, how could he be in Seattle? Oh man…what a mind-spinning clusterfuck.

He was a logical person; he could figure this out. Clearly he wasn't dead. If he were, then how could he even be trying to reason this out? Okay, what if he did die earlier today? Then what? Where did that leave him?

Was he a freaking ghost? A reincarnation? A figment of a deranged mind?

Nothing made sense. This was so totally incomprehensible that his head hurt trying to grasp it. Then, for a moment, this last thought seemed to hold some importance. An implication that might explain things. It vanished as he tried to bring it into mental focus. No, it was gone.

Call Reed. He was with you. He would know. He remembered Reed jumping up and down, waving at the helicopter appearing over the ridge. Sure, Reed would know exactly what happened. He reached for the phone.

Wait! Think about this. It was now early morning. Reed would be awakened by a phone call from…whom? What would he say? Hi, I'm Joel, calling to check on Chris? After all these years? Then Reed would ask, "Why call tonight?" *Because I got this really weird premonition.* That sounded like a good enough reason. But would Reed buy it? Not the Reed he knew. He wouldn't give out any information over the phone. In fact, he wouldn't put it past Reed to copy down the phone number and do a reverse check on the listing. Besides, he really needed to get his head straight before he talked to anyone. Everything was so confusing…

He killed the rest of the Talking Rain and dropped onto the lumpy couch they'd bought at St. Vincent's a year ago.

Think!

He started replaying everything that happened this morning. He and Reed drove up to the trail head, shrugged on their rucksacks, started out. Nothing remarkable there. Other than the discussion about getting the chance to live life over again knowing what he knew…

Jesus, is that what this is?

Could *that* really be happening? Sure seemed to be the case. But living life over as someone else just didn't happen.

Did it?

No…at least he didn't think so. But this…

Was he psychotic? If so why?

Well, that would be easier to explain. Simply chalk it up to a result of a cardiac arrest causing some severe brain damage. Hmm… Although that was the most logical way to explain this state, it just didn't seem right.

Why not?

Well, for one, my thinking isn't scrambled and fragmented like it'd be

37

if I were severely brain-damaged. Nor am I hearing voices or seeing things that aren't there. Right now, for example, I can think logically with well-organized thoughts. Not what I'd expect from a psychotic.

Then again, most people suffering psychosis couldn't appreciate how abnormal their thought patterns were. Most nuts picking up an axe to hack someone up believed they were thinking straight or, if not, believed they were following someone else's will. Yet, he just *knew* his thoughts were normal. But man, this situation...

Okay, so what else could this be?

Some bizarre Stephen King scenario in which an evil spirit or a good spirit—whichever—takes over a person's body? That's the sort of premise that makes a good paranormal movie but didn't actually happen in the real world. And what made this experience so strange was he wasn't in just anyone else's body; he was living in his son's body with his son's memories.

He leaned back and massaged his temples.

Aw, man, he'd just gone full circle without coming away with a speck of insight into what was going on. There had to be, just had to be, a rational, scientific explanation. One he wasn't yet aware of.

The only explanation that made a shred of sense was that he died on the mountain and was now reincarnated. Until now he'd figured reincarnation was only a belief of Shirley MacLaine whack-jobs. But he knew many people believed in it. Even some religions maintained that belief. Could all those believers be right, and he's the nutcase? After all, there was no real way to scientifically prove or disprove the belief. Maybe, like most religious beliefs, it contained an element of truth. At least reincarnation seemed more acceptable to him than being flat-out crazy.

The more he thought about it, a heart attack death at age fifty-five wasn't such a stretch. Actuarially, it did happen. And with his strong family history of cardiac problems—both his parents dead at relative early ages—and truth be told, he chose to specialize in cardiology because he feared the genetic cards were stacked against him.

So maybe that explained it: he died and his energy, soul, or whatever you wanted to call it was freed to transplant itself into Joel's body. That was an admittedly huge stretch, an assault on his beliefs, but what better explanation could there be?

Which raised another question: why come back as his dead son?

Well, now that he possessed Joel's memories, that one was easy to explain: Joel didn't die in the avalanche. Now that he thought about it, he—Chris—had never seen Joel's body. Where and how Joel died had always been an assumption based on two missing people and an abandoned car at the trail head. So if Chris did die, maybe his "soul" knew of only one place to go: Joel.

"Earth to Joel. Come in please."

Taylor was standing just inside the room, wrapped in her blue bathrobe and drying her short, amber hair with a towel. She wore it spiky, which he liked. She was a bit gangly in a boyish sort of way. Not beautiful, yet extremely appealing to him. He looked at her again, this time ignoring the acceptance familiarity breeds for the objectivity of seeing her anew through Chris's perspective. No, not beautiful. Certainly she wouldn't have been Chris's first choice. Their preference in women, he realized, was another difference between father and son.

He patted the couch to his right. "Come here, sit next to me. There's something I want to ask you."

She gave her hair one final rub, dumped the towel on the coffee table and settled in beside him. "What?" she folded both legs up under her.

"Do you believe in reincarnation?"

Head cocked, she finger-combed her hair. "Why do you ask?"

"Just curious."

She tugged the neck of the robe closed. "I don't know. Never really thought about it, I guess. Not seriously, I mean. Why, are you, like, serious?"

"Yeah. Do you believe in it?"

She thought about that a moment. "No. Not really."

"What about premonitions?"

She seemed momentarily confused. "Do I believe in them or do I have them?"

"Do you believe they happen?"

She shrugged. "Sure, guess so. I've never had a real one. Have you?"

"Yes. This evening, I felt this really incredibly strong premonition about Dad." *Jesus, how weird to talk about myself like that.* "That maybe he had a heart attack and died."

She reached over and took his hand in hers but didn't say a word. Maybe because she wasn't quite sure what to say. Or maybe because he'd never really gone into what had happened between him and Chris. The few times she'd asked about his family he'd explained that his birth mother died when he was young and that Chris remarried the Bitch From Hell, Janice, but divorced her years later. And as far as he and Dad went, there had been some major disagreements that resulted in them no longer speaking to each other. The few times she tried probing further into their relationship, he'd blown it off as something he didn't want to discuss. Mostly because he didn't want to tell her about the whole Ortega/Delgado thing, which of course would mean having to admit to dealing drugs. When he made the decision to walk away from the mountain, he vowed to start a new life. But suddenly the whole dynamic was upside down. Certainly, if he intended to call Reed Allison, now was the time to open that can of worms and explain the entire story.

He squeezed her hand gently, said, "Want a beer? There's a story I need to tell you." And suddenly it felt liberating to know he'd finally come clean about his past. Which, he realized was more characteristic of Chris than Joel. He'd always preached to Joel to do the right thing. In contrast, Joel always opted for the easy way out regardless of the consequences. His faked death served as a prime example.

She gave him a hesitant look. "I don't like the sound of that. It's not about *us*, is it?"

"No," he assured her, reaching into the refrigerator. "It's about me and Dad."

He brought over two Anchor brews from the fridge, uncapped hers, handed it over and did the same for his own. Seated again, he said, "This isn't easy for me, but here goes."

He described the avalanche and his decision to walk away from the mountain hoping that everyone would assume he died there. He couldn't bring himself to mention the drug arrest or the squeeze the DEA had him in. And this hesitation, he realized, was definitely Joel's personality. Taylor listened, beer in hand, never taking a sip.

When he finished, she said, "Oh my God, Joel...all this time I thought maybe you two just had an argument. It never crossed my mind he thought you're dead. So how do you feel about this now? I mean, what are you going to do?"

That look of hers.... *Is it disappointment for initially misleading her about Chris? Does she think less of me for walking away from Matt? I don't want to lose her.*

"I don't know. But most importantly, is it okay what I did? Leaving a friend like that?"

She seemed to notice the bottle in her hand and paused for a sip.

"Sweetie, I know you pretty well. If you could've helped him, you would've. Besides, I wasn't there. I have no idea what pressures you were feeling when it happened. It must've been terribly scary."

She'd grown up snowboarding, so knew all too well about mountains and avalanches. She had to have a sense of the very real danger an avalanche presented.

God, what a relief to finally unburden. At least partially. He leaned over and kissed her. "Thank you."

"For?"

"Not judging me."

"But what about your dad? What are you going to do about him? Call?"

"That's the thing. While you were in the shower I tried the condo. No answer. And that bothers me because he should be home tonight."

She cocked her head a moment. "Why do you think that? It's been five years. For all you know, he could be married again. Or vacationing in Hawaii."

Well, as of yesterday afternoon I wasn't.

He realized he should be more careful with what he said or he'd be quickly mired in a tangle of lies. "Yeah, you're right. It's just that he usually didn't go out on a work night. But back to the premonition…it was so strong, so real, that it really spooked me."

"That's easily enough solved. Call this friend right now and settle it."

"I will. But not tonight. Because when I do, I'll have to explain who I am. I don't want to do that until I'm more prepared. Besides, maybe you're right. Maybe it's nothing and Dad's just not home. Could be a hundred reasons. It's just that that premonition totally freaked me. I'll call again in the morning. If I can't reach him then, I'll call Mr. Allison."

She set down her beer. "Come here."

He moved next to her. She put her arms around him and held him tightly. "Let's go to bed."

7

Joel thought, *Oh man, what do I do now?* as he followed Taylor into the bedroom. He knew by her tone she wanted to have sex. Not because of being horny, but because of being either frightened or out of sorts from the events of earlier this evening. She simply needed to be held and loved. She was so different from Janice, his ex, that way. Janice sought out sex simply for the attention. And she tried hard to hide her lack of libido even though, in retrospect, it'd been so apparent. Her selfishness during foreplay, the glances in the mirror while on top of him, all those phony utterances, the faked climaxes, never gave him a clue to what really pleased her. If anything.

Taylor, on the other hand, was so different.

But Taylor was his son's mate. How was this going to work? It was hard to imagine going to bed with your son's girlfriend. Made him feel slimy even thinking about the act.

Then again, he was Joel now, wasn't he? That was the point of this…this situation. He was *supposed* to be living life again, right? Well then…

Still…just wasn't right, and he felt a spike of anger at being forced into this…this situation of living someone else's life. Okay, sure, he'd fantasized about doing exactly this, but that didn't include becoming your own flesh and blood. But right now, he needed to behave as normal as possible to Taylor. This situation wasn't her fault. And, now that he thought about it, she was simply an innocent victim. She didn't know that Joel's father had stolen her lover.

Slipping off his shirt, he said, "I'm really grubby. I need a shower," stalling the inevitable a few minutes, hoping for enough time to wrap his head around this.

Hot little stingers beat his back as his mind drifted back the first time he laid eyes on Taylor.

"Why do you want to work at Chez Pierre?" the manager asks.

It takes a second to realize he's been asked a question. He scrambles for some words. He looks the manager in the eyes, says, "For the experience. I can't imagine a better place to work, especially with this being my first job out of school." His attention snaps straight back to the woman setting up the bar.

When he walked through the door ten minutes ago, he was simply looking for a job. Now he wants to work here to meet her.

"Your grades and letters of recommendation are excellent." The manager continues to scan Joel's application. "What kind of wages you expect?"

"The money's not important. The experience of working here is."

The manager tucks the papers back in the manila folder and taps the spine against the edge of the table. "You're in luck. A line cook took off. Can you start today?"

That an offer? Joel takes his eyes off Taylor momentarily, unable to believe his luck, and asks, "You offering me a job as line cook?" He'd assumed if he were lucky enough to land any sort of job here, it'd be as a dishwasher or for some menial kitchen prep work.

"Yep."

The second night, Joel and Luther, the maitre d', are taking a smoke break in the alley when Joel asks, "The bartender. What's her name?"

Luther, a tall, good-looking black who fills out his tuxedo solidly, flicks ash off his Kool. "Name's Taylor. But if you got ideas of getting next to her, she's seeing someone."

Next morning the staff's in early for a meeting. Joel walks over to Taylor and offers his hand. "Hi, I'm Joel."

She shakes hands. "Taylor."

He glances at his watch, says, "Looks like we have about an hour before we need to start setting up. Want to grab dim sum?"

She seems to think about that a moment. "Hey, why not."

Later, as they walk back to the restaurant, he asks, "You free tomorrow evening?" Tomorrow being Sunday, the only night the restaurant closes.

She eyes him with a bemused smile. "I'm seeing someone."

He nods, says, "So am I. Let me know if your situation changes. I just had the best time in my life with a woman." Sounded stupid, but he means it.

Now they were together. Funny how things evolve. He turned off the shower and dried off.

As soon as he slid between the sheets, she had her arms tightly around him, head against his chest. "Hold me."

He felt strangely protective of her feelings. The last thing he wanted to do was upset her. He also felt Joel's love for her. He coaxed her on top of him, clinging to her the way she liked to be held when she got this way. "What's wrong?" he asked.

Nuzzling him, her chin brushing the side of his neck, she said, "You scared me to death today."

He relaxed his hug and just kept his arms around her. He could tell this was about closeness rather than sex. "When I fainted?"

She took a few moments to answer. "That too. No, it was when you didn't seem to know who you were. I thought maybe you'd had, like, a stroke or something terrible. I had this horrible feeling you were going to die. I was so scared..."

A little shiver rippled through her, so he began massaging away the tightness in her neck, starting with the left strap muscle that knotted up when she was stressed. "I'm fine."

She relaxed a bit, letting him work on the muscles.

"No, you're not. You're different."

Uh oh. "How so?"

"I don't know...just different. Your touch, for one thing...like what you're doing now. It's totally different. Gentler maybe."

She was moving her hand down to his hips, then, aw man, she had hold of him, making him hard.

"You first," he said, rolling her onto her back. He grabbed a pillow. "Here."

"What?" she asked.

"Raise your butt," he said and slid the pillow under her while moving onto his knees between her legs, his tongue tracing a line down over her belly.

"Feeling better now?" he asked. She was curled onto her right side, spooning, while he gently massaged her shoulders. All the earlier tightness was gone.

"Kind of, but not really." Her voice was softer but still not completely stress free, as if she still worried about something.

"No?"

"You seem so different...the way you made love right now, it's so *different*...like that pillow thing. You've never done that before. And, you could read me better. I didn't have to say a thing. I should be happy, I guess, but...and I don't know why...it worries me."

She was right, now that he thought about it. Joel didn't know the pillow trick.

"Don't be." He kissed the back of her neck. "It's been a long day and I'm just tired. And I'm worried about Dad."

She rolled over to face him. "I hope that's all there is to it," she said before kissing him. A second later she added, "Oh, God, I didn't mean it the way it sounded. I mean, I hope your dad's, like, okay. What I meant was this change in you. I hope it's just that you're tired."

"Love you." He kissed her again. She rolled away from him, onto her side on the right side of the bed where she always slept.

He ran his fingers down her back and over the side of her thigh, feeling the muscles so well developed from snowboarding. He knew that part of her story too. How she'd packed up her yellow VW for college, but on a whim, instead of driving to her dorm room at Reed, barreled straight through to Ketchum, Idaho to share a rental house with five other snowboarders. She waited tables during evenings to make enough coin for daytime lift tickets. She boarded the entire season, becoming a real hotdog, complete with wind-burned lips and goggle tan line. Everyone in that house skied or boarded with the devotion of monks.

She became very good, too. But not Olympic-good as she'd dreamed; that dose of reality came from getting blown off the hill at Nationals her senior year of high school, but she loved the sport anyway. Just wasn't as devoted to it anymore because what was the sense? So she'd spent a few winters hanging around Sun Valley and Ketchum, working her way up from waitress to bartender before moving back to Portland to live year-round. She made peace with her parents for abandoning her dad's dream of a college education and law school. She landed the plum job at Chez Pierre when the regular bartender, busted for possession, didn't show up for work one afternoon.

She was a classic underachiever. Had the smarts to "do more" with her life, but seemed content with bartending. And though she shared Joel's dream of one day owning a great restaurant, she didn't have the ambition to actually do something to accomplish that.

Taylor was so different from the women Chris chose to be with.

Chris's first marriage ended when Cindy died of weird, rapidly progressing lymphoma a year and a half after Joel's birth. The only good thing about her illness was how mercifully fast the disease progressed—only five short, confusing days between diagnosis and death. He was sitting in a chair next to her hospital bed when he noticed something wrong, then realized she wasn't breathing. There was nothing he could've done to change that part of his life. It'd been totally out of his control.

Janice was another matter that had been totally within his control, if he'd only been thinking straight. He married her for all the wrong reasons. In bed now, thinking back on it, he really did owe Joel a heap of thanks. Joel's death precipitated the divorce that he was too weak to initiate on his own. Yeah, he knew she was sleeping around on him, but he was too busy, too tired, had too many excuses to keep him from confronting her. Amazing as it now seemed, he'd rather be the cuckold people laughed about behind his back than go through all the hassle of divorce and starting over. How pathetic, knowing your wife is fucking your partner along with an unknown number of other guys, yet coming up with all sorts of rationalizations to do nothing about it. What did that say about him? Jesus!

Yeah, that pretty much described his life as Chris Holden. Forever held hostage by a conservative take-no-risk nature. Choosing medical school over what he loved most in life.

The Associate Dean of Admissions stares across the cluttered desk at Chris and asks, "What are your other interests?"

"Music," Chris says.

"You play an instrument?"

Chris lights up and nods. "Guitar. Bass guitar is my specialty. I'm pretty good at it too." He flashes on how arrogant that sounds, blushes and adds, "At least that's what I'm told."

The dean studies him intently. "So what makes you apply for med school? Why not try for something like Cornish or Julliard?"

Chris is at a loss for words. The thought had never even entered his mind. And if it had, was immediately dismissed as being foolhardy.

The dean is waiting for an answer, so Chris tells him, "There's no guarantee I'd ever be able to make a living at it."

"But you can as a doctor. I see."

Shit! Did he just blow the interview? He's compelled to justify his answer. "It's not the way that sounded," he says, but doesn't know what else to say without digging a deeper hole for himself.

"Oh?"

"Yeah. I mean, sure, everyone has fantasies that are way out of line with their actual abilities: being a star NFL quarterback, sitting in the Oval Office, your rock band selling out Yankee Stadium...I mean, what are the odds?"

"And so?" the dean asks.

"So, the key to success is to align your capabilities with realistic possibilities, then make the most of it."

And man, Chris Holden had done just that.

And in the process, had become single-mindedly goal-oriented.

Maybe that was too harsh of a description, but it pretty well summed it up. From high school he went straight into four years of pre-med at the University of Washington. Then into medical school followed by an internal medicine residency at UCLA, after which he returned to the UW for a cardiology fellowship. There he met the two senior cardiologists with whom he ended up in practice. He never indulged in any frivolous side-trips along the way like some of his friends: a year hitchhiking Europe or teaching white-water rafting on the Colorado. Never hung around bars trying to make a living playing third-rate guitar or writing lousy poetry. And unlike Joel, he harbored no dreams of opening a four-star restaurant.

Flat on his back, not moving for fear of waking Taylor, he stared at the dimly lit ceiling while mining his memory. In spite of being exhausted, his mind raced with the high-voltage energy of discovery. Instead of trying to understand how he could now be living in Joel's body—there wasn't any reasonable explanation—he explored Joel's memories. Especially the ones involving him, Chris.

At first—for a reality check (if that was even possible)—he

focused on events they'd experienced together. And though they'd both experienced the same physical stimuli, their interpretations of what happened were markedly different. He'd certainly underestimated Joel's visceral dislike for Janice. Had he known how strong it was, he might've filed for divorce earlier.

The thing that shocked him most was the realization that Joel had begun selling drugs in junior high. Eighth grade. Jesus! Only weed then, but still...now looking back on things, it should've been obvious. But with his nose millimeters from the grindstone he'd seen only the spinning wheel. Aw, man, what a disappointing parent he'd been.

And the Delgado thing...Christ! Unbelievable!

Worse yet was Joel considering to ask Reed for the money instead of him. Was he that bad of a parent? Then again, what would he have said to Joel had he asked? Good question. He'd.... no, that wasn't right. Now, with his mind able to see both points of view, there was no way to come up with an objective answer. Still, a part of him knew he would've told Joel no and justified it as being for his own good.

A sickening weight settled into his gut. He was still dealing drugs. He'd never stopped. He'd simply gotten slicker at the business. He and Luther were running a boutique pharmacy for select customers and friends. Cocaine, ecstasy, and whatever else they got their hands on that would move.

He'd tried to raise Joel with good solid life values. Obviously he'd failed. How had that happened?

Well, for one thing, he never appreciated Joel's opinions.

Wait a minute. That wasn't fair. How could he be expected to know Joel's opinions? Joel never voiced any.

Oh, really? Perhaps Chris never asked, or when he did, never listened?

Not true. He *had* listened.

Okay, how about baseball?

Baseball?

Yeah, think about it. On those rare evenings when you were free, what did you do? You parked yourself in front of the TV, made Joel sit next to you, and turned on baseball. No chitchat, no jokes, just a few expletives about the game. You thought it was good father/son bonding, but Joel hated every moment.

In retrospect, Joel never turned out for sports of any kind. Why?

Because he wasn't any good at them. Why? Because Chris never played with him. So instead Joel holed up in his room with the computer and video games.

Okay, point taken. Joel didn't like baseball. What else?

Well, for one thing, what about wanting to be a chef?

Yes, but that's...

That's what? Ridiculous?

Yes, exactly.

Careful to not disturb Taylor, he slipped out of bed and headed to the bathroom where Joel kept a stash of Ambien. He didn't like the idea of taking sleepers, but the way his brain kept clamoring, he didn't see any other choice if there was any chance for sleep tonight.

He opened the amber prescription bottle, shook one into his hand, thought about it, and dumped out another.

Back in bed, he chewed the first one into paste before swallowing the bitter sludge. One pill, he knew, wouldn't be enough, but he would wait for the first one to be absorbed before doing the same with the second.

His mind drifted back to his conversation with Reed on the mountain in the moments before his—heart attack? If given the chance to live life over again...

Was that what was happening? Was this his chance to redeem his prior life?

And Joel's. To give Joel the chance to start over too?

Meaning he, Chris, was really dead?

Most likely.

Tears, welling up between his lids and slid down the side of his cheeks as his loss began to sink in. Chris, the person he'd lived with for fifty-five years was gone, taking with him a life he dearly loved. The medical license he'd worked so hard to obtain was gone too, as well as all his long friendships. The body he'd inhabited since birth would be cremated and disposed of, becoming dust in the mountains. Now, looking back on that life, he realized just how much he loved it. Sure, he could start over again, but he was being forced into a completely different path than Chris had chosen. We are our experiences and he was now burdened—or perhaps not— with everything that had gone on in Joel's life too. And Joel's dream was to build his own restaurant.

The Ambien began to gently dampen consciousness, so he chewed the other pill to add to the dose and make sure of a deep sleep.

He told himself he should be happy because this was the chance of a lifetime to live a life with the wisdom of an older person. His fantasy come true. Yet he couldn't shake the heavy sadness of losing Chris.

8

He became aware of a gap in time and opened his eyes. The clock radio showed 7:09. Amazing.

He'd actually fallen asleep. Sound asleep too. Sounder than anything he'd experienced in years. Better yet, he hadn't had to go to the john two or three times during the night because of his enlarged prostate.

Mentally, he'd been prepared for one of those nights from hell, tossing and turning, mind zipping along like a rabid-insane bat, exploring Joel's memories and mourning his own death. Instead, he'd drifted into pleasant and restful—although chemically induced—sleep.

So what was the deal? What was really going on with him? Was all this spirit transformation experience real or had it been only a dream? He still couldn't come to grips with that one. Could he actually be in a coma from the heart attack? He glanced around their apartment: exactly as it looked last night, with Taylor still sleeping soundly next to him. Sure seemed real.

So, the question was: if he's here in Portland, what the hell happened to Chris?

Being careful to not awaken Taylor, he slipped from the covers, tiptoed to the bathroom, and closed the door to empty his bladder. Whoa, look at that stream! Like a damned racehorse.

While washing his face, he paused to study the stubble in the mirror. Thicker than Chris's. He glanced at the counter for his Gillette Track 3 but found Joel's Norelco instead. This…whatever this strange situation was, left him as baffled as last night. He shook his head, picked up the shaver but stopped just short of turning it on. The noise would wake Taylor. Instead, he replaced it in the charger. Interesting…Chris would've gone ahead and shaved.

He quietly made his way into the living room and shut the bedroom door with only a soft click of the latch. Pacing, he carefully scripted the story to spin to Reed. The best approach, he decided, would be simple and direct. The problem, of course, was that Reed was such a cynical bastard he'd have to be one-hundred percent convinced the person on the phone really was Joel Holden. If Reed didn't buy that from the get-go, he'd hang up. But more than that, Joel's miraculous resurrection would be hard to prove over the phone. He believed he had a way to convince Reed.

But before calling him, he should try a little harder to reach Chris. Still, a feeling in the back of his mind warned the effort was futile and ridiculous. Chris was standing right here holding the phone.

He dialed the Seattle condo and listened to the same recorded message as earlier. Not that he really thought he'd answer, but…

Next, he tried Chris's cellular. Got, "The Verizon number you called is not in service." Meaning the cell was either powered down or out of the service area. Chris was meticulous about keeping the battery charged and the cell on so the hospital could reach him any time, day or night.

He dialed his office's back line, a number only four or five close friends, like Reed, knew. No answer there either.

Well, that settled that. Time to call Reed Allison.

He dialed Reed's cell from memory, figuring at this time of morning he was either en route to the office or behind his modest desk sipping a latte and paging through the *Wall Street Journal*. Reed was a man of unvarying routines. He arrived at the office early regardless of how much or little sleep he'd had the previous night, because an early arrival assured that his first hour would be completely his: no one dropping by to ask questions and only rarely would the phone ring. If Chris had died yesterday, Reed would've been up quite late; meaning his voice would carry a degree of easily recognizable fatigue and stress. He listened to the call connect and ring.

Reed answered immediately with a prolonged, "Yes?" somehow turning a monosyllabic reply into, "Who the hell's bothering me at this time of morning?"

Joel said, "Is this attorney Reed Allison?" figuring that the question might establish the call as important business.

"Yes. Who is this?" Now sounding curious.

Do I sound like Chris or Joel?

If Taylor hadn't commented on a difference in his voice, most likely he now sounded like Joel. Now the hard part, the reason for rehearsing his lines.

"I know this might be difficult for you to believe, so bear with me a moment and let me explain. This is Joel Holden, Chris's son."

Dead air.

Pretty much what he expected.

Joel continued with, "I know. It's a shock. I'm supposed to be dead and buried in that avalanche up by Rachel Lake, but I'm not. And, if need be, a sample analysis of my DNA can prove that I *am* Joel Holden."

More silence. This time it felt like *shocked* silence. He could feel vibrations zinging over the connection at about 8.3 on the emotional Richter scale.

His own heart was racing with the harsh realization of not wanting to hear Reed tell him that he died yesterday.

Can't have it both ways.

Joel said, "The reason I'm calling is that several times yesterday I got these totally weird and strong premonitions about Dad. Then sometime late afternoon this real mind-blaster slammed me: I was sure something very bad happened to him. A heart attack, maybe. And for some reason, I felt sure you were there with him. I tried calling him last night, but he didn't answer his condo or cell phones. I just tried again and got the same thing. That's why I'm calling you. I have a really bad feeling. Can you help me out and let me know if anything's wrong?"

Reed was slow to respond, as if preparing a careful answer. "You specifically said heart attack. Why a heart attack, of all things?"

Ah, progress. At least Reed wasn't blowing him off.

"Because both my grandparents on Dad's side died of heart attacks. Dad always worried that the same thing would happen to him. It's one of the reasons he specialized in cardiology. But you know all this."

"Sir, I don't know who you are or what your intentions are by calling, but since it's a matter of public record, I can tell you that, yes, Christopher Holden did die last night. However, I will not divulge any more than this, so please do not ask for any more information."

Okay, that's settled. I died yesterday. Or at least my fifty-five-year-old body did. Probably by now it's in a funeral home. Bonnie-Watson Memorial, if Reed took care of it.

Joel said, "Please answer me this: what time did he officially expire?" *Did it correspond to his fainting spell at work?*

"What did I just tell you?"

"Mr. Allison, please don't hang up. I am serious. I *am* Joel and I know you're Dad's attorney. I'm in Portland. How about this: I'll leave here as soon as possible and drive up to Seattle so you can talk to me in person. If it helps, ask me right now any questions that are of such a private nature that only Joel would know the answers. Please, as Chris's lawyer for the estate, it's now your job to verify if there are any next of kin. Will you please do that for me?"

Reed hesitated, probably wondering if this could possibly be true.

Joel added, "Give me, what, three, four hours to get up there this time of day?"

Again, Reed hesitated, probably weighing things, wondering if this goofball on the line was a predatory opportunist who learned of

Chris's death and was trying to use it for an ulterior motive. Maybe even try to cash in on the estate. On the other hand, if by some miracle, this really *was* Joel Holden, then...

"I'll be in my office all day. You may have to wait, but I'll work you in."

"Thank you. You were Dad's best friend for years...even before I was born. So I'm sure you can think of ten really obscure things to convince you I really am Joel."

Reed gave a sarcastic grunt. "No worry. I already have a few."

"Oh, and one other thing. That trouble I was in before I left?" He kept his wording vague in case Taylor was listening.

"The Ortega case?"

"Yes. Can you find out what my status is with that? Please."

He knew Ortega had been convicted and was doing hard time. But the DEA wasn't able to nail all his crew, meaning several of higher-level lieutenants and numerous soldiers were alive and well, still prospering in Seattle's drug trade. Which could be a problem for him if he showed his face in the area.

"You're going to Seattle?"

Taylor stood in the kitchen doorway, tying the sash to her blue terrycloth robe. She'd rinsed her face and had cursorily brushed her short hair, making her look perfect.

"Sorry, did I wake you?"

"Yes, but it's time to get up anyway. What's up?"

"I just can't shake that bad feeling about Dad. I called Reed Allison, the lawyer. Dad died last night."

She came over, wrapped her arms around him. "Oh, no, I'm so sorry," she said and hugged him. "I know you guys had a few issues, but now that he's gone..."

He hugged back, stunned a bit by the impact of the reality. But it was such a damned emotional conundrum. Here he was, still alive, yet dead, making it so difficult to really wrap his mind around his existence. His lower lip trembled as he again thought about the life that was no longer his. She squeezed him again and murmured something he couldn't make out.

Making him feel guilty as hell for lying to her about who he really was. Should he sit her down right now and explain what had happened, that he was now a combination of Chris and Joel? How would that play? She'd freak, for sure. And if not, she'd certainly figure he was nuts. If so, how could he prove he wasn't? Couldn't see an answer to that one. What he *did* know for certain was that he didn't want to do anything that might risk losing her. So for now, at least, it'd be best to just roll with it. And as for the changes she sensed in him, well, his father's death was a perfect reason to be a little odd right now. After a few days she wouldn't notice any changes in him.

"—feel guilty for not saying your goodbyes," she continued, but he'd momentarily zoned out.

He hugged her again, just to reassure her, then let go and went to the cupboard saying, "Oh, man, I need a couple cups of strong coffee while I get ready. It's going to be a long drive." He hated driving long distances, and as far as he was concerned, anything over an hour dropped into that category.

She came over and put her hand on his shoulder. "Want me to go with you?"

He set the bag of coffee on the counter and considered the offer. Her company during the three-plus hours of mind-numbing freeway would certainly help pass the time, but the problem was not having a clue how long he would need to be in Seattle, so there was no telling when he'd get back to Portland. Could be later today, could be tomorrow. And the more he considered it, the more reasons there might be to stay overnight to sort things out. Hell, the trip could possibly turn into two nights. Everything depended on how smoothly talks with Reed progressed. Also, there were their jobs…

"Don't get me wrong. I'd love to have you along, but I don't know if I have to stay the night. Besides, think of what it'll do if we both call in to say we won't be showing up today?"

She nodded. "Valid point." She seemed to think about that a beat. "I'll keep my cell phone on. Call me, let me know you got there safely and what's going on."

Hugging her again, he marveled at Joel's choice of a mate. He'd certainly done well by choosing Taylor.

9

DOWNTOWN SEATTLE

Joel parked his car in the Nordstrom Tower garage, one of the many professional office buildings connected with Swedish Hospital, a large private medical center atop "Pill Hill." As always, he set the time-stamped ticket on the dash so he'd know where to find it, then waited by the bank of elevators. For some reason, the ones in this building were always glacially slow. And were always packed when they did arrive.

A moment later Jason Pratt, an internist with an office on the ninth floor, rounded the corner and stopped to his left. Even thought the call button was already glowing, Pratt thumbed it four times, rocked back on his heels, punched it two more times just to make sure the elevators realized an important physician was waiting. As if this would make it arrive sooner. Busy man. Meetings and such. He wore a knee-length white coat and the serious expression of someone with weighty options.

Joel nodded at him. "Morning, Jason."

Pratt shot him a puzzled glance. "Morning," he said and immediately turned back to glowering at the call button.

Wow, how totally weird. No sign of recognition. If Chris Holden were standing here, Pratt would chat him up, maybe comment on the Mariners or the weather, schmoozing a colleague to keep those all-important referral lines open.

Basically, Pratt was an arrogant prick.

"Estela doing okay?" he asked, surprised at being able to remember his wife's name.

Startled, Pratt studied him a beat. "Uh, yes. She is." He then pulled a smart phone from his belt and started thumbing it as if he'd just received a message. An important man with important messages. Rather than admit to not having a clue who Jason was, Pratt opted to ignore him. Fair enough.

Continue the game by asking about his son?

Naw, why make him more uncomfortable? But this chance encounter did serve as a good barometer of how others perceived him. Clearly, Pratt didn't recognize him.

The elevator finally arrived and they entered, pressed their respective floors, turned toward the closing doors and stood shoulder to shoulder not acknowledging the other's presence. At floor nine, Pratt hurried off, obviously relieved to be rid of any additional embarrassment.

Chris's office was on ten—the entire floor occupied by a single cardiology group. He'd signed on with two senior partners two days before graduating from his fellowship. Those original partners were long gone now, one dead—ironically from a heart attack—the other retired and shepherding a little white ball around sand traps and putting greens in Palm Desert. Both wonderful mentors, partners you could respect and admire. He missed their friendship and knowledge tremendously.

Then it struck him—who would assume the group's reins now that...

Aw Jesus, Dave Vosberg.

With Chris dead, Dave was, by only two weeks, the most senior partner in the group. And Dave was the kind of insecure, inadequate little shit who'd make damned sure everyone kowtowed to his seniority. Ironically, Dave's seniority hinged on a weird twist of fate.

The year Dave joined, the group hired two new graduates,

Dave Voseberg and Carol Abbott. Carol took a two week vacation before actually starting practice whereas the day after graduation, Dave was in the office seeing patients, which made his actual start date two weeks earlier than Carol's. Now, with Chris dead, the bylaws determined that the group's next chairman would be the most senior partner until a partnership meeting elected a new chair at the next annual meeting, which wouldn't be for months. Dave would be a colossal disaster.

Jesus, he should've planned for this, but didn't consider dying so young. This was the kind of transition that had the potential to blow apart a group. Once again his own death dragged him down.

Joel stepped into the tenth floor lobby.

The waiting room seemed exactly as it had when he left the office a few days ago. Well, except for now being full of patients. Rachael and Yolanda sat behind the front desk, one on the phone, the other handing an elderly man a clipboard with papers to fill out. Neither gave him a second look.

He waited at the counter for Yolanda to finish.

She turned to him. "May I help you?"

He leaned forward so she'd look directly at his face. "I was wondering if I could see Dr. Holden."

She hesitated. "Do you have an appointment?"

"No."

"Are you asking to be seen as a patient or for another matter?" She was adroit at screening out pharmaceutical company sales reps trying to wangle five minutes to pitch products.

"For a medical consultation."

She cast a nervous glance down at the desk. "I'm sorry, he's not available."

He lowered his voice slightly. "I know he's very busy. Is there any possible way you could work me in?"

She avoided eye contact. "I'm sorry but Dr. Holden is simply no longer seeing consultations. If you would like to wait, I'll ask one of our other doctors if they can work you in. It may take a while, so if it's urgent, you can be seen in the hospital emergency room."

As bad as he felt for pressing the issue, he needed to know if she recognized him. "No, I really would like to see Dr. Holden. When's his next available appointment?"

She hesitated, lower lip trembling, both eyes misting. "I'm sorry to inform you, but Dr. Holden is no longer with us. He died last night."

He returned to the elevator feeling slimy for being deceptive to one of his employees. But, paradoxically, felt strangely relieved that no one recognized him as Chris. It was one thing for Jason Pratt to blow right past without a blink. It was much more telling for his senior office staff to not recognize him. To the outside world, he was no longer Chris Holden. And as much as he mourned losing his past self, more and more it seemed like he had a shot at a new beginning to life. One in which he could really do things differently than either he or Joel had done the first time around. The more he thought about it, the brighter life seemed.

Reed's office was in one of those generic office buildings on Olive Way that you can pass each day without noticing. Yeah, the structure was there, but if someone held a gun to your head and demanded the building's name, you'd be hard-pressed to come up with it. Although he'd visited Reed's office many times over the years, he still didn't know the name.

He first met Reed in sixth grade, two days after the start of the school year, Reed's family having just relocated to Seattle from Spokane. During noon break they were out on the playfield. Something—long since forgotten—triggered an exchange of name calling—juvenile taunts back and forth—which, of course, precipitated a crowd of jeering classmates. The moment it happened their fate was cast: they had to fight. One of them— maybe Chris—took a swing, then came the inevitable clinch and a couple jabs and a bloody nose before the playground enforcer, Mrs. McNulty, hauled their asses up to the principal's office. Punishment was after-school detention.

In the same room.

By the time they left for the day, they were inseparable friends.

Being Catholic, Reed enrolled at Seattle University while Chris entered the University of Washington. They shared a dump on Capitol Hill until Reed moved on to Gonzaga after acing the LSAT. Chris stayed at UW, sharing the apartment with another med student.

He never understood Reed's attraction to law. Especially personal law, which had fascinated Reed from the start. Wills, taxes, estate planning, divorces. Snoozeville, far as Chris was concerned. Then again, any kind of law seemed tedious to Chris, particularly because he wasn't a detail guy. Couldn't imagine suffering through long butt-numbing, hours reading every damned word of every damned paragraph to verify perfect alignment. Then argue about it.

But he was grateful Reed could sort out those parts of his life. Like the divorce. On the other hand, Reed's detail-oriented personality would make it problematic to convince him he was Joel. Which was exactly the reason he offered to undergo DNA testing. That would be definite objective, non-arguable proof.

Reed's secretary ushered Joel into the corner conference room with a jaw-dropping view of Lake Union and the expansive urban development projects along its southern shore. A minute later Reed dragged in looking dog-tired, from little to no sleep last night. Typical Reed: crisp white shirt, rep tie, sports coat, and slacks.

He stifled the urge to hug him and say, "Hey, it's me, Chris, I'm back." Instead, he stood up and extended his hand. "Hello, Reed. It's been what, five years? Maybe even longer." And thought of all the life they'd shared, the intimacy of friends that was now gone forever. This realization saddened him.

Reed sized him up, studying him from one angle then another. Maybe searching for evidence of make-up, as if this were some fantastic hoax. Apparently satisfied, he shook hands, but Reed's grip carried a definite vibe of distrust.

"Have a seat." Reed waved to one of the conference table chairs. "I must admit, you do look like Joel." The lawyer dropped into chair directly across the table.

Joel ignored the suggested chair for the one next to Reed.

"How's Betty Ann?" He figured a question about his wife was a good place to start.

"Doing well, thanks. It's been how long since you saw her last?"

Not too long. Only about two weeks. "Must be close to six years."

"She's very interested to know how this turns out."

Reed still wasn't convinced.

"That makes two of us."

"She always liked you. She's happy to know you're still alive."

"Where do you want to start?"

Reed slipped off his glasses, started digging at the corner of his eye with his little finger. "An explanation of what happened the day you supposedly disappeared seems like a good place."

He described the avalanche. How he'd walked away, hitched to Portland where he stayed in a homeless shelter until landing a job at a McDonald's. How he started over by doing what he'd always wanted to: go to cooking school. He told how his hard work had paid off with a job at Chez Pierre. He detailed all of yesterday's weird feelings, how they came and went, finally culminating in one climax—the crushing chest pain and the certainty that Chris was dying of a heart attack. That during this final episode, he flashed on the avalanche site but instead of being early spring when it had swallowed his friend, Matt, it was summer with most of the snow melted.

When Joel finished the story, the room became eerily silent,

Reed sitting there with a thousand-yard stare, apparently deep in thought.

Finally, Reed said, "You always did have a fascination for cooking and food. I remember when Janice taught you how to make Eggs Benedict and you served it for us. How proud you were of that."

Yeah, he remembered that one too. Only it wasn't Eggs Benedict. It was seared tuna with a tarragon-flavored béarnaise sauce. And it wasn't the Step-mom from Hell who taught him the recipe. He picked it up on the Food Channel.

Janice hated his fascination with cooking, suggesting the only reasonable explanation was that he had to be gay, or if not gay, less manly. She didn't buy that many great chefs were male. The puff-puff fashion designers she loved so much were the ones who were usually light in the loafers.

He laughed at Reed's test. "Sure, I remember that meal well. But you're wrong. It wasn't Eggs Benedict I served."

Reed's eyebrows raised in mock surprise. "No? Then what was it?"

He told him. Reed nodded in agreement.

"Ah, yes, that it was."

Silence.

"You have no idea," Reed continued a moment later, "the mental pain you put Chris through, deceiving him as you did."

The hell I don't.

He suspected something like this would come, but hadn't quite decided how to handle it. "Actually, I think I do. But as you well know, there were extenuating circumstances."

"Yes, all that unsavory DEA business."

Reed removed his glasses and knuckled his right eye. "Even so, that really doesn't justify your actions." He sighed. "But I guess that's in the past and there's no sense dwelling on it."

"I appreciate that."

"I did some checking today after your call." Finished with his eye, he replaced his glasses. "Tell me, right after you fled to Portland, did you check the newspapers to see what happened when you disappeared?"

"Not sure I understand the question. If you're asking did I look in the papers, yeah, sure, why?"

"You didn't rate much attention, did you? In fact, only your friend's name was mentioned in the context of the avalanche. Did you wonder why?"

Joel nodded. "It crossed my mind."

"That was the DEA's doing. As you know, you were under surveillance that day. When you didn't return to your car, they went looking for you and guess what, you were missing and presumed dead. They hid that particular bit of information from the press—not that it was a front page story anyway—to use for the purpose of weaving a fabricated story of their own that they leaked to the street. They claimed you cut a deal with federal prosecutors: to trade everything you knew about Ortega's drug organization for the witness relocation program. It was a total lie, of course, but it did encourage a few soldiers in Ortega's crew to roll over. Once that started, Delgado and his other investigators just worked up the food chain until they had Ortega. See, whether you intended to or not, even without testifying to the Grand Jury, you were instrumental in sealing Ortega's ultimate conviction."

Joel chewed on that a moment, unable to decide if this was good or bad news.

"Okay, but where does that leave me? With the Feds, I mean."

"One very lucky young man. No charges were ever filed. Because of your deal with the DEA, they held off filing formal charges until you testified in front of the Grand Jury. But then, after you were apparently killed in the avalanche, there was no reason to move forward with any charge, so your case simply went away, disappeared. By now, the statute of limitations is expired. Bottom line is, you're free and clear."

Yeah, but there was no statue of limitations on the hard

feelings with whichever of Ortega's crew was still out there on the streets. Those dudes would hold him responsible for Ortega's conviction. Then again, five years was a lot of time for things to blow over. Maybe.

Reed pressed steepled fingers to his lips and blew a long contemplative sigh. "Now the issue is to determine if you really are Joel Holden."

"I take it that you don't believe me."

Reed gave a sarcastic grunt. "*I* do, but you see, too frequently, when a person of financial substance dies, people come crawling out of the woodwork to lay claim to the estate. As executor of your father's estate, why should I not scrutinize you just as closely as I would any other opportunist?"

That hurt. Hadn't he just proved who he was? Then again, he should thank Reed for being conscientious. Attention to detail was why he'd chosen him for the job.

"Because you know in your heart that I am. You knew me before I disappeared. You must have a feeling about me or you would've thrown me out a half hour ago."

Reed just studied him, looking into the depths of his eyes, as if recognizing something familiar in there.

Joel wanted to say, "It's me, Chris." Instead, he said, "Here's the deal. I appreciate you being protective of Dad's estate. But you're making it sound like he was Bill Gates. Which we both know isn't the case. Okay, sure, he owns the condo free and clear, his car, a modest portfolio, but that's about it. And let's not forget, I *am* the legal heir. What do you expect me to do, stand back and watch the entire estate go to the medical school? Because that's the instruction in the will and is exactly what will happen if I don't come forward."

Reed appeared surprised. Having the estate revert into the medical school scholarship fund was a revision made *after* Joel disappeared.

Reed said, "You disappeared five years ago. How do you know

the contents of the will? How can you even be so sure one exists?"

Shit! His mind raced for a reasonable excuse.

"Because Dad and I discussed it a month before I vanished. The last time he revised it, he planned on giving Janice only enough to make certain she couldn't contest the outcome. The rest went to me. There's a provision that should he survive me, my share would establish a scholarship at the medical school."

Reed held his glasses by the stem, swinging them back and forth, eyes drilling into him. "Are you sure?"

"Mr. Allison, I don't want this to become adversarial. If you claim I'm an imposter, then I guess we'll have to take this to the next level. We do, you know you'll lose. So why not get on with the DNA verification."

Reed slipped his glasses back on. "I arranged for a blood sample and cheek swab to be done."

"Let's do it. But first, tell me, where do we go from here?"

Reed pushed back his chair, walked to the north window and turned to face it, hands stuffed in his pants pocket. "If the DNA results show that you are in fact Joel, you will collect your rightful inheritance." A slight pause. "Do you mind me asking what you plan to do with the money?"

"I have no idea." Which was a blatant lie. During the drive up from Portland he'd fantasized about using the money to fulfill Joel's dream. But he couldn't trust Reed's allegiances or biases quite yet. After all, he'd been Dad's best friend and knew Chris's feelings about Joel's restaurant dream.

With a sigh, Reed turned, swept a hand toward the door. "Well then, come with me and we'll get this unpleasant business over with."

"Before we do, there's one more thing. I need the key for the condo. I plan on moving back here. I believe you have a copy. May I have it?" He knew damned well Reed had a copy because he'd given it to him shortly after the divorce.

"Certainly."

He reached out, placed his hand on Reed's shoulder. "Wait, one more thing."

Reed raised his eyebrows.

"You know the thing Dad wanted most for me was to be a success—at whatever I did. Our problem centered on my choice of careers. In particular, my dream of being a master chef. Whatever I do with the estate, I *will* make him proud of me. You won't believe this, but I *know* he's watching me right now. He'll be proud of what I do."

Reed appeared doubtful. "We need that DNA sample."

10

DOWNTOWN SEATTLE

Joel sat on a concrete bench watching a Border Collie nip at the neck of a Rottweiler three times his size, the Rott on his back in mock submission, legs pumping in the air. Two other dogs played "catch me if you can" as their owners chatted.

Several years ago the city enclosed this patch of cracked cement, weeds and piss-yellowed grass on the corner of Second Avenue and Bell Street with cyclone fencing, transforming it from a homeless campsite and open air drug market to an urban off-leash doggie park and open air drug market. Good for the downtown pets, just okay for the pushers and junkies. He knew it well. It was one of the places he picked up product when first starting out. But that stopped when he moved up the ladder as Ortega's "restaurant connection." It amazed him how many line cooks and chefs worked blasted night after night. Including himself.

During the walk here, he'd bought a Mariner's cap at a Walgreens and wore the bill low over his face. A disguise, especially necessary for this corner. But things change. He wasn't sure which dealers owned which block, but saw transactions taking place. No mystery there. Across the street two buff bicycle cops in spandex shorts and black Kevlar vests, their trail bikes propped against a utility pole, sipped lattes while chatting, keeping a lazy eye on foot traffic. Urban policing.

The sun was out and the sky blue. Life didn't get much better. Except for all the confusion rippling through his mind. The neighborhood was Belltown. A once trashy cluster of blocks had been transformed into one of Seattle's prime high-density vertical residential areas. Ultra expensive high-rises mingled with soup kitchens and low-income housing, making it a poster child of the politically correct urban blend. A haven for empty-nest baby boomers fleeing poetically named suburban neighborhoods, strip malls, and long fuel-gobbling commutes. The neighborhood of choice to launch his dream.

The hood was also notorious for the highest concentration of popular restaurants in the Pacific Northwest, catering to an eclectic assortment of tastes spanning wine bars to bistros, white linen, jazz, classical Spanish guitar, or residual grunge. Which, depending on your point of view, was either good or bad. Good, because a presence here gave instant credibility (assuming the menu and décor passed consumers' fickle tastes). Bad because of cutthroat competition for diminishing discretionary dollars in an anemic economy. A point underscored by the high percent of establishments that were forced to close within a year of opening. He knew the statistics cold, having meticulously tracked Seattle's volatile restaurant scene for the past five years.

Well shit, want to be published? Go to New York.

Want to establish one of Seattle's best restaurants? Open in Belltown or South Lake Union.

Like most things, reward remained proportional to risk.

He reflected on this last thought.

What would it cost to open the place of his dreams? A ton of bucks, for sure. Which also depended on a ton of variables, like how much remodeling would be needed. Did his portfolio have enough money to swing it? He doubted it did, meaning he might be forced to take out a business loan, which would be difficult now with the credit market still tight.

Which brought up another thing. It'd been fun to fantasize

about his dream restaurant when things still remained hypothetical. But now in a position to actually have a shot at it, he had to ask himself: did he really have the balls to lay down every cent of the estate—and perhaps then some—on a dream?

Throughout his life, he'd learned the value of money and how hard it was to come by. Even harder to hold onto and grow. Early on, he'd started salting away a small amount every month into a retirement account, saving for his future. Establishing a restaurant by wiping out his entire monitory worth would run counter to his tendency toward fiscal conservatism.

Which brought up that conversation with Reed again, the one on the mountain...Reed telling him that if given a chance to live life over again, he'd be held hostage to his underlying personality. This was a prime example. Chris's basic personality was hindering him from even considering leveraging himself. Well, the only way to do things differently this time around would be to do exactly what he felt uncomfortable with.

Gave him pause. But hey, wasn't that what this new life was supposed to be all about? Living differently. More than that, he owed Joel a chance to fulfill his dream. He saw the karmic symmetry to it: Joel had given him a new life, so the least he could do in return was to fulfill his dream.

Eyes closed, he leaned against the cyclone fence, visualizing his future creation. Eager door personnel in black bolo jackets and open-neck white shirts waiting at the passenger zone to park customers' cars. A spotlessly washed and waxed Mercedes, BMW, or Porsche—maybe all three—parked at the curb, selling the image that their affluent owners chose to spend time and bucks here. A car pulls up. Valets immediately open both passenger and driver's doors and say, "Welcome to..."

Welcome to...what?

Aw man, have to come up with a totally awesome name.

Strange, never thought about that.

Nothing with Chez in it, that was for sure. Hmmm...

Oh well, just one of a thousand little details needing to be decided. Taylor would be great at helping him.

A double-door entrance, each door with an eye-level porthole window like right out of Casablanca. The entire interior—walls and ceiling—painted flat black. A tiered floor, like a 1930s nightclub. Banquettes along the upper level. A long curving bar with ultra cool hidden lighting.

Yeah, lighting could create a hugely important effect. Just another place to not cheap out during the remodel.

He made another mental note to line up a really good lighting company.

Christ, he could hardly stand it. This was it! Putting the package together to fulfill Joel's dream would be his new life's work, something radically different from the stodgy practice of medicine.

A heady rush—one not felt since being accepted for medical school—swept over him. So invigorating and vibrant, infusing him with an energy he hadn't experienced in decades. Had he become that jaded? Was jaded even the right word? Perhaps a better word would be blasé about life and its opportunities? How is it we lose the excitement of youth? Is it a function of the collateral damage from myriad failures and disappointments accumulated over the years? Hard as we try, no one leads a charmed life. Everyone's road contains potholes.

He shook his head and refocused on the planning his new venture required. But so much would depend on the space and utilities available. Specifics could come once those had been nailed down.

He'd make it the spot to be seen. Not only would he have a killer menu, it'd be the place for young upwardly mobile singles to be noticed and find each other, a place where established money could count on excellent food with only a modest markup on premium wines.

He'd handle the kitchen, Taylor the bar. But every good

restaurant needs a smooth talker, the slick one who regularly mixes with customers, chatting up the regulars, always developing alliances. No one was better at that than Luther. And, in a way, he owed him. Assuming Luther would be able to walk away from his sweet deal at Chez Pierre.

He sits across the table from Daniel Walsh, the owner/chef of Chez Pierre, the high priest of Portland's restaurant scene. They're in the main dining room, a short-haired beauty working behind the bar. He can't keep his eyes off her. A black dude in tuxedo pants and formal shirt is working the counter in front of the coat closet.

"And your reason for applying here?" Walsh asks.

Oh, shit, a trick question? His stomach does a back-flip as sweat sprouts across his forehead. The interview so far has been a disaster. He flashes on Dad's story of his medical school interview, how he played into the interviewers' egos. He has nothing to lose by trying it.

He smiles at Walsh. "This is the best restaurant around. I want the experience of being part of the team. But more than that, I can learn a lot from you."

"For what purpose? You have visions of moving on in, oh, five years to start your own bistro? You look the type."

Jesus, what would Chris say to that?

Just then a guy says, "Dude, aren't you Joel Holden?"

The black guy is standing by the table now, all friendly-like and smiling.

"Ah, yes," Joel says, wondering: have I met you before?

"You work at Trade Winds?" Then, to Daniel, "I was over there a couple weeks ago—this dude's duck l'orange was totally awesome, simply awesome."

On his way out Joel stops by the desk to talk to the black guy.

"Have we met before?"

Dude smiles, extends his hand. "Luther Rabb. Heard him offer you the job. Congratulations."

Joel is embarrassed because as far as he could tell it was Luther's endorsement that landed the offer for him. "Seriously, have we ever met?"

"No."

"Then—"

"Overheard you two talking, was all. Him giving you a hard time, like that. Thought I might help you out a tad."

"But—"

"Yo, don't think twice about it. We family here, we look out for each other. Just remember, get any filets sent back, ask if I've eaten before you toss 'em. You feel me?"

"Yeah."

"Aw right then, we good."

Yeah, Luther was good with people, the best: a jive-ass nigger to rappers, a refined butler to gentry, and a godfather to most of the crew at Chez. He took good care of people. If he liked a waitress, he'd make sure her station filled up first. The little things he did for staff was good for morale. He provided the added benefit of quickly sorting out the assholes from the good ones and quietly encouraging them to move on.

But, if Luther were to join him in the new place, their drug business would have to stop. There'd be none of that here. Which was why he was certain Luther would turn down the offer. Still, he had to give him first refusal...

Luther would be so perfect for the new place that he'd hand him the best offer possible. Forcing Luther to seriously consider it.

Dizzy with excitement, he strolled from the park. Yet another part of him—the Chris part—warned that too much excitement caused errors of judgment, that over-confidence was a younger man's foible. Then again, he was supposed to be living differently, right? A young man's enthusiasm with an older man's wisdom. What could be better?

Before heading back to the car, he decided to spend two, maybe three hours meandering the neighborhood, checking out commercial rentals. As long as he was here he might as well check it out, because the moment Reed received the DNA results and legally acknowledged his identity, he planned to walk out of Chez Pierre, pack up his meager belongings and move back to the condo. What had Reed said, the results would be back in four or five days?

Soon as that happened he'd work in earnest on fulfilling Joel's dream.

This was staggering, an opportunity of a lifetime, one he couldn't let slip away.

Then again, how long would this new life last? Would he be able to shepherd Joel's dream to fruition?

He stopped to think about that. Chris had never considered that he might die before reaching old age—whatever age that might be. Certainly not as a man in his mid-fifties. But he *had* died. And that taught him a very important lesson: you never knew when or how death was coming, but the possibility always loomed on the horizon. Sure, if you had a terminal disease, you had a better fix on your allotted time, but otherwise...

Short of suicide, death was one of the few things in life left to fate and fate alone. You accepted its eventuality but didn't dwell on it.

These aren't productive thoughts. Put them aside.

But he couldn't.

11

I-5, SOUTHBOUND

"I'm almost to Olympia now. Traffic's a bitch, so don't know how much longer it's going to take. Could be a while." With his earpiece in one ear, the cellular between his legs where he'd dropped it after dialing, Joel drove the middle lane, cars on both sides of him. Traffic had been bad enough getting out of Seattle but then it congealed into a clot halfway to Tacoma. An ocean of frustration and impending road rage remained stalled bumper to bumper while tires cooled for thirty minutes. A KOMO helicopter reported a two-car pileup in the HOV lane one mile ahead. But mercifully Joel remained so wrapped up in thoughts about the restaurant that he wasn't forced to deal with his usual impatience.

Finally, the State Patrol managed to get two lanes moving. Then progress consisted of stop and go all the way past Fort Lewis. Now he was zipping along at a blistering 40 mph.

Taylor asked, "You dropping by the restaurant?"

He could hear the usual background clatter and pictured her crouched behind the bar pretending to search for something while sneaking the call.

At the moment, the last thing he wanted was to face people at work and hear their condolences about his father's death. Besides, a party of ten was booked for tonight. It'd be crazy busy around there, meaning he'd only get in the way.

There were so many things he wanted to share with her, but they could keep until later when they were face to face and not rushed. More to the point, he just didn't feel like talking. What he wanted was to be alone in a quiet room with a beer or maybe a glass of wine and think things over without the constant distractions—traffic, people, noise—all around. He needed a good dose of solitude.

"Naw. I'll wait to see you. I'll pick up some takeout at the Golden Dragon. We can eat at the apartment," he said, though his excitement submerged any hunger. But that, he figured, would change by the time he pulled into Portland. The only time he didn't enjoy food was when ill with the flu. "Want me to pick you up anything?"

"No. I'm poaching dinner here. Okay. Gotta go. Call when you hit home so I know you made it safe."

The way things can get—so busy at the bar—she didn't need any distractions. "Tell you what, put it on vibrate and don't bother answering. I'll text you."

"Ohhh, I love it when you talk vibrators." She made a kissing sound.

"Love you." He disconnected.

Now moving along the inside lane at sixty, behind a FedEx truck, he compared Taylor's way of ending calls to Janice's way. So different.

Janice. How could he have missed so many red flags? But he had. Maybe the saying "love can blind you" is true. Or maybe it was just hard to be objective about someone so close to you. Like a wife. Or maybe he just couldn't face the reality that he really hadn't been in love.

He waits in the physicians' lounge, chatting up another cardiologist when Tom Holmes enters the room. Tom stops at one of the coffee urns to fill a Styrofoam cup before ambling over.

Chris says to the colleague, "If you'll excuse me, I need to discuss a consult with Tom."

Tom nods. "Daryl, Chris," then says to Chris, "You want to grab a coffee before we start?"

"No, I'm fine." His stomach is too sour to add coffee anyway.

He and Holmes move to chairs in a discreet corner, out of earshot of the ongoing coffee klatch.

Chris says, "Thanks for coming over last night."

He'd invited Tom and his wife, Hanna, ostensibly for dinner. One of Janice's strong points was cooking and she loved to show off her talent. But Chris's true motivation for the evening was for Tom to assess Janice's personality. Both men were well aware of the shortcomings of such a devious tactic, but Chris needed an objective opinion.

"Thank you. It was a fantastic meal. Especially with the '92 Sterling Cellars."

Several silent seconds tick away.

Chris says, "Were you able to form an impression?" Although he's not sure he wants to hear what Holmes has to say because it will probably simply confirm his own diagnosis.

Tom nods, nervously rotating the Styrofoam cup in his hand. Uncomfortable with this approach, he'd finally agreed to it only because Chris was a good friend and the marriage seemed headed for disaster.

"I can see why she might resist an evaluation. Keep in mind I'm basing this on limited, very informal observation and don't have benefit of a private interview. But I agree with you. She's a narcissistic personality. The only question is whether or not she meets enough criteria to be diagnosed as a personality disorder."

Chris feels slimy for asking Tom to evaluate Janice this way. But dealing with her "issues" is becoming increasingly difficult. He figures that, like most medical problems, effective treatment begins with an accurate diagnosis. And before taking this step, he'd seen Tom for three personal sessions, hoping their marital issues might be his problem—making it easier to correct.

He says to Tom, "I reviewed the diagnostic criteria again this morning. A diagnosis requires five or more of the nine possible traits."

Tom seems to relax now that Chris hasn't shot the messenger. "Right."

Chris pulls a slip of paper from his white coat. "I wrote down the ones that fit her." *He glances at Tom to make sure he's attentive. Tom nods for him to continue.*

"A grandiose sense of self-importance."

Tom nods. "That's obvious."

Chris sucks a deep breath and moves to the next one. "Preoccupied with fantasies of beauty."

Again Tom nods. "Agree."

"Believes she's 'special' and unique."

"Appears to be the case."

"Requires excessive admiration."

"That too."

"Interpersonally exploitative."

Tom holds up an index finger. "I'll have to take your word for that."

Chris thinks back to all the examples he's seen. "Believe me, she does. Lastly, she lacks empathy."

"Again, that's something I couldn't evaluate last night. But you've made your point. She qualifies."

Well, at least it's a relief to have an official diagnosis. At least one of them. There are maybe two more, he fears, making Janice difficult to deal with personally as well as psychiatrically if she were to finally agree to seek professional help. So far she's refused to even consider an evaluation, much less treatment.

"What can I do for her, how do I treat this? It's killing our marriage."

Tom sets down his coffee and massages his forehead. "Unfortunately, and you should know this if you're up to speed, you're facing a very difficult situation. Personality disorders are tough to treat. Especially because it's hard for the sufferer to acknowledge they have a problem. To them, everybody else has the problem. What makes her case worse is she won't agree to an evaluation. This said, it's going to be impossible to do anything about it."

Joel was past Olympia now, debris from at least a couple truck tires scattered along the shoulder of the road, a green and white interstate sign announcing Centralia up ahead, triggering memories of another time he'd seen that sign...

"Here, you do it."

Chris hands him the line, the dangling trout sill flipping its tail back and forth. Although only seven years old, Joel hates this part: seeing the fish die. The fish's struggle for air makes him hate the sport. But the thing he dearly loves about this is being alone with Dad, just the two of them. No Janice. It's their time. Dad loves to teach him these things, even if he doesn't like them. But he'd never tell Dad that...

Out of pity he takes the slimy wiggling fish in his small hand and carefully removes the hook like Dad did with the last one, then cuts off the head, putting the poor soul out of its misery. They've caught their limit. Or at least Dad has. He hasn't caught one. Had a few bites but has yet to actually hook one.

Then they're sitting on a log, the stream twenty feet away, a sky-blue REI dome tent another ten feet in the other direction over by the Volvo station wagon. He hears the hiss of the Coleman stove, the sizzle of the frying pan. He smells pine needles and butter. His toes are still freezing from being in the water, even though he had boots on. He's starving. Or at least it seems that way.

Why can't they always be like this, just the two of them? He notices Dad smiling at him and he spontaneously cuddles up next to him and leans into his side, watching him cook the trout.

"Son, time to get our dishes and forks," Dad says.

Joel comes back from the tailgate carrying the metal plates and hands them to Dad.

Dad spoons up the trout into both dishes and hands one to Joel. "It's hot. Let it cool a bit."

He sits on the log, the heat of the plate radiating through his jeans to his thighs, but the air is chilly so it won't take long before it will be eatable.

"Here." Dad hands him a lemon wedge. "Squeeze a little on your fish."

Joel watches Dad do it and mimics him, but the lemon flies out of his fingers and lands on pine needles. They both laugh. Dad takes another wedge and squeezes juice over Joel's fish.

He takes a bite and can't believe the taste. Can't remember tasting anything so good. What's even more amazing is this is the first time he's seen something that came directly from nature made into food. Stream to plate. It's pure magic. And nothing has ever tasted this good. Sure, Dad showed him how to make toasted cheese sandwiches, but all the ingredients came straight out of the refrigerator. And the trick with the lemon, boy did it enhance the taste. Pure magic.

Centralia. He passed that turnoff now with the road to the river where they'd camped. God, if he'd only known how much those times had meant to Joel, he would've made a point to create more of them instead of devoting time to Janice. Perhaps if he had, Joel would've turned out better than a damned dope dealer. But he'd had other worries too, like developing his career. Couldn't be a successful professional and have too many distractions.

Really? Was that true? The more he thought about it, the more he could point to colleagues who seemed to have accomplished both. Truth was, he was driven to not just perform an acceptable job. He wanted to develop one of the best cardiology practices in the area. And he had. And because of his singular focus, parenting didn't fare as well. And what about being a good spouse? Well...

Janice and Taylor were so completely opposite personalities, making him marvel at the polar opposites father and son had chosen for mates. But, he had to remind himself, our minds were forged from our experiences. Two people never experience life in exactly the same way, even if presented with the same stimuli, a finding proven repeatedly by studies of identical twins. Chris and Joel developed very different skills for dealing with all the curve balls life throws. Joel inevitably chose the easy way out. Chris often delayed gratification for what he perceived as a greater reward. But, did living life over with the wisdom of age necessitate turning your back on the rules you'd previously lived by?

The more he thought about it, the more he realized that Chris had let circumstance dictate major life choices. At age twenty-two he was so hyper-focused on med school, he never moved in with Cindy, a nurse at University Hospital. Her apartment was big enough, but at that time he considered living together on a par with an engagement ring and he wasn't ready for that level of commitment. How can you be sure a person is the one you could spend your life with when all you're doing is trying to survive a crushing schedule day after day? It was nuts back then. So instead of moving in with Cindy, he opted to share a one bedroom dump with Frank, a master of sloth and Tuna Noodle Casseroles.

Along came graduation and his internal medicine residency. Not only did this mean moving to San Francisco—a city so foreign to him it might as well have been Moscow—but Cindy laid down the big one: without a ring on her finger, he'd be moving solo.

He caved.

Now, experiencing Joel's love for Taylor made him question if Chris's feelings for Cindy could even be considered love. Or had his reason to marry her been a carbon copy of his reason to marry Janice: a good solution for the moment. Hard to tell after so many years and with such a generous layering of defense mechanisms.

Not that he hadn't been happy. They were too damned busy to be unhappy. He and Cindy were working full time, making it a tag-team marriage with respites of weary comfort in each other's arms.

Joel was born. Then one day a year later, Cindy got the flu. Or at least that's what they thought during those first twenty-four hours. She got worse. Then a lot worse, ending up in the ER dehydrated and febrile. The diagnosis turned out to be acute leukemia. Which was the last thing he'd considered. And him, an internist. Jesus!

She was dead within a week.

Only after she was cremated did he realize how much he loved her. But then, of course, the question was how do you distinguish love from loneliness especially when you relied on the other person for efficiency in dealing with a busy life rather than emotional sustenance. He didn't have an answer for that. But he still kept her ashes in the drawer of the bedside stand.

Her death put him right back in a vortex of circumstances. There he was, in the middle of a cardiology fellowship, "in the barrel" every third night, while raising a three-year-old with the help of a nanny. That and all the other crap he needed to do just to stay afloat day to day.

Janice seemed to offer everything: knockout good looks, classy, sufficient in bed, supportive. She seemed to love Joel. And, guess what? She wanted to marry a doctor.

He was too blinded by the need for help managing his life to be his usual objective, self-disciplined self.

The irony was laughable.

Now he was in his twenties and living with Taylor. Well, at least he was doing this part of life differently and not making the same mistake twice.

Which brought up the other thing again. How did this transference—or whatever the hell you'd call it—happen? Not knowing the answer was disconcerting as hell. But what difference did it really make? Probably none at all, so why not simply accept the gift and enjoy it?

Well, for starters, he couldn't get comfortable with the idea. It was too damned strange...and when would it end? Then again, we live life never knowing for certain when the end might come, so why worry about it? And wasn't he simply tacking on time to his fifty-five prior years?

He suspected he could accept this weird situation *if* he could prove to himself it was actually happening and wasn't some sort of weird psychotic delusion. No, he couldn't accept that possibility. Still, it was worrisome. He needed more objective evidence, a second opinion that he was sane.

Which brought him full circle to Tom Holmes.

In a day or so the DNA would prove his identity. Soon as that happened, he'd give notice at Chez Pierre, pack up, and move back to the condo.

Once there, he'd make an appointment with Holmes for an evaluation. Sure, he'd have to modify the story a bit, but not enough to not allow Tom to evaluate him. Yeah, before he could *really* enjoy this new life he had to know for sure whether or not this was real or nothing but a delusion. Tom was the only person he trusted for an honest answer.

12

PORTLAND, OREGON, 11:42 PM

He awoke with a start, wondering.

Where am I?

He glanced around, the room lit only by weak street light angling through the Venetian blinds, the interior muted grays like a classic black and white movie. *Ah, yes, of course, the living room.* Must've fallen asleep on the couch. But why Portland?

Oh right...this is my apartment. This dual life was definitely confusing at times.

He'd arrived home after a quick stop at the Chinese place at the end of the block for takeout lemon chicken and broccoli with oyster sauce. Empty white containers were scattered over the coffee table and the air smelled of soy sauce. It'd been a long tiring day, considering the drive up to Seattle and back. So he'd stretched out on the couch for a quick nap before Taylor came home. Apparently, it'd turned into an hour of dead sleep. The familiar splatter of water on the molded plastic shower stall was sneaking under the closed bathroom door. Okay, she'd obviously come in and he'd slept right through, or she'd purposely not wakened him.

He glanced at his watch. Must have been a slow night after all, even with the big table booked. Slow at the bar too.

He flicked on lights, grabbed a Talking Rain from the fridge and was returning to his warm spot on the couch when Taylor padded from the bedroom in her terry-cloth robe, toweling off her face.

"Sorry to wake you. Long day, huh. How you doing?"

"Tired. Driving does that. You got off early."

"For good behavior."

She laughed, drying her hair. The robe fell open, exposing her body. She gathered it back together without a hint of embarrassment.

"I wanted to get home, see how you're handling things. What happened with the lawyer, how'd that go?"

"Pretty much as expected. He didn't believe me at first, but by the time we finished up, I think he was on my side. I ended up having to give a blood sample, but figured that would happen."

She folded the towel and draped it over the arm of the couch, then finger-brushed her short hair. "You were legally declared dead?"

"I don't really know. I never asked that specifically. Interesting question, though. I suppose so."

"How about a beer?" Which, in Taylor-speak, was a request, not a question.

"Sure." He headed for the fridge and capped the bottle of water.

She called after him. "How does that work? I mean how do you legally become not dead?"

He grabbed two beers, noted that only two remained in the fridge and made a mental note to pick up another couple of six-packs tomorrow. Better yet, maybe a nice single malt too, now that he could afford it.

Single malt?

Yeah, single malt scotch. *You like it, Joel doesn't.*

He uncapped a chilly bottle and handed it to her. She took a long pull, sighed with pleasure and leaned back, stretched out her legs, plunked her bare heels on the coffee table.

"I'm not sure. Maybe I should ask Mr. Allison next time we

talk."

"Mr. Allison. That sounds so...formal. Old." She sat up again, leaned over to inspect the callus on her right foot before picking up a pumice stone to smooth it. Grinding one down was one of those little personal things you never let anyone other than your partner watch.

They both sat drinking beer, the muted TV still playing the movie. Jimmy Stewart or some male lead from the era when men with Vitalis-slick hair wore hats and double-breasted suits, smoked pipes, and said *swell* instead of *awesome*. Though Chris was too young to have experienced that time period, it held a certain appeal to him because of the simplicity and civility that now seemed gone from our evolving culture.

"Let me ask you. You think any less of me for what I did? Walking off the mountain like that?"

She glanced up from the pumice stone. "We discussed that. I wasn't there, you were. You made a decision based on what was in your mind at the time." She shrugged. "What can I say?"

That wasn't what he wanted to hear. Then again, he purposely left out the part about being forced to testify to a grand jury. He wanted absolution from her for the guilt eroding his stomach— which seemed worse now that he had Chris's psyche—guilt that grew every time he thought about his walking away from Matt. He needed to know she didn't think less of him because of it all. But her tone carried the same guarded neutrality as had Reed's earlier in the day. He'd wanted both of them to understand he'd been powerless to help Matt. He wanted them to exonerate him, to say they would've made the same decision. This was Chris's need, he realized. It hadn't eaten away at Joel the same way. And he realized age brought increased compassion and empathy, and that the more you fathom your own mortality, the more you cared about the legacy you leave behind.

"Let me put it this way. You think I'm a bad person because I left Matt?"

She downed the rest of the bottle, rocked the empty back and forth. "I'm getting another. You?"

"Sure." Why did she dodge an answer?

She collected the empties and headed for the fridge.

"Do I think you're a bad person? No. Because I know you. Do I think there might've been another way to treat your father than make him believe you were dead? Absolutely. But no two people will ever perceive a situation in exactly the same way because we've all been molded by our experiences. No two people ever experience life identically. Understand what I'm saying?"

He agreed with her logic, but she hadn't really answered the question hammering away at his mind. And, the more he thought about it, the more her answer intensified his guilt.

She uncapped a beer and handed it to him. "I guess the next question is, what are you going to do now? How does your father's death change your life?"

Another wave of guilt came over him. He was living a lie by not telling her who he really was. Then again, there was no way to possibly explain this when he didn't even understand how it happened. Besides, it was too preposterous for anyone to believe.

"I really miss him," he said, blinking away a tear. So true. So confusing, mourning a death that wasn't. In spite of not talking to each other for years, he—Joel—had enjoyed a subtle stability in knowing that no matter what, Chris was there for him, serving as an emotional touchstone of sorts, a life stabilizer. Chris's death had cut the anchor chain. "But," he added, "I think he's given us a wonderful opportunity."

She tossed the bottle cap on the table. They both watched it spin into a widening dying spiral until it flattened out and stopped. Then she settled into the chair, feet tucked under her. "Opportunity?"

"To start the restaurant we've always dreamed of."

She took a pull from the beer. "No kidding? Right now, I mean, like, right away?"

"No kidding. Look, I'm the sole heir of the estate. That should give us enough money to finance it."

She tore along the center of the bottle's label with her fingernail, ripping it in half. "Why right away?"

Well, for one thing, he didn't know how long this...new life?...would last. In one moment he was Chris, in the next moment he was Joel in an emergency room. Why couldn't he suddenly find himself on a mountain trail dying from a heart attack? She was too young to appreciate how tenuous our hold on life is, or to appreciate the fact that the future we eagerly anticipate only brings us closer to death.

"Because...it's something I've always wanted to do. You know that. We've fantasized about it often enough. Why not now? We may never have another chance."

"You know, I find this conversation very interesting."

Uh oh. Didn't like the sound of that. "What do you mean?"

"Your dad's body isn't even cold and all you can talk about is your inheritance. I mean, come on, sweetie, don't you feel the least bit sorry he died before you guys had a chance to reconnect and smooth things out? I mean, he died believing you'd died in an avalanche. That's *so* totally sad."

"You don't understand."

She cocked her head and studied him a moment. "What don't I understand?"

He opened his mouth to explain who he really was, then stopped. What was the use? She wouldn't believe him. And if she did, she'd freak. If she did that, he'd risk losing her forever. One thing Chris had learned in his fifty-five years was it was sometimes better to say nothing, just cede a potential argument, and take your losses. He stood, finished off his second beer in one big gulp, said, "I'm going to bed."

She was back to working on her foot. "That's the way you're going to deal with this, by going to bed?"

He faced her. "Taylor, look. It's been a very long and trying day, and I've seen this reaction from you before and know where it's headed. An argument. I don't want to have to deal with that on top of everything else right now, so yeah, I'm going to bed. But before I do, I want to say one more thing. There are things you do not, and will not, ever know about my relationship with Chris. So please don't be judgmental."

She glanced at him with defensive bemusement. "Judgmental?"

"Yeah, I'm sorry you're disappointed in me at the moment, but you either do or don't believe me when I say you can't possibly know all that's going on with me right now. There's no way I can explain it."

She set down the pumice stone. "You can try. I'm listening."

For a moment, he considered it again but ended up back at the same place as a moment ago. It was a dead end road. Best to just walk away from any further discussion and take his lumps. Go to bed looking like a total asshole.

He bent down, kissed her forehead. "Good night," he said, before heading for the bedroom.

Hands clasped behind his head, he lay on the futon staring at the dark shadowy ceiling, Taylor still in the other room watching TV with the volume low, his mind drifting over Joel's memories.

On a field of dandelions and a potpourri of grasses Dad carefully assembles the kite and then carefully strings the parallel control lines for fifty feet before setting down the handles. Joel watches every move as growing excitement tingles his fingers. The west edge of the field is a short steep bank into cold saltwater. Off to the west are the San Juan Islands and Canada. The summer sun is high, but the gusty breeze off the water pleasantly cools his skin.

"Okay, son, where's the wind coming from?"

Easy question. He points at the Straits of Juan de Fuca and the Pacific Ocean beyond. "From out there."

"Right. And which way is the kite line lined up?"

Ah, he hadn't thought about that. Now he sees. He sticks a finger in the opposite direction toward a hill packed with modest one- and two-story houses, windy streets and buried power lines.

"Get it?" Dad asks.

Joel nods, suddenly afraid Dad's going to ask him to do something he doesn't know how to do.

"Okay. Now go to the kite and when I tell you to, pick it up like this"—he mimicking the movement he wants—"and throw it straight up in the air like this. Let's see you practice it once here before you really do it."

Joel goes through the motions.

"Perfect. Now remember, as soon as you toss the kite up, step back and come here."

Facing Dad, Joel bends over and grabs the edges of the kite, suddenly feeling the force of the wind against him. He steps back just as Chris tightens slack from the line. For a moment he forgets exactly how he's supposed to throw it but hears his father yell, "Put it right up over your head."

He does. The kite—the shape of a swept-wing arrow—pulls from his hands to take flight. He stands frozen in amazement.

"Step back," Dad yells.

He stands next to Dad, watching him use both hands to guide the kite in tight figure-eight patterns, back and forth, left to right, hands working deftly, like a magician.

"Okay, now you do it."

Suddenly he's afraid. Afraid of crashing the beautiful blue and yellow kite, afraid of being pulled off his feet, afraid of not being able to hold on and letting the kite fly off to wherever, tangling the lines into an unmanageable mess, afraid of failing in front of Dad.

"I...I...can't."

"Sure you can. Here." *Dad kneels down, arms still extended, holding the two controllers.* "Put your hands on mine and feel how I do it."

Tentatively, Joel does as told.

He feels Dad's strong hands guide the kite through various maneuvers.

"Okay, now your turn. When I say go, take the controls."

"But..." He knows there's no way out. He will have to try even if it means destroying the beautiful kite.

Then he's gripping the two handles, forgetting everything he was just shown.

"Pull right," Dad says.

A gust hits, the sudden pull almost topples him over. "I can't hold on. I'll fall."

Then Dad is behind him, arms around his chest preventing him from being pulled over. He loves that feeling of being hugged and wishes it would happen more often. But more and more Dad turns his attention to Janice. And Joel hates that. And he knows he shouldn't. She's supposed to be his mother. He's supposed to love her. But she isn't his mother and he hates her. His mother died years ago.

13

FOUR DAYS LATER

"I'll get it." As Joel reached for the phone, a strong gut-nudge warned that the call was for him and was important.

"Hello." He was ensconced comfortably on one end of the couch, Taylor on the other end, legs tucked under her in her typical posture, sections of the day's *Oregonian* scattered between them—the newspaper their only concession to outdated technology. (Joel refused to read the paper on his tablet, which Chris thought was weird). A carafe of coffee on the table.

A male voice asked, "Joel Holden?"

Ah, Reed Allison. He recognized his old friend's voice immediately. "Yes, Mr. Allison, it is," he said, finding it difficult to remember to address him so formally.

Taylor set down the sports section and raised her eyebrows at him expectantly. There could be only one reason for this call: the DNA test results proved he was Chris's son. He'd mentally visualized this moment for the past several days, the test results representing more than just access to his assets. They would validate his identity. An identical match proved he was Chris. A close but not identical match would prove he was related. Would they look that closely? If they were identical, no one would believe he was Chris. Would they? Interesting dilemma.

A feeling of weightlessness blew through his gut. He licked his lips.

"I was presented with the results of the DNA analysis a few minutes ago," the attorney said crisply.

He waited, but Reed didn't continue. Joel smiled. Reed had a tendency toward the dramatic, so this could only mean one thing: it proved his identity.

"And the results are?" he asked, playing Reed's little game.

"They confirm you are related to Chris Holden. Given our interview last week, I can reasonably and legally conclude that you are Joel Holden."

He gave a silent sigh of relief. Now he could pursue Joel's dream. On the other hand, it bugged the hell out of him not being able to understand how he ended up in Joel's body. And that was extremely unsettling. How long would this situation last? Simply put: without knowing how this happened, he had no idea if it might come crashing down on him in the next minute, leaving him…where? Another good question. Was this life? When it ended, would he die? Or did we keep coming back until we got "it" right, whatever "it" was?

"That's good news," he told Reed. "Thanks."

"It's a comfort to know that legally this makes several issues easier for us to handle." Reed's voice now carried the friendly tone familiar to Chris. "But there is one wrinkle. As I mentioned during our visit, according to the law you are dead. Before you are allowed to receive any moneys from the estate, I—assuming you want me to continue as your lawyer—will have to petition the court to reverse that ruling. Given the test results and your story, that should not be a problem. It occurs. In fact, these cases happen more than you might think. Someone goes missing only to show up years later. But the process will require some time. Having said all that, personally I remain extremely upset over the effect your shenanigans had on your father's emotional well-being. On the other hand, Betty Ann and I admit to being pleased in the knowledge that a part of Chris lives on. I want to see you live up to that promise you made during your recent visit to my office."

"Believe me, I will."

"Oh, one more thing before we hang up."

There's always one more thing. "Yes?"

"The funeral home needs guidance as to how you wish to dispose of the body."

Easy answer. "Unless Dad gave you different instructions, he wanted an open-casket funeral followed by cremation. Bonney Watson was his choice of morticians."

"Exactly." Reed seemed impressed by Joel's intimate knowledge of his father's wishes in this arena. Too many families never discuss this topic, for some reason figuring it's a taboo subject, something that will bring bad luck.

Well, hell, I should know his wishes.

"Since you've already talked with them, would you be kind enough to call and make the arrangements for me? I understand you're busy, but it would help me tremendously if you'd do me that favor."

"I am delighted to help out. I'll arrange for the service to be held at the end of this week if that meets with your approval."

"Thanks so much." He made a mental note to buy Reed a bottle of his favorite twenty-five-year-old Macallan as a thank you.

Today was Monday. The weekend had been spent planning his Chez Pierre "exit strategy." In truth, ninety percent of the planning had been done during the return trip from Seattle. Most important was to not leave any ill feelings in Portland. In the restaurant business it wasn't unusual for cooks to walk off the job at a moment's notice. Or just not show up. Being considerate enough to hand in a two-week notice very seldom happened. But the good thing was that because of being home to an excellent cooking school, Portland overflowed with potential replacements. For Chez Pierre, the loss of Joel Holden would be a simple inconvenience instead of a hardship.

Reed said, "Is there anything else or are we squared away for now?"

"One more thing. I plan to move into the condo when I come back for the funeral. You see any problem with that?"

Reed hesitated a few seconds. "Nothing I can think of. I will notify the manager to expect you. Oh yes...I left my set of keys with him. But until we formally resolve your legal status, you may not sell any of your father's belongings or place the apartment on the market."

Sell it? Hardly. *I love the place.* After all, he designed it. "Thanks for the warning, but I intend to live there."

"That's what I expected, but it is my responsibility to make this point absolutely clear."

One of Reed's strong points, checking every little detail off the list.

"Thanks. You have. I'll contact you soon as I move in. Oh, and about what you said a moment ago, about upsetting Dad? I want to try to smooth over any hard feeling you have toward me. You were his best friend. I hope we can get together and share a bit of scotch, perhaps develop our own friendship. I want to hear what kind of a man Dad was, from your perspective. Talking with you might help me to connect back to him." Over the weekend, the reality of hanging with only twenty-two year olds had begun to sink in. Yes, he loved Taylor dearly, but he also longed for the companionship of older people. In particular his lifelong friend. Thank God Taylor didn't talk with the high, adolescent, nasal voice so many of the twenty-something girls used now. He didn't understand this affectation. Just like he didn't understand the easily recognizable universal tone some gays fostered.

It was one thing to sit in Starbucks and watch a group of twenty-year-olds interact. Quite another to actually try to fit in when your cultural frame of reference was at least one, possibly two, generations removed. Rap served as a good example. He couldn't get into it, yet Joel's tablet was crammed with it. Taylor's too.

And the differences went further than music. Tastes in movies, topics of conversation, historical perspectives on politics. Taylor's generation knew little of the Vietnam War or the first Desert Storm. On and on. It shocked him to realize just how far removed he was from Joel's generation.

Taylor folded the sports section, dropped it in the pile between them. "You're moving back to Seattle? This week?" She made it sound like a revelation. They'd only discussed this, what, maybe fifty times?

He leaned over, refilled both coffee mugs. "You sound surprised."

She flashed thin-lipped irritation, arms folded. "I *am* surprised. Okay, sure, we talked about the possibility, but giving notice and leaving in the next couple days? It just feels like rushing things a bit. Maybe too fast for me. Besides, if you expect me to join you, we need to clarify a few things."

Uh oh.

Until Chris's coronaries congealed into ropes of cholesterol plaque and clot, Joel's relationship with Taylor had been drifting along in a steady state. Like a carefully balanced chemical reaction, it would remain in that state until some perturbation triggered a change, causing the ingredients to form very different bonds. Truth was, a change in Joel happened the moment Chris's mind entered his body. He and Taylor both knew it. The difference was that she sensed it without even the remotest clue as to what had happened.

She jabbed a thumb at her chest. "What about me? Us? All the plans we've discussed about *our* restaurant?"

He brushed the newspapers off the couch, drew her close, and hugged her. "I'm surprised you have to bring that up. You and me, we'll do this together."

She pushed away from him. "That's not what I mean and you know it." She slid off the couch and walked to the window, keeping her back to him and her arms folded. "What about *us?*"

The inevitable question. The inevitable need for commitment

to ensure the relationship. She was right—things couldn't continue in limbo. They both knew their relationship had just reached a critical crossroads. Now what?

Two weeks ago he might've proposed, knowing she wanted to marry him. But in reality they'd never discussed some big-ticket issues like having kids. Did she want to? If so, when? Now or wait a few years? For Joel, these questions really didn't matter. He'd greet each day as it came. But Chris approached life entirely differently, planning for the future and sticking with it unless faced with a compelling reason to do things differently. But now? Kids? Been there, done that. Right now his most important priority for Chris was to fulfill Joel's dream and, in the process, live life differently than before. So yeah, maybe a few dynamics of their relationship had changed. Big ones too. Regardless, he wanted her with him.

He asked her, "You mean something more permanent? Like marriage?"

She must have read a message in that, perhaps subtle body language or a tone, because her eyes riveted to his. "No, not that."

Liar. "If not that, what?"

She threw up her hands and turned away. "I don't know."

He walked over to her and took her hand in his. "You don't know? Sweetie, one of the most important things in a relationship is communication. Being able to tell your mate what's on your mind, good or bad. You're a great communicator. Saying *I don't know* isn't you. Something's wrong. Tell me what it is."

"I'll tell you." She spun around to face him again. "Ever since your dad died you're a different person. It affects you more than you realize. You've changed. You know it too. And this change is forcing both of us to reevaluate what we are together, as a couple. On the one hand I don't want to lose you. On the other, I'm not sure I want to give up everything here in Portland to run off with someone I don't feel I know anymore. That may sound crazy, but it's what I feel,"—she thumbed her chest—"deep down in here. Can you understand what I'm saying?"

He moved closer and tried to wrap his arms around her, but she pushed away. "No. Don't treat me like that. As long as the subject's come up—and I'm glad it has—we need to discuss it."

He returned to the couch and settled back in, wrestling with the appropriate words. There had to be a way to let her know that even though he was a different man, he loved her. If anything had changed, the intensity of his love had increased.

"You're right about several things. I am different. But to me, the difference is positive. Maybe that makes it hard for you to decide about moving to Seattle, but why not at least give it a try? A couple months. Things don't work out, come back to Portland. You'd have no problem getting your job back. And think about the up-side of coming—we get a shot at fulfilling our dream. Isn't that worth a gamble?"

She sat on the couch looking at the wall, saying nothing. Finally, "I don't know. What I *do* know is that I'm not going to be able to make up my mind before you're out of here. Can you accept that?"

"Do I have a choice?"

She shook her head. "No."

The both laughed. Which made him feel good.

He *had* to move forward. Waiting for her to make a decision served no purpose. Right now the most important thing in his life—even more important than Taylor—was to turn Joel's life around. It killed him that Joel was still dealing drugs. That needed to change. So maybe spending a few days, weeks, or months away from Taylor might not be a bad thing. She would either eventually come around or she wouldn't. With all his heart, he wanted her to come with him, but his love for Joel trumped that. And, in the end, if she didn't join his restaurant venture it would mean only one thing—they weren't meant to be a couple. And this logic amazed him. It seemed so...mature.

He shrugged. "In that case, I guess I have to. But you realize that no matter what, I'll be leaving Thursday. Understood?"

101

She nodded, asked, "So what happens now? To us."

"Nothing. Except I'll be in Seattle working."

She nodded. "The restaurant thing, okay, I understand you wanting to do that. I do too. But the thing I don't get is why the hurry? Sure, there's the funeral, but just take a day or so off and then come back. Why pick up and move now?"

He wanted her to understand this. "Look, this is more than just the restaurant. It's about a total change. I need to get my life back on track in several ways. The drugs, for one."

"Really?" Her eye brightened hopefully.

Drugs: a big bone of contention between them. She used alcohol and caffeine but nothing more. She didn't approve of him using or of him and Luther selling product to other restaurant workers at several Portland hot spots. They'd argued about it countless times.

"Really."

She hugged him tightly. "That makes a huge difference. A huge difference. But I'm still not ready to decide."

"I know that." He guided her into the bedroom.

14

CHEZ PIERRE, LATER THAT DAY

The entire crew—line cooks, dishwashers, waiters and runners—were scattered around the kitchen listening to the chef spew his daily pep talk and update before they opened for the day. Joel stood over by the dishwashers and Taylor on the opposite side of the room, neither one making eye contact with the other. Earlier, they'd gone to bed, but Joel wasn't in the mood for sex. They hadn't really talked much since, both of them trapped in their own thoughts of adjustment. They moved around the apartment not exactly ignoring each other while at the same time not chatting as they usually would. Joel dressed early and left the apartment in time to catch the bus, giving Taylor the car and a few extra minutes to get ready. Besides, he wanted as few distractions as possible to think about all the issues buzzing around in his brain. Like trying to make sense out of the betrayal he felt because Taylor didn't jump at the chance to actualize their dream.

Although intellectually he understood her reasons, emotionally they were hard to accept. More than that, suspicions began to form. Were things not good between them? Had something happened that he was unaware of? He'd heard of guys caught completely off guard, coming home to find their wife or girlfriend gone and a note on the kitchen table. Was this her way of dumping him? Even though he believed she'd be straight up with him on something that important, he couldn't help but wonder.

Okay, even if they weren't going to stay together as a couple, she still shared the dream. Why not grab the opportunity?

It dawned on him: she didn't have any money. Meaning, if she wasn't part of him as a couple, the place would be his, leaving her as only an employee. That made sense, but still...

It'd be a great opportunity. She'd have free rein in managing the bar. Which would mean ordering and buying all the wine and liquor. He would oversee the kitchen, organize the menu, order everything else. The responsibility for running the place would be equally divided. What was not to like?

Stealing a glance at her, he caught her looking at him. He smiled before he realized what he was doing.

Just then, the chef finished up with, "Any questions?"

There was that moment when everyone glanced around, looking for someone else to raise a hand or speak out. No one. So the group broke up, everyone heading to their respective jobs, making final preparations before the manager unlocked the deadbolt, officially opening the doors to the happy-hour trade.

He caught the chef's eye. "Have a moment?"

The chef folded up his half-height reading glasses to slip into his breast pocket. "Sure. What's up?"

Sucking a deep breath, he thought: *this is it, the start of everything.* "I'm giving notice."

The chef did a double take. "Notice? As in, leaving notice?" From the look on his face, it was clear what the chef was thinking. Of all the Portland restaurants, this was the best one for building a name. And he had voiced suspicions during the hiring interview that this was Joel's primary goal for working there. But even if Joel suffered from delusions of grandeur, it would be premature for him to leave now. His reputation needed to build for a couple more years, at least, to reach the status Joel sought.

Serve your time in the minors before getting called up to the Yankees.

Even then, only a few actually continue on to become stars.

"Yes," Joel said with sincere regret. His time spent in this kitchen had been extremely productive, teaching him more than cooking school. Some days he felt almost guilty for being paid to learn so much.

The chef's expression softened from shock to sympathy.

"This have anything to do with your father? Hey, you need a few days off, I'll be—"

Joel waved off the suggestion. "No. Thanks. It's not that. Well, not directly, it isn't. I decided to move back to Seattle."

"Oh."

The chef nodded as if he understood, which Joel was sure wasn't the case at all.

The chef said, "So what are we talking, two weeks?

Now came the hard part. Letting down a man he respected and admired. "No. I won't be back after tonight."

Glancing around, probably mentally counting heads, the chef sighed. "Fuck me...man, that's going to leave me in a bind. You couldn't possibly wait until I line up a replacement, could you?"

He started to say okay. And really wanted to. But caught himself. Because he knew where this would lead. Likeable as the chef was, his biggest liability was procrastination. Two weeks from now, he'd be pleading for two more weeks. Same thing in another month, until one day Joel would realize that a half year had passed with nothing to show for it but more earnings on his W-2.

"Here's the deal, I'm sorry. I really am. I can't explain it to you, but there are things I have to do that need doing soon as possible. They can't wait."

Joel dropped eye contact and ran his hand through his hair as a way of avoiding the chef's eyes. No way in hell could he begin to explain the intensity of his obsession of fulfilling his dream. Hell, it was confusing to him in spite of living with it. Equal parts love and fear. Love for Joel. Fear of suddenly discovering that this new life was nothing more than a sick joke and that he really was dead. He needed to prove to himself he could take this through to completion and do a good job in the process. A goal Joel had never accomplished before. For if he did, it would be a tangible demonstration of truly changing his life.

The chef nodded again with obvious disappointment. "Out of curiosity, these plans of yours? They don't include another job up there, do they? Got another gig lined up?"

Rather than lie, Joel felt he owed him an explanation.

"No, nothing like that. It's a couple of things. For one, Dad's funeral is Friday. After that, I plan to stay there and open my own place." As a chef, his boss should understand. He hoped so.

He flashed Joel a bemused expression. "You talking what, a café, a little bistro?"

"No." What made him feel so apologetic? "I want to create a major statement. Like this." He gave a sweep of his hands.

But better.

The chef scoffed with an edge of superiority. "Really! You think you have enough experience to set up something like this?"

Well, hell, that was the question, wasn't it? "I better. I'll be gambling my own money." Soon as he heard those words fly from his mouth, his confidence sank. Other than to Taylor, this was the first time he'd actually confided his dream to anyone. It sounded, well, grandiose.

"You mean your inheritance?" The chef seemed to catch himself. "No offense, you understand. Just curious."

Joel felt his face redden. "This is getting way too personal. Are we done here?"

The chef slowly shook his head. "All I can say is good luck, man. I mean it. Putting something like this together is harder than you obviously think. Trust me."

He watched the chef who'd taught him so many cool tricks turn and walk away. And felt like a jerk for letting him down. But, he reminded himself, turnover was part of the business.

Well, that was over. And, it turned out to be just as difficult as he anticipated. But it was the first step, leaving him with a strange brew of elation and dread. He knew the statistics for restaurant start-ups: very much stacked against the entrepreneur. Ninety percent fail within the first year. Of the survivors, only a few make money, the average lucky to pull in maybe a ten-percent profit margin. Especially now, with the economy in the toilet, those dismal odds were probably optimistic.

And you had to know so freaking much: state health codes, labor law, accounting, locating and managing good suppliers. On and on and on.

But hell, wasn't that what this new life was all about? Taking a few chances? Might as well go for the gold.

"Dude, couldn't help but overhear your conversation."

Luther Rabb was standing next to him, smiling, shooting the sleeves of his white tuxedo shirt. Joel didn't notice him approach. African-American, 6'2", a beard cropped close like his hair, he filled out the tuxedo well. Handsome, with a deep resonant voice and a scary memory for people's names. Definitely one of Chez Pierre's assets.

Without thinking, Joel held out his fist and did the fist bump thing with him.

Luther asked, "Got a moment?"

"For you? Always. Out back?" he said, figuring Luther had a taste to start the night with.

He followed his good friend through the kitchen to the alley door, excited about having made the first move in changing Joel's life. His next move would be to tell Luther he intended to be clean from now on.

They stood in the alley door alcove, just enough room to stay dry in the light rain blackening the asphalt and enlarging puddles. Luther pulled a small baggie and tiny spoon from his tux, offered it to Joel.

He waved it away. "Pass."

Luther shrugged, started to open the bag. "What's this shit about you leaving?"

"I was going to mention it to you later. After closing when we're having a drink. But yeah, going to open my own place. Can you believe that shit?"

"Here in Portland?"

"Naw. Seattle."

"Here, hold this." He handed Joel the bag, plugged one nostril, inhaled a spoonful through his other. Held his head back, swallowed, cleared his throat. "Lord have fucking mercy. This is some righteously wicked shit. Sure you don't want a taste? Just a tad?"

He waved off the offer. "If I thought there'd be any chance of getting you on board, I'd offer you a job, but…"

Luther folded the bag and replaced it in his pocket. "But?"

"You got too much going here to start over. I'd love to have you along on this if you're willing."

"Dude! You and I's a team. You get a place for me, we'll talk. I'm always willing to talk."

"Yeah, so you say now. But first you need to know a few things. Most important, the rules gonna to be different there. I don't think you'll like them."

"Like?"

"No moving shit out of the place. Nothing at all."

Luther's eyes widened a bit. "Fuck! You serious?"

"Nothing personal, yo. It's that I'll be fronting the money. Every cent I own. I can't take a chance on losing it."

"And starting your own place ain't risky enough?"

"Different kind of risk. You know that."

Luther ran the back of his hand across his nostrils, sniffed again. "Still, what I say about us being a team's real. You serious about this place, you give me a call. Never hurts to talk. Feel me?"

15

DOWNTOWN SEATTLE, TWO DAYS LATER

Joel had the key halfway in the deadbolt when tightness encased his chest and a chill burrowed though his stomach. He slowly withdrew the key and stared at the four numbers on the door: 2101. They were small and silver; a classy font that he would never in a million years know the name for. The font was a minor, yet stunning, touch, contributed by some nameless perfectionist in the architectural firm that designed the building.

Another wave of apprehension washed over him.

For Christ's sake, this is my home. What's the problem?

He heard the click of a door open behind him. A male voice asked, "May I help you?"

He turned, saw his neighbor Maynard Wong slip on a navy blazer, apparently preparing to leave.

"You must be Mr. Wong." Joel walked over, hand out. "I'm Chris's son, Joel."

Wong was allegedly a wealthy businessman who'd immigrated from Hong Kong years ago. Far as he knew, Wong didn't really work, just seemed to hang around drinking coffee and reading the *New York Times* at the Starbucks down the block.

Wong shot him a questioning look before collecting himself and accepting the extended hand.

"Terrible news about your father." He nodded toward the

door to Chris's apartment. "You'll be putting the unit on the market, then?"

"No. Actually I'm moving in."

"Oh." Wong's face flushed with embarrassment. The obvious assumption being that a man Joel's age couldn't afford to live in such an upscale condominium. "Yes, of course. How silly of me."

"Don't worry. No loud parties, if that's your worry." Which he knew was Wong's hot button during association meetings, always complaining about the noise from directly overhead. "I'll be working too hard for that."

Relief flashed over Wong's face.

"Welcome to the building."

"Thank you."

"Well then, I must be going now." Wong stepped to the elevators.

Reluctantly, Joel opened the front door, still puzzled over the anxiousness chilling his gut. To his right, past a small coat closet, was a hall with a door to the guest bedroom—and beyond that the master bedroom and bath. To his left, the hall entered the living room. Dead ahead was the kitchen, dining area, and sliding doors to the balcony, the dining room contiguous with the living room.

Other than having slightly stale air from days of being shut up, the interior seemed untouched since the morning he walked out the door for his last hike, the day he died. He stopped to think about that a moment. Was his life now an afterlife? That was something to consider.

Chris had never been a "believer," totally disregarding the image of a bearded old man in a flowing white robe sitting on a throne passing judgment on people who lived life victimized by circumstance. He couldn't buy into the "life force" concept either. Too much science supported the expanding universe theory. But then again, he couldn't wrap his mind around the idea that every bit of matter came from one unitary chunk that, for some unknown reason, exploded to form the universe. Leaving him a skeptical agnostic. In other words, he never heard an explanation for "being" that made sense. It was, he supposed, this ambiguity that forced people to cling to religions filled with deities.

He wandered through the living room to the dining room. Out on the balcony the chaise he routinely sat in still had a slight cushion indentation from his evening hours of admiring the view with a scotch in hand. In the kitchen he rinsed a cereal bowl he'd left in the sink days ago and placed it in the full dishwasher, added soap, clicked the on switch. He remembered thinking about starting the washer before leaving for the hike but hadn't wanted to run when he wasn't home.

He opened the Sub-Zero and removed the carton of milk. Sour, of course. He dumped it down the drain. The rest of the food could be sorted out after putting away his Portland clothes. He leaned against the granite counter and glanced around as his earlier anxiety segued into an amorphous emptiness. Why? Well, for one thing, he still mourned his own death. Sure, he was now a younger, stronger man, but as his eyes wandered the apartment he'd so carefully put together, he couldn't help but miss his old life: the practice he'd worked so hard to develop, the pride his medical license instilled in him, his friends, the various little scars his past left on him.

And there was also Taylor. He missed her already. Missed her a lot, now that he thought about it. Her humor. The way she could weasel things out of him. Was it wrong to move back here alone? Was starting the restaurant more important than nurturing their relationship? Good question. And this singularity of drive was definitely Chris.

Confusing life's priorities had been the primary reason Chris messed up. Was he now making the same mistake? Was this a prime example of Reed's belief that we're held hostage by our personalities?

Then again, who was to say Chris's prior decisions were mistakes? Even with the help of a retrospectoscope, there was no way of knowing. At the time, his choices felt right. Maybe they were. Maybe not. But this time around, fifty-five years of life experience was giving him a much different perspective, allowing him to explore other options. He should welcome the opportunity to live a different lifestyle, even if doing so produced some anxiety. It was probably normal that it might.

After the funeral, should he head straight back to Portland and Taylor and abandon this Don Quixote dream of starting his own restaurant? What would Chris have done? He wasn't sure.

Damn, how confusing. How do you do things differently if you're not sure what you would've done in the first place? Living now, with Chris's life experience, was totally fucking up his perspective, especially as the delineation between Chris and Joel blurred.

He meandered around the fifteen-hundred square-foot apartment with a bizarre mixture of familiarity and first impressions. He loved this place. Contemporary, sleek, exactly his taste. But why shouldn't he love it? He was the one who put it together. He'd love living here again as a touchstone of his past. Taylor would love it too. And he knew that Joel loved it. So why not stay the course and work on convincing Taylor to join him?

Back down in the garage he loaded one of the rolling carts with clothes from the Hertz rental he'd driven up from Portland. Having Chris's Benz allowed him to let Taylor keep their beat-up Toyota. Hopefully by working downtown—if he was lucky enough to find a space in the neighborhood—a car would seldom be a routine necessary. Certainly, not like in Portland.

After making room in the walk-in closet for his clothes, he sorted through Chris's things, selected his favorite suit, and tried it on. A little roomier in the waist and chest, but a good tailor could easily alter it. Most of the other clothes could also be used, although they were a bit stodgy for his present tastes. Sorting them out would be a good job for another day.

He brought only essentials from Portland: iPhone, laptop, tablet, and toiletries. He left Taylor everything else. Didn't want any of it: second-hand furniture, mismatched dishes, all the kitchen crap. He'd miss the espresso machine, but the one here was pretty good.

Could Taylor afford to live alone in the apartment after three years of sharing expenses? If not, she'd probably find a roommate. Female, hopefully. The thought of a male living with her, platonic or otherwise, brought him down, made him jealous.

He checked his watch. Time for a beer. Damn, the Sub-Zero didn't have any.

No, of course not. Chris didn't drink beer.

He poured a glass of ice water and took it out to the balcony to settle onto his chaise for a few minutes, admire his beloved view, and reflect on Joel's life. In particular, the hours surrounding the avalanche with its bitter irony: walking away to start life anew. This also was a fresh start. How many people had two chances to start over? Very few.

Okay, so much for reflecting. There was work to do. Better get moving.

Back in the kitchen he did a quick inventory. The perishables in the fridge had done just that—perished. So, he bagged and tossed them down the garbage chute. He jotted down a list of items to pick up at Whole Foods for the next few days. More extensive shopping could come at another time.

Shopping done, the condo back in order, he wandered the streets as he had during the last visit, getting a better feel for the Belltown neighborhood. Chris never walked downtown like this. Always too busy driving to and from the hospital, seeing friends, meeting someone at a restaurant, or making a quick run to Macy's for something. Never took the time to just explore his hood and check out the myriad shops.

Amazing places, some of them, mostly unnoticed by Chris. A store filled with used CDs. A pet store. A bike shop. Vintage dresses. And a ton of suspiciously similar small convenience stores with barred windows, narrow aisles, lotto ticket readers, beverage coolers, and at least one ceiling-mounted security camera behind the counter. How they all survived selling identical merchandise was one of life's mysteries.

Well, this part of town was dense with high-rise condominiums, making it a perfect place to launch his dream.

And the density of people benefitted him with anonymity, lessening the chance of running into someone from Ortega's crew. Then again, Seattle was big and this neighborhood wasn't close to Ortega's operation. Besides, time dulled memories, so maybe he'd be just fine here. No need to routinely glance over his shoulder here. Still...

He stopped in at Mamma's Mexican Kitchen for dinner, one of the few remaining bargains in the area. He downed a black bean burrito with guacamole and sour cream before heading home, happy with how the day had gone.

Kicking back on the chaise, he soaked in the view. He found it strangely comforting to know which windows would be glowing this time of evening, which flat-screen TVs were big enough to see, to hear the familiar ebb and flow of traffic, the occasional blast of a ferry at the dock, and to smell the crisp saltwater air. Although comforting, they also underscored one harsh reality: his death had absolutely no effect on the rhythm of the world. Not that he had ever expected it would. Still, the thought became sobering. Did it mean his life had been useless? The world skipped a beat for the death of one of its leaders, but didn't miss a beat when a commoner shuffled off.

He hated to think Chris's life had been meaningless and wanted to believe his skills as a highly competent cardiologist had benefited numerous patients.

Or had the negatives of his life outweighed the good?

Joel, for example. He'd raised a drug dealer. How good was that?

And as much as he despised Jan, what role did he play in how she turned out?

Oh, man, I need a drink.

He pushed off the chaise and headed for the kitchen.

Tumbler of scotch in one hand, portable phone in the other, he returned to the chaise, took a moment to organize his thoughts and rehearse his lines, took a sip, then dialed Taylor's cell. She typically kept it muted during work so he figured on leaving a message.

Correct. It rang through to the recording.

He started to say something but somehow, what he wanted to say just shouldn't be left in voicemail.

He dialed Chez Pierre and asked for her even though he knew she'd have little time to chat. He didn't need much time for what he wanted to say.

"Hello?"

"It's me, I'm at the condo. I know you're busy, so I'll make this short. Just one question."

"What?"

His fingers were tingling, his heart skipping with nervous apprehension. He closed his eyes. "What can I say to persuade you to come up here and help me start Orcas?"

"Orcas?"

"Yes. That's the name I came up with. What do you think?"

She laughed. "About the name or your question?"

"Both."

"Aw man...look, it's nuts here. It's impossible to think about

115

anything right now except getting out this next order. Let me call you when I get back to the apartment. We can talk then. You okay with that?"

"I'll wait up for your call."

16

The alarm went off at 1:00 am.

He splashed cold water over his face, toweled off, grabbed the portable phone and padded into the living room to sit on the couch facing the view straight down First Avenue from twenty-one floors up. There was a surprising amount of traffic this time of night.

Seven minutes later, the phone rang. Right about when he suspected it might.

"Taylor?"

"Orcas?" she said. "How'd you ever come up with a name like that?"

Did that sound like approval? Sort of. Regardless, it was wonderful to hear her voice.

"I wanted something Northwest and simple. It seems to fit. You like it?" Nervousness began building inside him.

"Strangely enough, I do. It's just, like, not what I expected from you."

"And that would be?"

"I'm not sure. It's just that Orcas never would've come to mind. But now that you mention it, it's cool."

Enough skirting the issue. He wanted to know where she stood on *them*. "Glad you like it, but that's not really what I want to know. Where do we stand on you moving up here?"

"Aw, jeez...after you called, that's all I could think about. It's lucky it wasn't a *really* busy night, or I would've been totally hosed."

"So?"

She giggled.

"Here's the problem" she said. "I can't decide. And this isn't a decision I can make right this minute on the phone. I love that you called to ask. I mean, I wasn't sure what you wanted. I thought maybe you were doing this restaurant thing as an excuse to get rid of me."

His heart sank. Get rid of her? What had he done to make her think that?

"Oh, Taylor, nothing like that."

"Anyway, here's the deal. I'll decide soon, but the commitment thing is no longer part of the deal. I either come or I won't. If I do, it's without any expectation of attachments. You okay with that?"

"No. That's one of the things I wanted to say. I want you up here with me. That means I want us to have more commitment. Let's get married." There, it was, he'd gone ahead and asked The Question.

She sighed. "No, that's not part of it anymore. You made me realize that the last time we had this discussion. If I come, let's just see what happens to us. Simple enough."

He didn't understand. There was a time when she'd subtly pushed for more commitment. "What's changed?"

"Oh, sweetie, we've been through this. You have, Joel."

True. He had. In more ways than she realized, because he hadn't told her the truth.

A thousand things zipped through his mind, none of them the right one to say. He opted for, "So, what do we do now?"

"Keep on keeping on. That's all we can do. I'll let you know soon as I sort this all out." She gave another quick laugh. "Believe me, I want an answer just as much as you do."

How disappointing. Especially after getting his hopes up. Still, it was comforting to hear her voice.

"All right, then. I'll wait for your call."

She said, "Good night. I love you."

Her words felt good, giving him hope that she'd come to Seattle.

"Love you."

He dropped the phone back into the charger, returned to the bedroom, slipped between cold sheets, his warm spot long gone.

Taylor—what if she didn't come?

Well, he could always move back to Portland.

No, not really. Not if what she'd said was true, that the change in him was the sole reason for the change in their relationship. That'd remain the same regardless of which city he lived in. He'd never be the Joel he was before Chris entered his body.

Meaning there was probably little he could do to influence her decision. And he really shouldn't try to force it.

He was struck by the irony. His fifty-five years of experience weren't much help to him now, other than to give him enough patience to wait for her decision. Thirty years ago he might have tried to intervene, to force and sway her decision. And more than likely, that would've worked against him.

He turned over on his side and tried to relax. But couldn't stop thinking of Taylor.

17

Joel was just about to leave the condo when the phone rang. He immediately thought of Taylor. Could she have reached a decision so soon? If so, it could only be bad news. It rang again.

Can't just ignore it. Answer the damned thing.

As he picked up, his breath caught. "Hello?"

"Mr. Holden?"

A female voice. One he didn't recognize. What a relief. In a way. He started to say yes, thought, *hold on, does she mean Chris?* "Yes, but which Mr. Holden do you want?"

"I'm calling for Mr. Joel Holden."

"Okay, that's me."

"This is Cyndy Nguen at Bonney Watson funeral home. I need for you to drop by whatever clothes you want Christopher to wear during the viewing and funeral. Preferably today. Tomorrow morning at the very latest. Is today convenient?"

Conversation finished, he disconnected the call but remained at the kitchen counter holding the phone, thinking, go ahead, call now, make an appointment. It's probably going to take a couple weeks before he could get in anyway.

He got the number from his laptop, jotted it on a piece of junk mail from the stack next to the phone, dialed while wandering into the living room.

"Doctor's office."

He stood at the floor-to-ceiling window, peering down on

First Avenue. "I need an appointment with Dr. Holmes." He wanted to add "as soon as possible," but didn't. Instead, he gazed at the view south toward Qwest and Safeco Fields. He loved this perspective. It had been a strong selling point the first time he entered the unit.

"Are you a patient of his?"

"No."

"Has doctor seen you previously in consultation?"

"No."

"Is this an emergency?"

"No, not really, but I'd like the earliest available opening. My schedule is extremely flexible, so I can be there any time." Which, being unemployed, would be easy.

In the background he could hear the clickity click of a keyboard and figured he was talking with an answering service remote from Holmes's office. Like most shrinks, his staffing requirements were minimal with no front desk other than a white-noise maker to keep waiting patients from hearing what was being said in the doctor's office.

"May I ask what this is concerning?"

Yeah, delusions of reincarnation.

"I need help dealing with my father's death." Well, sort of. And it sounded better than the first option.

"Oh, I'm sorry to hear that. We have an opening at three o'clock this coming Monday. Will that work for you?"

Great. Sooner than he'd expected. "I'll take it."

"Is another doctor referring you? Are there records we should request?"

"No. I'm referring myself."

"Please arrive at the office fifteen minutes before your appointment to complete the paperwork and insurance forms. And don't forget to bring your insurance card."

Of course.

Aw shit, do I even have insurance? Have to think about that.

Allen Wyler

BONNEY-WATSON FUNERAL HOME

The instant the heavy glass front doors closed, the outside noise from buses, trucks, and cars descended into heavy stillness, encasing him like a tomb. He glanced around the deserted lobby. Not another soul in sight. He saw an interior of muted colors, soft lighting, and plush sound-attenuating carpet. The air was scented from lilies. Giving him the same creepy feeling the echoing shadowy cathedrals of Europe had years ago.

A bald middle-aged man with a pinched face and rimless glasses materialized from nowhere. His smile—probably intended to be comfortingly empathetic yet professionally serious—seemed overly practiced and insincere.

"May I help you?" he asked, hands clasped at mid-chest, which only added to a Bela Lugosi ghoul effect. His pale forehead glistened in the soft light.

"Here." Joel handed him a hanger with his charcoal pinstriped suit, white shirt, and anthracite tie. "I'm Christopher Holden's son. His viewing is tomorrow. Ms. Nguyen asked me to bring these for him."

"Oh yes, of course." He took them from him.

Silence.

The man cleared his throat. "Thank you."

More silence.

Joel asked, "May I see him?"

The man pursed his lips a moment. "Of course, but you see, he's not dressed or prepared for viewing. It might leave you with a better memory if you wait until after he's been made a bit more presentable. Perhaps, the public viewing?"

"If I can, I'd like to see him now." A public viewing wouldn't provide the privacy he wanted.

"I'll be right outside the door." The mortician shuffled from the room, softly shutting the door, leaving a silence even weightier than

122

the lobby.

Chris's naked body lay supine on a stainless steel shelf pulled from a refrigerated locker. Joel stood back to look at his body. And found it difficult to comprehend what he was seeing, to objectively recognize himself lying there. Days ago that had been *him*. Now, instead of intimately familiar, the body seemed alien, as if it were a perfectly crafted wax model. His face looked as it had from years of seeing it in mirrors and photographs, yet seemed a bit too small. But still…was that really him?

He walked around the gurney, studying the corpse's face from one angle, then the next, fascinated with seeing himself from the perspective of outside his own body, as others saw him in 3 dimensions. It was weirdly fascinating.

His body appeared at peace. Or was it just because his face lacked the minor tension of dozens of muscles that never really relaxed? Interesting question.

Regardless, it made him wonder what death was like. Not the act of dying, but the actual physical state of being dead. Nothingness, probably, like the state he experienced five years ago while under general anesthesia for a hernia repair. In the first seconds do you become aware of having no heart beat, the sensation so familiar that it becomes noticeable only when absent? Of course not, he reminded himself. Consciousness requires a certain core of very primitive brainstem activity, and it's only after that mass of neurons permanently ceases to function that we die. He'd always scoffed at the belief that death was, instead, determined by a lack of a heart beat. It was still a debated concept for some people, one that some still didn't accept and, in turn, subjected severely brain-damaged victims to meaningless existences on ventilators solely to keep their hearts beating. Karen Ann Quinlan had served as a prime example.

He didn't believe in an afterlife or that a soul levitated from the dying body to float through the universe or ascend to some magical place called heaven. Yet there was an inexplicable peaceful aura to his face that he found unnervingly appealing. So peaceful, in fact, it beckoned him.

His reason for this time alone with his body now seemed pointless. And for a moment the Chris part of him vanished, leaving only Joel looking at Dad. Then it hit: *I'm looking at the body of the man who had brought me into life. He's gone forever.* Cold emptiness filled his chest. He felt alone and abandoned. He had to remind himself that he was the one who deserted his father, and for the first time understood Reed's admonishment.

Although he had chosen to spend the past five years away from Chris, a part of him knew that no matter what, Dad had always been there for him. That he could explain what happened and, in return, receive love, understanding, and forgiveness. That unconscious emotional backstop was now gone forever and he was on his own. He missed Chris terribly.

Joel leaned down and whispered, "I don't know how this happened, but I'm going to make the most of it. I'll make you happy. I swear to God I will."

18

FRIDAY, BONNEY-WATSON FUNERAL HOME

Joel pushed up from the hard oak pew into the aisle and made his way slowly to the podium.

So far he'd been unable to decide what to say, much less how to say it. But time had run out. He figured, what did it matter anyway? Screw up and they'll chalk it off to a grieving son. Pull it off and you're a good eulogizer. And, by the way, what are the rules for giving your own eulogy? He smiled at that conundrum.

He glanced at the open coffin and realized that he still wasn't completely emotionally recovered from his episode the other day when viewing the body.

Chris was stretched out in the coffin, hands crossed on his chest, impeccably groomed and at peace. Regardless of the mortician's skill, no amount of make-up could hide that pasty hue of death. On the other hand, he loved that suit and tie combination. Always looked good, even under the present circumstances. He'd bought it two years ago at the Nordstrom yearly sale.

He turned to scan the crowd and was deeply touched by the turnout. Bigger than he would've expected. Mostly colleagues from the hospital and his practice. He didn't have a huge number of close friends. People he liked, he saw frequently. Those he cared less for, well, he didn't socialize with much. His rationalization was that his practice was so exhausting that on his nights off call he preferred to kick back with a bowl of popcorn and a good movie.

His gaze stopped at Reed Allison. With a stiff-upper-lip-be-brave smile, Reed nodded for him to begin. Strange, that one small movement gave him a feeling of their old connectedness and that pleased him.

Across the aisle from Reed sat Janice, drilling him with her characteristic stern-faced look of disapproval. Jesus, she never disappointed. Nor did she ever give up. He half expected her to stand, point an accusing finger at him and inform the group of what a bastard of a son he'd been.

He cleared his throat. "Without Mr. Allison's kind introduction, I'm sure most of you wouldn't know I'm Chris's son. And those of you who do know about me believe I was killed five years ago in an avalanche." The emotions he'd experienced during his private viewing began creeping back, making it difficult to keep his voice from cracking. *Come on, don't lose it.*

"Today is about Chris, not me, so why do I bring this up? Because I feel I owe it to him to publicly apologize. So bear with me, please."

He paused to clear his throat again and rein in his composure.

"The day I disappeared I was snowshoeing with a friend. We were stupid enough to be traversing a known avalanche area. So what happened? An avalanche, of course."

He tried to ignore his misting eyes and to hold his emotions in check.

"I was lucky. It missed me. My friend wasn't so lucky. Afterwards, when I tried to climb down to where he was buried, the snow started shifting and I couldn't risk another slide. A person buried like that has only seconds to live. You're either saved or suffocate. Matt died because I was too frightened to risk my life for him.

"I stood there humiliated at not being able to do anything. And because of this, I didn't want to face anyone. Especially Dad. So what did I do? I turned and walked off the mountain and deceived everyone who loved me. Especially Dad."

Well, partly true. Sure as hell wasn't going to mention Ortega and Delgado.

He looked at the open coffin and addressed Chris with, "I realize now that my reasons for deceiving you were completely selfish."

Emotion overwhelmed him and fighting it only made it worse. He wanted forgiveness for hurting him. The only way to obtain it would be through confession. To Reed, to his father's associates, even to that bitch, Janice.

"All you ever wanted for me was what any parent wants for his son. A safe, secure life that was better than your own. What breaks my heart is that you died with the belief that I was dead. With all of you as my witness, I ask for your forgiveness."

He swallowed hard. What he was doing made no sense, especially now that he understood both sides of the story. But he also knew firsthand the pain his actions had inflicted.

He sat in the pew staring at his hands clamped between his knees as the service continued around him. He should've prepared something witty, something to reveal a side of Chris that friends and associates would find endearing or special or enlightening. But hard as he'd tried, nothing had come to mind. So instead, he'd blathered on about personal issues. Which ended up becoming an embarrassing emotional meltdown. Jesus, how inappropriate. He felt like a total shit.

Worse, Janice's eyes continued lazing a path across the aisle, burning a hole in his shoulder. He knew damned well what was coming. She'd wait for the church to clear before blasting him with a few heavy-duty verbal shots. What the hell, she'd been the problem in the marriage, so why expect anything different now?

Eleven-oh-three pm, dog-tired from sweating through an operation—an emergency stent of a left coronary artery—he closes the front door to the apartment and wearily hangs his coat in the closet. The third night in a row of pulling call. Unusual, except that one of his partners is out of town on an emergency, so he's in the barrel.

"Well, hello sailor, want a drink?"

In the bedroom doorway, Janice strikes a provocative pose wearing only a lacy baby doll halter, one he's never seen before, but hey, she has several.

She says, "Go take a shower and while you freshen up, I'll pour you a scotch."

Not exactly what he had in mind for tonight. Or any other night, for that matter. Not after his discussions with Reed about moving ahead with the divorce. Why he's waited this long to do something about it is, well, symptomatic. And pathetic.

"Not tonight, Janice." *He starts toward the bedroom but she doesn't step aside.*

"No?" *She reaches down to fondle his crotch.*

He pulls her hand away. "I said not tonight."

Her lips get that little girl pouty look, her typical response when not getting her way. Her voice turns cold. "What's the matter, Limp Dick, need a Viagra?"

Although Reed advised him to wait a few more days before dropping The Bomb, this last comment brings to a boil two years of cumulative frustration and humiliation.

"Do you wear that for Richard?" *with a nod at her negligee.*

Obviously shocked, she's quick to recover. "Richard?" *Her tone all innocent.*

"You remember. My partner? The one I'm taking calls for?" *His anger is fully erupting now.* "I mean, why couldn't you show me some respect, like you did with the other ones you were fucking? Why did you have to do one of my partners?"

He'd tried to understand the cause for infidelity, but she'd never given any reason other than the lame excuse that he spent too much time at work, leaving her alone. As if that justified trampling their marriage vows. The way he saw it, the world was filled with hard-working people whose spouses remain faithful. So, he didn't buy that one. Instead, he suspected it was an insatiable need for attention, to be sexy and wanted, adored and idolized.

128

He'd seen pictures of her as a child, her father's "princess."

Attracting attention had always come easy for her. Stunningly beautiful with a body one notch up from anorexic, she was a magnet for jealous appraisals from females and sexually hungry stares from males. An asset or liability, depending on your point of view. As far as their marriage went, it had been an obvious destructive force.

Joel stood at the doorway, shaking hands, thanking people for coming, when he noticed Taylor off to the side of the vestibule, hanging back. She looked more attractive than usual, dressed appropriately in a simple black suit he couldn't remember seeing before. He hadn't expected her to attend the funeral nor had he noticed her during his disastrous podium breakdown. Then again, he hadn't scrutinized the crowd in any detail while at the podium. She must've been sitting in the back.

Reed and Betty Ann Allison also lingered, allowing others go ahead of them, and, just as predicted, The Bitch was doing likewise.

Soon only the five of them remained; the Allisons, Janice, Taylor, and himself. He held up a just-a-minute finger for Reed, went to Taylor and hugged her. He savored the familiar feel of her in his arms and missed her even more.

"Thanks for coming," he said, not quite sure what her presence meant. Was she making an appearance out of respect or did she reach a decision she preferred to not discuss on the phone?

He introduced Taylor to Reed and Betty Ann, then asked Reed, "You two have time to for a latte? There's a Starbucks on the next block." Hoping to keep them here to buffer his impending encounter with Janice. She still waited her turn to speak to him, just off to his right, her rattler shaking.

Reed shook his head, cast a quick wary glance in Janice's direction. "Thanks, but I have to get back to the office. We'll take a rain check, though."

Shit, totally fucked. Joel said, "I understand."

Betty Ann expressed perfunctory condolences, leaving him

with the distinct impression she still hadn't quite forgiven him for his vanishing act. The Allisons walked out, leaving him with Taylor and Janice.

"Are you ignoring me?" his stepmother asked.

As a matter of fact, yes.

"Just saving the best for last, Mother Dearest. Taylor, this is Janice, my stepmother whom you've heard so much about." No shit.

And, of course, Janice recognized sarcasm when she heard it.

"Nobody likes a smart-ass, Joel."

Taylor started for the door, "I'll wait outside," she said, leaving them alone.

From one corner of his mind a little voice whispered, *you want to do things differently this time around? Well, here's a perfect situation. You never could pass up a chance like this to be caustic; how about just letting it go? She's a bitter, self-centered woman. Knowing that should be enough for you, shouldn't it?*

He ignored that wisdom and said, "Your tone and body language say it all, Janice. You're pissed and looking for a fight. Why would I want to put up with that if I don't have to?"

She jammed her fists on her hips, elbows akimbo. Joel couldn't believe it. Choreographed and all.

"How do you expect me to feel after what you put your father and me through?"

C'mon, just walk away. It'll be a good test of character.

No, I have to deal with it.

"Oh please! What I put *you* through? You can't possibly be serious. My disappearance didn't affect you at all. I was something you had to endure to get close to Dad. The only thing you wanted from the relationship was to be the wife of a successful physician, to be able to play the Mrs. Doctor trump card. Raising a family was a nonexistent priority. I suspect that my no longer being underfoot was a godsend for you."

She stabbed a finger at him. "*That* kind of attitude is a perfect example of why there was so much friction between us. Okay, you made it quite clear you didn't care about the effect your actions had on *me*. That's understandable. But stop and think about how selfishly you hurt your father. You actions eventually resulted in our divorce. You never liked me. I can understand that. It's a common reaction children have toward stepmothers. But with you it was worse because you were so jealous of the time I spent with Chris. I loved him deeply and you destroyed our marriage, you self-centered little brat."

Joel let out a sarcastic laugh. "Oh, really? Then it had nothing to do with Don Tharp or Richard or the other guys you were fucking?"

She recoiled as if slapped in the face. A very specific clause in the divorce papers stated that only she, Chris, and their lawyers would be privy to information about her peccadilloes. It further stipulated that the pictures and other evidence accumulated by the private investigator be kept sealed.

Dark, raw anger painted her face. "Who told you that?"

"I know a lot about you, Janice, more than you think. So unless you want your new husband to learn about your dirty little secrets, GET THE FUCK out of my face."

Her cheeks and forehead turned an even darker crimson. "You have no idea what you're talking about."

"C'mon, Janice, get real. You weren't exactly discreet about it. It was—excuse the pun—a fucking joke. You saw the pictures the private investigator took. Besides, when it was going on, everyone knew. It started years before I disappeared. What was so humiliating was how long Dad put up with it." He turned to go find Taylor.

Furious, Janice wagged that finger at him. "Believe me, you little shit, you'll regret this."

Her tone unnerved him. But, he assured himself, *there's nothing she can do to me now.* Still, it left an uneasy queasiness, one impossible to disregard.

19

He and Taylor were stretched out on the two balcony chaises enjoying the magnificent city view, a bottle of Sterling Vineyards cabernet on the table between them. All afternoon, sodden pewter clouds drifted in from the Pacific, engulfing the Olympics, blanketing Puget Sound in gloomy, misty rain. But with lightweight coats, the mild summer temperature and lack of wind allowed them to sit outside and enjoy the evening. After leaving the funeral home they'd stopped by a Thai place for some takeout dinner. Now three empty cartons lay on the kitchen counter.

He sipped the wine, savoring the tannins and hint of blackberry before allowing it to slide over the back of his tongue. Aw, good wine. So superior to the Anchor beer Joel favored. "If you want, we can drive down tomorrow and pick up the rest of your clothes."

Hands clasped behind her head, Taylor seemed lost in the view. This was, he reminded himself, her first time here, so the view would be especially engrossing. Funny how, over the years, he'd become rather blasé about it. Made him reflect on just how lucky he was to live the life he had and just how much he had taken for granted. His own death had driven this point home, causing him to cherish his life even more dearly and enjoy the fruits of Chris's hard work.

She said, "And the rest of our stuff?"

Our stuff. He liked that. Sounded like something a couple would say.

"Most of it was second-hand when we got it. It's junk. Anything you really want, keep, the rest we can put in the storage locker downstairs if you want. Everything else we can donate to Habitat for Humanity. If we leave first thing in the morning, we could be back here Sunday afternoon at the latest."

She swirled the wine in the glass, sniffed the bouquet. "You haven't mentioned a word about the restaurant. How's that going? Or have you been too busy getting all this settled," she said, sweeping her free hand toward the condo interior.

Which brought up a more important question. "Does this mean you're in?"

She turned to face him. "That depends on what you mean by *in*. You know I don't have money to invest, so if you're talking about a financial stake, that's out of the question."

"No. No money. I'm talking about helping me get it set up and then run it. It'd be the same arrangement as the Chez. You handle the bar, I take care of the kitchen."

She set down the wine glass. "You expect me to answer without knowing more? What are your plans? Like, what've you put together so far?"

He sank back into the chaise, swirled the wine, and started describing the concept he'd roughed out in his mind. Just generalities. Tangible specifics would come after securing a space. He finished his description and glanced at her. She starred back at him.

He said, "That's a strange look you're sending me. What's it mean?"

She glanced away self-consciously. "You think your concept might be a bit, um...ambitious? I mean, it's your first restaurant. It sounds hugely expensive."

At least she didn't use the words unattainable or impossible. "Ambitious, sure. Out of the question or impossible? No."

She studied the back of her hand, started massaging a knuckle injured in a boarding accident years ago. "But that's going to cost a small fortune. You have that kind of money lined up?"

"Not yet, but I will. I plan on taking out a bank loan. I don't want investors telling me how to do things. This will be our project. Ours alone."

She flexed her fingers. "That's nuts. What bank is going to loan you that kind of money?"

"I can use the estate as collateral."

She stopped fiddling with her hand and turned to face him. "I don't believe it. You've never done a place like this before. How can you risk everything you have, and then some, on it?"

He liked the edge to her tone. It had, what, a touch of admiration? "Hey, life's about taking chances. Way I see it, if I don't jump at this, I'll regret it. The rest of my life." He thought of Joel, of how much he owed him. He thought of Chris and how he never would even consider such a risk.

"Could be, but what if you lose everything? You'll regret that, too."

He shrugged. "Maybe. Maybe not. But I'll never know if I don't try."

She shook her head in disagreement—making him feel the need to justify his position.

"Okay, sure, losing everything can happen, but there's also a good chance—and I emphasize good one—that it could be a huge success. And say I do lose. I'm young. I have the rest of my life to make up the losses. The longer I wait to do this, the less likely it is that I'll ever try. It's like people who always say they're going to finish school after dropping out; they never get around to it. No, this is something I *have* to do. And can do. If I don't give it a shot..."

She shook her head and sighed. "I'm not suggesting you don't do it. I just think it might be smart to start out small and learn from experience. I mean, this concept of yours is way huge. Why stack the cards against yourself?"

So much for that tone of admiration.

"Hey, it's not exactly like we don't know what we're doing. Between us we know a ton about this business. Besides, it's not all that complicated. You make good food and provide good service and people will come back for more. It's not a difficult concept to understand."

She didn't look convinced.

He said, "How many times have we gone into some place and tried their food, looked at their service, their décor, and predicted they'd be under in three months. We've always been right. Always. How many times did we go to a place that we *knew* would be a success? Again, we've been right. The point is we have a knack for this. We both know it. I'm telling you we can do it."

She still didn't seem won over.

"Look at it this way," he continued. "Until a week ago I had nothing but some second-hand furniture and a beater car. All of a sudden I have money I never counted on. If I lose it all I'm not really out anything. I never counted on Dad's estate as part of my future. Especially after I walked away to start over. To me it's worth the gamble."

She held her wine glass up to study its color in the light. "Who else is going to be involved? I mean, any of your friends?"

"Does that make a difference?"

"Are you kidding? Absolutely. I want to know who I might be working with."

"Like I said—I'm not planning on any investors other than the bank. It's going to be just you and me."

"Come on, sweetie. I'm talking about the other employees. Cooks and such that we know."

He saw where this was headed and wondered why she just didn't just flat out ask about Luther. "I was thinking of asking Luther, of course, but I doubt he'd leave the Chez."

She obviously wasn't pleased to hear that. "Luther Rabb?"

"Do we know any other Luther?"

"Joel! I thought you said you were straightening out the drug thing. That isn't going to happen if he's around. And you know it."

"I mean it when I say I'm done with that. Have a little faith."

"Oh, man..." She finger-combed her hair, then shook her head.

He said, "Hey, look, you know he's talented. He's extremely personable, and, you have to admit, a terrific maitre d'."

"He's a *drug* dealer, Joel. That's how he makes all that money he burns through so easily. Think he's going to give that up just because *we* want to build a good restaurant?"

"Let's get something clear. If he works for us, he's not doing anything I don't approve of. And I wouldn't approve of dealing. That's a risk I just can't afford to take. How much clearer can I be about it?"

Shaking her head, she turned away from him toward the view.

He said, "Hey, see if this makes any sense. Sure, okay, so he and I snort a little blow at work. Most of the guys in the kitchen do. So? No big thing."

She pressed the fingertips of both hands against her temples. "But they're not *dealing*. That's the difference. That's a felony."

No shit! Tell me about it. "Will you just listen to me a minute."

She shook her head.

Joel said, "Forget the drug thing for a moment. What we want for Orcas is a moneyed, 'now' clientele. He's perfect for developing that. Smooth, clever, charismatic. He remembers everybody's name. He's a natural."

She stretched both arms overhead and yawned. "That's probably true. But you're not listening to what *I'm* saying. I'll repeat it, so pay close attention. He's trouble. Capital T. I'm warning you, you have him play for our team, you'll regret it."

"Sweetie, if I'm prepared to risk everything on this, I want to hire people I've seen in action. He's handled some pretty gnarly situations, and handled them well. And you have to admit, he brings that touch of class. We need those qualities in a maitre d'."

"Got your thoughts on that the first time. Hasn't changed my opinion one iota."

He said, "Make you a deal. We find someone better, we'll take them. If not, we offer Luther the job. Hey, like I said, he probably won't even consider it." He held out his hand. "Deal?"

She looked him in the eye. "You mention this to him already?"

Fuck. "No," he lied.

Reluctantly, she shook his hand.

"Does this," he said, looking down at their clasped hands, "mean you're in?"

"Yes."

"Thank you." He picked up his glass in a toasting motion. "Here's to Orcas."

"To Orcas."

They settled back into their chaises. Today was truly significant. Chris's body had been put to rest and Taylor had moved in. Now, with those two things taken care of, he could direct all his efforts into finding the perfect spot to build Joel's dream. A dream that had never been Chris's. But now, strangely enough, he was getting into it and could relate to Joel's excitement for it. More than that, though, he would fulfill his dream too: a better life for Joel.

20

SWEDISH MEDICAL CENTER, SEATTLE,
MONDAY

"Mr. Holden?"

He dropped the three-month-old *People* magazine he'd been paging through while fretting about this appointment back on the end table. All day he'd been wrestling with ways of framing his questions without coming across as a total nutcase. Tom Holmes stood in the doorway to a short hall to his office. There was, Chris knew, another exit from that hall so patients could leave without being seen by, or seeing, the next appointment. He nodded and stood.

"Chris Holden's son?" Holmes held out his hand. A hulking man, about six-two and portly, hunched through the shoulders. Round face, a crescent of salt and pepper hair, twinkling eyes that gave him a leprechaun look in spite of his size. Which, Joel believed, helped disarm emotionally defensive patients. He dressed in a psychiatrist cliché: tweed sports coat, white shirt, black slacks, round rimless glasses, and a bowtie for a crowning touch. Chris always figured Holmes was *The Man* if he ever needed to see a psychiatrist. Well, here he was.

"Yes." He shook Holmes's soft, warm hand.

"My condolences. Your dad was a fine cardiologist."

Holmes nudged him on the shoulder, moving him from the

small waiting room toward his office. The door closed behind them.

"Thank you. I know he thought a lot of you."

He followed Holmes past the other exit. Unlike a cardiologist's practice, solo psychiatrists needed little to no office help. No fancy equipment, no nurses, no behind the counter staff. So it wasn't surprising to see no one else here.

They entered a small, nicely decorated office of warm wood furniture, one window with a westerly view of the downtown business district, a modest-sized desk with a living-room style table lamp. One wall filled with bookcases. A Tabriz knockoff on the floor. Unlike the offices of more egotistical physicians, there was no trophy wall of diplomas, licenses, and pictures of Holmes shaking hands with important people. The ambience cleverly softened the reality that you were seeing a mental health professional for emotional problems, which for some patients was difficult to admit. It was fine to see a doctor for physical pain, yet it was a sign of weakness to see one for emotional pain. Far as Chris was concerned, you saw whomever you needed to see to get well.

Holmes offered him his choice of chairs. After Joel took one, Holmes settled into the other one so they faced each other. Holmes held up a manila folder with a Post-it on one side. "Says here you want to see me about your father's death?"

Joel shifted to a more comfortable position, crossed his legs, and started into his planned introduction, although he still hadn't formulated how to ask the most important questions.

"This is rather difficult to explain." He exhaled, still nervous. "Before Dad died, we hadn't been in contact for several years...sort of a disagreement thing. I was living in Portland..." He swallowed and cleared his throat. "But here's the point: the day he died I had this extremely strong premonition that something bad was happening to him, maybe even a heart attack. Which, it turned out, was exactly what did happen. Even the timing coincided. Okay, that's happened to other people, I guess. That's not really the problem, although at the time it really freaked me out. The problem now is that from the moment Dad died, I feel like he cohabits my mind." Cohabits. He'd searched for that word for several hours. It seemed to be the only one that felt right without actually saying what really happened.

Poker-faced, Holmes asked, "Cohabits your mind?"

"Yeah, I know. It's a totally weird word. But what I'm experiencing *is* totally weird. It's the only word I can use to describe the sensation. Well, it's not really a sensation like touch or feel...it's more like a perception. It's like Chris is in here"—tapping his right temple—"with me. It's like I'm thinking his thoughts in addition to my own."

Holmes furrowed his brow. "Can you give me an example?"

"Well...we had very different personalities. He was very conservative in everything he did. Skiing, driving, investing, politics. He tried to raise me to be the same way, but I didn't turn out at all like he wanted. I'm just the opposite. Now, whenever I'm faced with a major decision, I hear him talking to me. Not like hearing voices that are external to my being. It's very different from that, like he's right inside my brain controlling my thoughts. But the really weird thing is, he's totally different now. Now, he's the one who wants to take the risks and I don't. It's like we've flip-flopped. He thinks it's what I want and is trying to please me. Sounds, nuts, huh?"

Holmes frowned, obviously confused. "I'm not completely following this. Are you saying you're hearing your father's voice in your head?"

"No, not actually hearing it. That's the weird thing. It's not an audible voice like a hallucination. It's more like his thoughts are now in my brain and they come into my consciousness and I know they're his thoughts, not my own." And here was his chance to really lay it out. "I know how crazy this must sound to you, but it's like the moment he died, his consciousness left his brain and migrated into mine."

Aw shit, is this being recorded?

140

Holmes remained expressionless. "Do you mind if I ask you a few questions?"

Okay, here it comes, the mental status exam. He'd wondered how long before he'd get to it. "Whatever it takes."

"What is today's date?"

Holmes listened and asked questions for forty minutes, taking few notes. Never once did he sound judgmental or biased, simply objectively interested. Finally, he set down his pen, closed the chart, and folded his hands.

"I'm intrigued with your story but I'm afraid I don't have an explanation for what you're experiencing. This feeling, if I understand correctly, is that your father is merged into your mind. What you describe is really quite unique. On the other hand, the premonition you experienced the day of his heart attack was probably very real and understandable. Premonitions do exist and are not uncommon. But if that's all that you experienced, well, you wouldn't be here, would you?" Holmes smiled.

"No, I wouldn't. Am I'm crazy?"

Holmes began tapping the pen on a pad of yellow paper next to the chart.

"Crazy as in psychotic? No. Nothing suggests that. But I strongly suspect that the avalanche that killed your friend—which you witnessed and was a near-death experience for you—may have more to do with this than you give it credit for. Do you think that perhaps you underestimate its significance?"

Okay, there's his way to blow this off.

"I don't know. I really hadn't thought about that before now. But offhand, I'd say no."

Holmes set down the pen, clasped his hands together and studied his interlaced fingers a moment before returning to Joel. "I wasn't there, obviously, but it seems as though you did have a near-death experience. Those can be—quite understandably—very traumatic. They often result in flashbacks. Do you understand these

141

terms?"

Okay, this was something new. He hadn't considered a near-death experience, maybe because he knew so little about them. "No, not really."

"Let me explain. First, do you understand what a near-death experience is?"

"The name is self-explanatory, isn't it?"

Holmes smiled. "Yes it is, but tell me what it means to *you*."

Joel shrugged. "I guess if a person survives an event that, under slightly different circumstances, would've killed them, they've had a near-death experience. Being pulled out of the water while you're drowning would qualify, I guess."

"Excellent example. In your case an avalanche missed you by mere inches and buried your best friend instead. I can assume you were terrified during and immediately after the event. Correct?"

"Terrified doesn't even come close to describing it."

Holmes spread his hands as if to say there-you-go. "At the very least, it's fair to say this traumatic experience changed your entire life from that point on. After all, you used it to quite literally start a new life."

True, but..."Go on."

"It's common for near-death survivors to claim that during the seconds before they *would* have died, their life flashed before their eyes. Others describe the same experience as time slows and during those moments, their entire life is replayed in flashes. These aren't just isolated stories, mind you. Thousands of people have experienced them. So it does seem to be a valid phenomenon. So how do we explain it?

"Some medical experts think the total life flashback may be a way for the mind to cope with the impending trauma and that once the accident has passed and the threat of death is no longer imminent, the flashes stop but the memory of those flashes stays embedded in your brain as a memory of the flashback."

Interesting stuff but still off point. "But how does that explain what I'm feeling?"

"It doesn't. Not directly, but indirectly it may explain a great deal. I hypothesize—for lack of a better explanation—that during the avalanche you flashed on your father's life instead of your own. And now you're recalling those embedded images but interpret them as Chris's voice. These flashbacks might convince you that he's now inside your mind."

Not even close to what was he was experiencing. Then again, had he really expected Holmes to be able to explain his transformation? No. But this interview did serve one purpose: a psychiatrist whom he highly respected didn't diagnosis him as crazy. A minor consolation.

"But I don't remember considering it a near-death experience at the time."

Holmes shrugged. "That's understandable, but what else would you call it? Fact is, you *did* come this close," he said, holding his thumb and index fingers a fraction of an inch apart, "to being killed. Think about what I've said." He glanced at a clock on the desk. "I see that we're out of time. If you need another appointment, just call and I'll work you in. But I believe you really wanted to see me to test your sanity. That seems to be very much intact."

Smiling, Joel stood. "Know what? This has helped a lot. Thank you."

Holmes offered his hand. "Again, sorry for your loss. Chris Holden was a good man."

21

He and Taylor stood on the sidewalk in front of Pampas—a restaurant that had gone bust three months ago—waiting for the real-estate agent representing the space. They'd purposely arrived a few minutes ahead of time to walk the block and get a better feel for the immediate neighborhood. He thought the location was perfect. The block comprised an eclectically cool mix of retail shops and residential buildings, the businesses being mostly funky boutiques and restaurants. The one he was now standing in front of, for example: two commercial spaces—Pampas and an Asian import shop—on the first floor with the remaining eight floors residential. He remembered reading that the building housed fifty condos.

The failed restaurant's theme had been South American cuisine featuring imported Argentine beef. Although he'd searched the *Seattle Times* archives for as much of the restaurant's history as possible, the exact reasons for bankruptcy remained murky. In asking around, neither he nor Taylor could dig up a consistent story in spite of several opinions. What he did learn was that Pampas's opening—actually two: one private, one public—had been heralded with extraordinary hoopla and fanfare. The exclusive gathering included mostly investors (several local pro sports celebs) who loved being blinded by flashes while stepping out of shiny late-model Benzes. Also included were the usual heavy-hitter television hotshots, two top-of-the-totem-pole food critics, and a wide assortment of the city's beautiful people, all easily recognizable from routine appearances in *Seattle Magazine*.

Pampas's chef ran two other wildly successful, markedly different, downtown restaurants, both still going strong. Which made the murkiness surrounding Pampas's bankruptcy even more vexing.

He'd nosed around, talking to the manager and chefs of other nightspots in the area and heard explanations that ranged from a collapse of financing to customer fickleness. The only part of the story that remained consistent was that initially, at least, Pampas was a huge hit. For the first half year even the mayor couldn't score a reservation sooner than three months out. The bar was a constant mob scene featuring the hip younger singles crowd. It immediately became the sole Belltown restaurant that didn't have to stoop to half-price happy-hour drinks and a cheap bar menu to pull in customers. Sure, you could eat at the bar, but you paid full fare off the regular menu. Initially too, the food was good.

That wasn't the problem.

Then, near the end of its first year, Pampas began a death spiral. Some claimed it simply fell out of favor, as can easily happen with trendy places. Apparently, nobody understood the reasons for the reversal. Over the course of six months traffic shrunk from the *in crowd* to a trickle of walk-ins. And you can't support horrendous overhead on those meager pickings. For months the chef limped along, cannibalizing profits from his other two places to keep Pampas afloat. But it didn't take long for the investors to act on diminishing returns. Pampas closed and the space was put on the market for immediate lease.

That was that. One day Pampas's front door was open for business, the next day the dead bolts were secured. No obituary, no postmortem in the *Puget Sound Business Journal*. All very strange.

"Good location, I think," Taylor said, eyeing the high-rise across the street.

"Except for parking." He noticed the small lot across the street and a half block south. He made a mental note to find out which company ran it to see if they could cut a deal for valet parking. If not, he'd have to scour the neighborhood for other options.

Taylor nodded. "Have you walked the streets around here to see what the neighborhood's like after six?"

That was exactly what he'd done the night before the funeral. "Yes. It's great. The entire neighborhood is nothing but condos, so there's a lot of foot traffic and density. For someone who lives in the 'burbs', this appears to be downtown but in reality, it's residential." His own home was only five blocks further south along First Avenue.

"Mr. Holden?"

A straight-backed thirtyish Asian female—Pakistani maybe—was offering her hand to him. So engrossed in their conversation were they that she'd walked right up to him without being noticed. Well, he noticed her now. Yes, indeed.

"Yes."

"Latasha Khan." A round silver stud protruded from her right cheek just above the bone. A small, but unavoidable, eye magnet against her flawless brown skin.

He introduced Taylor.

"Do you have any questions before we go inside?" Khan pulled a set of keys from an expensive leather portfolio, started sorting through them.

"Yes. About the previous restaurant, Pampas. You know why it failed?" Taylor asked.

Khan rifled through the portfolio, found a sheet of glossy paper, handed it to him. It listed square footage and other useful information but not the rent or sale price.

Khan said, "I've heard several stories but don't know how valid they are. The best I can tell is the chef became embroiled in a huge ongoing fight with the building's homeowners," she said with a wave of her hand. "It turned quite bitter, and as a result the homeowners put pressure on the city to shut it down." She held up the key. "Shall we?"

He was anxious to see the interior. "Yes, please."

Khan opened the door and ushered them in.

Joel asked, "Can you give us any more details than that? How did they do that, shut down a restaurant?"

Khan closed the street door and engaged the deadbolt. "This is so we'll be able to visit without worrying about someone wandering in." She laughed. "That's exactly what happened the last time I showed commercial property." Another sweep of her hand. "Please, feel free to look around. And while you do, I'll talk."

A large bar area with high cocktail tables filled the area to the left of the entrance. To the right was a small waiting area with a receptionist stand. Further to the right were the restrooms. Dead ahead, a wide hall led deeper into to what appeared to be a large, main dining area with low-backed booths on the right and open cooking area to the left.

Joel liked the space so far. Liked it a lot. One appealing feature was that the original build-out had been designed to accommodate a restaurant instead of a retail space. Remodels from retail to restaurant always resulted in city code issues; things like proper ventilation became problematic. This space only required minor redecorating to fit his concept.

"Are you familiar with Snake?" Khan asked.

"The snake?" Joel watched Taylor slip behind the bar, inspecting it with a bemused expression, imagining, he suspected, what to change if it became hers.

"Snake. It's a block or so over that way." Khan pointed. "Over on Western. A nightclub that attracts mostly gang-bangers and banger-hanger-ons. I'm a bit surprised you haven't heard about it if you're in the business."

"I'm into restaurants, not nightclubs. Big difference," he corrected. "Sorry I interrupted. Go on."

"About a year ago there was a shooting in the parking lot adjacent to Snake. One man killed, another critically injured. All because of a fight that started in Snake and then spread outside. For months they'd been having problems, so when the murder

147

occurred, the liquor board slapped them with a three-month suspension. So, of course, their regular customers had no place to party, but loved the neighborhood. So, they started hanging out here. And, as you might imagine, their presence had a cascading negative effect. Customers stopped making dinner reservations, leaving only the drinkers. If you intend to run a bar that's great, but in Pampas's case, this led to problems. You know the type: fights and yelling at two in the morning, car alarms going off, an occasional gunshot fired, guys relieving themselves in the various doorways. It turned into a mess very quickly. The homeowner boards in this and the surrounding buildings complained to the manager but he simply blew them off." She began a slow three-sixty turn, inspecting the walls and ceiling.

She continued with, "What happened next was highly predictable. The homeowners united and organized a massive retaliation. They would call 9-1-1 every time a problem arose, no matter how big or insignificant. They formed a group to pressure city council members. After all, if you consider the amount of revenue these people pay the city each year in property taxes, it's significant. To say nothing of the votes they cast at reelection time.

"In turn, the city council pressured the police, and the police started coming down on the management, but by this time Pampas's only customers were bangers. When the cops couldn't control the situation, the liquor board set up an undercover sting. In one week alone they were able to slip ten underage agents into the bar. The kids were buying drinks without ever being asked for ID. Another undercover cop took video of the bouncer allowing in a banger with a gun. From what I hear, it wasn't even a concealed weapon and the kid didn't have a permit."

Joel blew a slow whistle.

"Next thing you know, the liquor board suspended their license for six months." She shrugged. "That was the end of it. They had no place to go but under. That's the story I heard and the one that makes the most sense. I've heard some of the others, but they don't add up." She addressed him directly now. "If you want my advice, this isn't a place to launch a nightclub. Find a spot that's not in the same building with residences that start at half a million."

Behind the bar, Taylor dropped below the counter, probably inspecting the refrigerators or shelves or plumbing. He wasn't sure she'd even been listening to Khan's story.

He strolled past the counter where diners could eat while watching the grill and salad cooks work. He continued back to the main dining room, a spacious, high-ceiling area interrupted by three weight-bearing concrete columns. The concrete ceiling had been left exposed but painted, with all the necessary ventilation ducts and conduits in clear view. Although it made a hip look, it was a big mistake because without soffits or other sound attenuation measures, the bare ceiling would transmit noise directly into the living quarters above. That would have to be fixed for sure.

The back wall was contiguous picture windows highlighting a view out over Alaskan Way Viaduct—a landmark Seattle eyesore—to the harbor beyond. Banquettes upholstered in nauseating burnt-orange leather lined the walls. Tables for four were scattered across the floor, allowing for excellent spacing between them. Apparently all the previous furniture remained, but most, if not all of it, was unusable for the motif he envisioned. The banquettes were seriously cool but would have to be reupholstered in a more pleasing color. But these were all simple cosmetic changes.

He opened the door to the men's room. Looked like hell. Same with the women's toilet. Graffiti and gang signs covered the walls and all the stalls had obscenities scratched in the paint. His rule of thumb was if management couldn't keep the johns clean, imagine what the kitchen looked like. The fixtures and tiles were fine, so a little paint would fix both rooms.

In contrast, the kitchen was great news. Top of the line appliances that needed only a good cleaning to be functional. A door from the kitchen opened into a back stairway that split; running up to the residential floors and downward to a steel fire door. He and Khan walked downstairs, almost slipping on grease caked to the cement, and pushed open the door to the alley. He noticed a steel plate welded across the outside of the lock to overlap the door jamb to prevent it from being jimmied. Urban defense at its best.

"Who owns the space?" he asked Khan as they trudged back up the stairs to the kitchen.

"Morris Werner, the building's original developers."

"And the rent?"

"They're asking forty per on a three year. That includes water and sewage but gas and electricity are metered separately. Oh, and there is a garbage fee too. You'll probably need at least three pick-ups a week."

He glanced at the spec sheet for the square footage. Jesus, it was larger than it seemed from the outside, a shade over 5,000. At forty per square, that came to two hundred grand a year. His heart took off galloping. Sweat beaded under both arms. He hadn't budgeted that much. Taylor was eyeing him from behind the bar.

"Forty per, huh?"

"That's what they're asking, but I imagine if you signed a five-year lease, they might be willing to negotiate a few dollars in your favor. Certainly doesn't hurt to ask."

He did a 360-turn like Khan had done earlier. The place had definite potential. A little larger than anticipated, but very real potential. He loved it.

"I'll think it over and let you know tomorrow morning."

She smiled at him. "Tomorrow will be fine, Mr. Holden. Talk to you then."

22

Back outside on the sidewalk, Joel and Taylor watched Khan lock the front door of Pampas.

The real estate agent turned and smiled at them, said, "I'll wait for your call," before dropping the keys in her portfolio. She walked away with a crisp, professional step.

Taylor began to say something, but he cut her off. "Wait. Don't say a thing. Let's mull over our impressions and thoughts before we discuss it, okay?"

She appeared puzzled at this. "Why?"

"I just want to organize my thoughts first." He reckoned that sometimes it was best to reflect on things before getting tangled in a discussion.

"Fair enough. What now?" She was looking around, as if searching for a distraction.

He checked his watch. Too early to eat. Besides, he couldn't eat now, not with all these things on his mind. A Starbucks was directly across the street, but he didn't want any more caffeine. Didn't want to go to the condo either. Jesus, what a huge decision, this Pampas thing. He'd really underestimated the anxiety this would evoke, but now that he'd come face to face with the actual expenses...man, just the rent for this space was huge. "Let's just walk around, check out some stores." He wondered if maybe he should start on smaller-scale project and work up, as Taylor had suggested.

They began strolling up to Second Avenue and then headed

north, toward the Seattle Center with its landmark Space Needle, no particular place in mind, just wandering.

They came abreast of a store dealing in secondhand CDs and Taylor stopped to peer in the window. "Let's go in. I want to see what they have."

He strolled the aisles, randomly flipping through rows of disks stacked on edge and crammed into chopped-down cardboard boxes, not really paying attention to the artists or content, his mind consumed with sorting through pros and cons of the Pampas space. Two aisles over, Taylor appeared to be searching for a vintage Smokey Robinson CD she wanted, but he could tell she wasn't really fully focused either. It amazed him how much she got into Motown and old R&B when it was generations removed from her.

It was 5:30 when they were passing a tapas bar and he caught the whiff of roasting lamb. It made him aware of just how hungry he actually was.

"You hungry?" he asked Taylor.

She grinned. "Smells too good. I am now."

"I read a review of this place last week in the *Times*. It just opened and they gave it a pretty good rating."

"Let's try it."

The place was packed. But just as they entered, a couple stood up from a table against the back wall, the man shoving a credit card into his wallet. Joel took Taylor's arm, said, "C'mon," and started leading her to the space being vacated. The table had barely room enough for two wine glasses and a few small plates.

The menu was interesting and the wine list extensive but it featured only Spanish wines. He handed the list to Taylor. "Recognize any of these?"

She shook her head. "No, I'm like you. I know mostly the West Coast and French ones."

The waiter, a portly man with his black hair in a ponytail,

started clearing the table. "You folks want something to drink?"

Taylor ordered three small plates. They both ordered two glasses of a 2005 Ricon de Navas Crianza Rioja. Soon as the waiter left, they fell back into contemplative silence, their minds focused on Pampas.

Halfway through their meal Joel's gaze drifted toward the front door, stopped and locked onto a face. He froze, the bottom of his gut falling out of him.

One of Ortega's old crew was standing at the door, his arm around a woman with spiky hair, tats, and enough piercings to trigger a metal detector.

Joel almost didn't recognize him because of ugly large blue tattoos over both cheeks and the flashy oversized diamond stud in his left ear. But shit, there was no question the banger was one of Ortega's. His eyes were scanning the room for an empty table. Joel turned away.

"Joel? What's wrong?" Taylor asked.

Fuck!

He gave her an almost imperceptible head shake. She stopped chewing to stare back. They stayed frozen this way for several moments.

Joel said, "Just take a sip of wine and be cool."

She continued to study him two long beats before picking up her glass and taking a long slow sip. Instead of glancing around to see what was wrong, she held up the wine glass as if studying the wine's color, then moved the glass toward the front of the restaurant as if to get better light. He did the same with his glass but the movement felt exaggeratedly slow and awkward.

An uneasy silence settled in between them in spite of the typical clatter of a busy restaurant.

Another beat passed until a primitive self-protective urge forced him to look at the doorway. The banger and his girlfriend weren't in the entrance. Joel spun around to see if he was elsewhere in the place, like approaching the table with a gun, but he wasn't.

"What's wrong?"

Momentarily, he was at a loss for words. Didn't want to open up the Ortega mess. He said, "Thought I recognized someone from years ago. I really didn't want to get in a conversation with him." True. Sorta. He picked up his wine and took a slow sip, no longer hungry.

She shot him a skeptical expression but diplomatically dropped the topic.

He and Taylor walked hand in hand back to his place, Joel trying to shake the scare of the near miss. Had the guy seen him? If so, did he recognize him? And say he did. Then what?

When they got back to the condo he needed a stiff drink. How the hell did he ever make so many bad decisions and end up in the Ortega mess? He should've known better. Chris was right.

I stand next to the bike rack admiring Troy Miller's midnight black Trek, equipped with full suspension, special seat, ultra cool grips. And fantasize about owning one, riding it to school, envy so obvious on my friends' faces—envy as strong as I feel now.

The real pisser is Dad won't buy it for me. Instead, he insists I earn the money. Keeps preaching about how much more it'll mean to me if I work for it, how when he was growing up that's what he had to do. Blah, blah, blah. Shit! Why is Dad such a scrooge? He has the damned money. Besides, it'll take me a gazillion years of mowing lawns and washing cars to put together enough coin. Meaning no way I'll have it by the end of summer when the school year starts.

Unless...

The thought has been flitting around the edges of my mind for the past week. I have an older friend, a very cool dude who, by the way, introduced me to weed. In turn, I started a few of my closest friends smoking some now and then. And now they don't have any connections, so they pester me for more. Okay, so what's wrong with selling them a joint or two? At maybe at

*a little more than it costs me. Isn't that the American way? Capitalism.
Profit from ingenuity. See a business opportunity and act on it?*

Sure it is.

*It's not like the other kids are forced to buy a joint from me. It's their
choice. They can buy it from someone else, right? I'm just there to make it
easier for them. Nothing wrong with that.*

*I stand back and admire the bicycle again, thinking, yes, maybe it just
is possible.*

"What'd you think of the bar?" he asked Taylor now that they're
kicking back on the deck chaises enjoying the view, sharing a nice
bottle of cabernet from the wine closet, more relaxed now that
more time has passed since seeing Ortega's soldier.

She was holding up the glass to the light, checking the wine's
color. "The tapas place?"

"No, Pampas."

"Are we free to discuss that now?" She held the glass under her
nose to sniff the bouquet.

"Sure. I just wanted both of us to give it some thought. We
have."

She took a moment to savor the wine, nodded appreciatively,
set down the glass. They were developing an appreciation for good
wine, but he still believed there was a high bullshit level involved
past a certain price point. He vowed to never be one of those
insufferable wine snobs who claimed subtleties in flavor that simply
didn't exist. Or existing only in the minds of those who wrote the
advertising copy.

Taylor said, "It's certainly enough room. More than I
envisioned. The décor sucks. But, hey, with a little work it could be
more along the lines of what I think you have in mind. What about
the kitchen?"

He'd been considering the amount of renovation needed.
Having finally walked through the space gave him a much clearer
idea than peering through a dirty window. But as was always the

case, the closer you looked the more problems you found.

"Not laid out the greatest. Whoever designed it was forced to work around some very real space limitations. It's clear they maximized the dining area at the expense of the cooking area. The good news is they have great appliances."

She laughed. "That's it? Great appliances? That's not the most enthusiastic response I've heard you give."

"What can I say? It needs a lot of work. Lot of work."

Taylor laughed again. "No shit. Did you get a load of that upholstery?" She stuck her index finger in her mouth, like triggering a gag reflex.

"Oh, Jesus, the banquettes? You wonder how any self-respecting gang-banger could hang there."

For a moment she seemed to be watching a 737 over the harbor turn south on its approach to SeaTac, then asked, "So what are you thinking?"

"Like you said, it's a ton of space. Especially at that rent."

She swirled the wine in her glass, put it to her nose again. "But?"

He hadn't touched his wine yet.

"The pro is, it'd be a remodel, not a build-out from scratch. Also it was originally designed as a restaurant. Meaning we don't have the headache of figuring out how to rig good ventilation for the cooking areas, things like that. The con is its history. We'd have to go out of our way to make nice with the homeowners in the neighborhood."

She flipped a dismissive wave. "Easy enough. Hold a grand opening and invite everybody, serve a respectable wine and finger food and smile and kiss ass. The only hard part might be keeping the wrong kind of people out."

"That shouldn't be a problem. We just don't make it banger friendly." Which had the added advantage of diminishing the likelihood of running into anyone from Ortega's crew.

They sipped their wine, slipping back into their own thoughts.

He watched northbound traffic along First Avenue thicken and figured the Mariners game must've just finished.

Taylor collected the empty glasses and wine bottle. "I'm going to take a shower and go to bed. Want a sweater or coat?" She was rubbing her arms to warm them.

"I'll get it. I'm going to the kitchen for a nightcap anyway. Want one?"

She shook her head and, with her foot, shoved the slider open enough to step inside. "Come wake me if you want to talk about it some more."

Deep in thought, he followed her into the kitchen, grabbed a tumbler from the shelf, filled it with ice chips from the fridge door, added an unmeasured amount of scotch. He stopped to inspect the bottle. An expensive single malt. Not Joel's taste. At least not until recently. Same with the wine tonight. Chris's choices. Taylor seemed to approve of these changes, pointing the out they were just another indication of how different he'd become since his father's death.

He shrugged on a jacket and headed for the balcony again and nestled back into the chaise, his spot now cold.

Jesus, what a decision. Back when this had been nothing more than fantasy, it was fun and exciting. Precisely because it was a dream. Now, facing the decision of whether to rent a space that expensive, he had to stop and consider the risks. Taking on a tangible financial debt scared him shitless.

The lease was huge. The reality daunting. Carrying such large debt was, well, intimidating. To top it off, the cost of the renovation was a total unknown. Jesus, it suddenly became staggering.

All the countless hassles. The hundreds of little problems associated with starting a business. Everything from petitioning the state liquor board for a license to setting up a credit card reader.

He was sweating, he realized. Having difficulty getting enough air into his lungs.

A strong déjà vu hit. He was back on the mountain, thinking, *I'd live life differently. I'd take chances I never would've considered before.*

Well, this was his chance, his opportunity to do exactly that. A unique second chance at life. A fresh start.

He *had* to live it differently this time around. Which meant he *had* to sign that lease tomorrow and take the gamble. Otherwise, what was the point?

He owed it to Joel.

The feeling of déjà vu intensified.

His left shoulder began to ache just like it had...*aw shit, Reed is looking at him, saying, "Jesus Christ. Don't move. I'm calling 9-1-1."*

The paramedics are stretching him out...the sound of the helicopter rotors winding up...

And he wonders: is there a God? An afterlife? He's suddenly afraid that all his life he'd been wrong, that perhaps maybe, just maybe, he would be...

Suddenly, the pain and memory vanished, leaving telltale goose bumps on his arms.

Shit! What was that all about?

He shook his head and downed a slug of scotch, realized the sweating and shortness of breath were gone.

A stress reaction is all... from seeing Ortega's guy.

Okay, he decided, it's settled. Tomorrow, after his appointment with Reed Allison, he'd sign the Pampas lease. Everything would work out.

This time he'd do it right.

23

NEXT DAY

Joel couldn't believe it. "This is a joke, right?"

Across the desk Reed Allison was giving him the same sympathetic smile he himself had given patients while delivering bad news. Empathetic, yet clinically separated. I feel your pain, but this-is-how-it-is type of look.

When Reed didn't answer, Joel knew the answer and within seconds anger began displacing dismay. The bitch!

Then again, he wondered, why be surprised? He flashed on the encounter after his funeral. Her threat. If he could just grab her neck and squeeze it down to the diameter of a garden hose...

Reed sat waiting.

Joel inhaled slowly, struggling to regain control of his emotions. Raw anger distorted reason, he knew. Young men shot from the hip. Older, wiser men took aim. At the moment, what he needed was to think clearly and assess what the situation really was.

Finally, he got it together and said, "Go through that again to make sure I have all the facts."

Reed leaned forward, hands clasped tightly together, forearms on the desk, locking eyes with him. He spoke slowly and clearly, "The estate is frozen." Reed sat back, cocked his head to one side. "I can imagine this catches you very much by surprise. I was a bit shocked myself. But there it is. It's unavoidable. We now have to deal with it, which I am quite prepared to do."

Okay, he got it right the first time, even though it didn't make sense. "Thing I don't understand—because I know the wording of Dad's will—is that *I'm* the sole inheritor. That was absolutely clear. She can't do that."

Reed pushed out of the chair, stepped around to the front of the desk and sat his butt half on the edge. He removed his glasses and started massaging the bridge of his nose. "Explain to me why you are so confident that you know the exact wording of the will? Do you have a copy that I don't know about?"

Because you and I hammered it out together a year ago. But he couldn't very well say that. Any attempt to explain that now would only lead to bigger legal problems. Like, how the hell does a son inherit his father's estate if he's the father who everyone knows is dead but is living in his son's body? Then again, who the hell would believe him? If anything, they'd claim he was a raving nut-case, giving Janice the perfect opportunity to declare him incompetent when he made the will and unfit to control the assets.

"I explained that to you before. The days before I disappeared Dad and I had several very personal conversations. And, as you also know, we had a few disagreements. One of them was I wanted to use the money that was earmarked for my education to pay for cooking school." He coughed out a derisive laugh. "Dad didn't consider culinary school worthwhile training. During those talks we discussed several things. He may not have told you all of them." Which was a lie. He confided everything to Reed.

Reed's eyebrows shot up. "For example?"

"His marriage to Janice, for one. It sucked. But you know this because he talked to you about getting a divorce. He knew she was screwing around on him. I mean, Jesus, all the signs were there. He hired that investigator to document it. The crowning insult was her constant complaints about him not being around enough in spite of being quite content to spend the money he made."

Reed's expression sobered. "I'm surprised he discussed Janice with you in such detail."

"We discussed it all. Hiring the private investigator. The evidence that'd be needed in divorce court to limit what she'd claim in the event he died before the divorce was granted. You know firsthand what a complete mess things were during those days."

Eyes distant, Reed nodded agreement. "You're absolutely correct."

"That's why I can't understand why or how the assets can be frozen. Things were locked down. You two arranged it so that when he finally divorced her—which happened shortly after I split for Portland—she probably had to sign an agreement. At least, that was his intent." In fact, at the time it gave him spiteful pleasure to see her sign. It was a petty emotion, he freely admitted, but served as minor compensation for the humiliation of being a cuckold for years.

"Remember two very important rules, Joel; just about anything can be challenged in the courts. But keep in mind that even if Janice didn't contest the will, state law still requires me to meet several fiduciary responsibilities—probate being one—before I may legally release the estate to you. Just so you know, I started probate as soon as possible, so that's already underway." Reed's expression softened. "I assure you that Janice will not prevail. At most, she can only delay your eventual inheritance."

He felt the pressure spike between his temples. The bitch!

"What grounds does she have to contest it?"

Reed held up both hands in surrender. "Take a few slow, deep breaths and calm down. I just said she doesn't stand a chance of winning. All I said is that she *is* contesting the will. She claims that since you were legally declared dead, how can you possibly inherit the estate? The DNA analysis proves you're Joel, but until the court hears both arguments, there can be no *major* distributions of funds. That part is very clear."

Without money he couldn't to afford to start Orcas. Okay,

sure, he could delay it until the money became available, but who knew how long that would be. By then, the Pampas space—one he dearly loved—would likely be gone.

Joel's cell rang. He dug it from his pocket and checked the number. Khan, the real estate agent. Probably calling to ask for his decision about the lease. He held up a finger. "Just a second."

Irritated at the interruption, he connected with the call. "Hello."

"Mr. Holden, Latasha Khan. How are you this morning?" Her voice crisp and professional.

"Rather busy at the moment. May I call you back?"

"You may, but I feel it only fair to let you know another party is interested in Pampas, the space you looked at yesterday."

To Khan: "Hold on a sec."

To Reed: "Give me a second."

Reed shoved off the desk. "Alone?"

Joel waved the question away and said, "No. Really. This will be over before it starts."

He said to Khan, "Let me guess. The other party made an offer, right?"

"I know how this must sound, but, yes, they have."

Clearly a pressure tactic. How maddening. Sure, he was young, but young didn't necessarily equate to stupid. Did she really think he'd fall for it?

"What a coincidence. Yesterday I walk the property and today you have a competing offer. Know what? I really take offense to such a cheap shot."

"I'm sorry you interpret this that way. The other party looked at the property twice before you did. Remember when I locked the door, I mentioned someone walking in off the street? That happened the last time they inspected the space. The only reason I didn't mention their interest until now was because I wasn't sure if they would be able to secure financing. But apparently they have. I'm serious when I say they're very serious."

He still didn't believe her and gave a sarcastic laugh.

"Fine. If they take it before I call back, tough luck for me. Now, like I said, I'm in a meeting. Goodbye."

He thumbed off the call and blew out a long frustrated breath. His fingers, he realized, were trembling with anger at both Janice and Khan. "Jesus."

Reed returned to his perch on the edge of the desk and crossed his arms. "I can't tell you how much you remind me of your father. Just now, for example. It's amazing."

He waved that away too.

"What was that all about?" Reed asked.

He explained.

When he finished, Reed said, "Here's what I can do: I can arrange a monthly stipend to defray your living expenses, if that will help. It can continue until this mess is cleared up and the balance of the estate can be released."

That would help, but didn't solve the immediate problem of financing a restaurant.

"Thanks. I appreciate that. I could certainly use the money. And as long as we're on the subject, will the estate continue to pay the condo expenses?"

Reed nodded, turned to his desk, jotted a brief note on a yellow legal pad and then nodded. "I'll make certain it does."

What a relief. At least he now had a place to live and enough money to buy essentials. He stood up, anxious to leave Reed's office so he could mull things over. There had to be a way to get his hands on Pampas while the will was in probate. He extended his hand to Reed. "Sorry I yelled at you. That was uncalled for."

Reed shook his hand warmly. "Not to worry. I can imagine how stressful this is for you, especially if you intend to start a new business."

Out on the sidewalk, heading north along Fourth Avenue in the direction of the condo, he retrieved Khan's number on the cell and connected.

She picked up with, "Latasha Khan here."

"Ms. Khan, Joel Holden. I apologize for my reaction earlier, but I was in an important meeting and didn't have time to talk. I do now. So, about the space, I'm interested but need to arrange financing first. How much flexibility do you think the owners might have in negotiating a lower price?"

An awkward pause echoed over the phone.

"I'm sorry Mr. Holden, but as I said earlier, another party was interested. They signed the papers for the lease just minutes ago."

He stopped in stunned disbelief. He'd been convinced her call was nothing more than a pressure tactic to force his decision. After all, it was one of the oldest tricks in the selling game.

"No way."

"I wasn't joking then, Mr. Holden, and I am not joking now. That space is taken. Now if you're still interested in finding a property, I'll be delighted to show you some others. I should be free later this afternoon."

24

"Mr. Holden, if you'll follow me, please, Ms. Lee will see you now."

Joel dropped the recent copy of *Newsweek* on the end table. He'd been thumbing through it, barely registering the pictures, making a pathetic effort to divert the anxiety eating away at him. He followed a man he guessed to be his age but better dressed toward the back of the bank. Joel was wearing Chris's charcoal gray worsted wool pinstripe. The suit was a half inch short in the sleeves and showed too much sock, but Joel's only suit had been in desperate need of dry cleaning for months and was now at a cleaners a block from the condo.

The man stopped beside an open office door and waved him in.

Ms. Lee sat on a svelte black leather chair behind a contemporary desk of thick plate glass or acrylic supported on a high-gloss stainless steel frame. No drawers. The phone and computer monitor cables were beautifully concealed in the tubular legs, making the desktop a minimalist statement of taste and power. He couldn't even guess how much a custom piece of furniture like that cost, but suspected it'd be more than his annual Chez Pierre salary.

He did a double take when first seeing her. He'd assumed that the family name Lee was Chinese or Korean. Instead, the banker was a round eye, about fifty, with short salt-and-pepper hair, wearing a teal Hillary Clinton pantsuit. So much for living in

Seattle. In Atlanta, that last name would evoke an entirely different expectation.

He recognized the light blue report binder her hands rested on: His business plan.

She glanced over the tops of her rimless reading glasses at him. "Please, Mr. Holden," she said, gesturing at the two chairs in front of the desk. She told her secretary, "Thank you, Michael."

So much for offering him coffee or water. Should he take it as a bad sign? He dropped into a chair, clasped his hands at his waist, and swallowed hard.

The door to the hall opens and one of the other interviewees steps out with a stressed look, says, "You're next."

Chris glances at the paper in his hand, then at the number beside the door, making sure this is the right room. Of course it is.

As the other student passes, she whispers, "Martin Luther King."

Confused, Chris turns to her, "What?"

But she's hurrying down the hall to her next interview, out of earshot.

The tightness in his gut knots up harder. He enters a conference room with a table and twelve chairs. Three men and two women in white lab coats sit at one end, a pile of manila folders before them.

"Christopher Holden?" one of the men asks. He has a crescent of short white hair below a bald glistening scalp, oversized glasses, white shirt with a burgundy bowtie. The air is too hot and stale, making it hard to breath.

"Yes?"

"Please shut the door and have a seat."

Which chair should I take, he wonders, afraid of making the blunder of sitting in the wrong place. He picks the chair farthest from the group and slowly sits, back rigid and straight.

Each of the white coats opens a folder and busies themselves reading while the one with the bowtie says, "No need to be nervous, young man, you've made it this far."

Yeah, but he's heard horror stories about disastrous interviews, how sometimes the committee throws a few trick questions at you to see if you

166

know the answer or are trying to bullshit your way through. You never know their intent for certain. And he's heard that they can be extremely fussy, temperamental, and capricious.

"Do you mind if we ask you a few questions?"

"No."

"Excellent. Please describe the Krebs Cycle."

A wave of relief hits. Easy, right out of organic chemistry 101. He spends the next few minutes explaining how glucose is metabolized.

"Very good." The professor nods, sucks on the stem of his glasses. "Can you tell us who won the Nobel Peace Prize in 1964?"

Shit!

He has no idea.

He opens his mouth to say he doesn't know but hesitates. No way!

Then wonders, how can I be sure?

"Mr. Holden?"

Time to gamble.

"Dr. Martin Luther King."

The one with the bowtie says to the group, "Amazing. He's the second one today to know that."

Ms. Lee held up his binder. "I read your plan. Pretty ambitions, don't you think?"

Now there was a trick question if he'd ever heard one. Say yes, you admit to delusions of grandeur. Say no, and you disagree with the person you're trying to suck up to. Instead, he opted for a compromise, one that would help sell his concept. "Ambitious, yes. Doable? Absolutely."

With a barely audible sigh, she flicked a fingertip against the binder. "This is ambitious," she said before dropping it back on the desk. Fingers knitted together, elbows on the desk, she studied him closely. Every ounce of her body language underscored the image of corporate efficiency. "Remind me. How old are you?"

Shit, guilty by age!

"Twenty-two." He resisted adding, "Almost twenty-three,"

because that would sound juvenile and defensive.

"And how many years have you been in the restaurant business?"

Another trick question. Letting her to continue along this vein would condemn him to a no-brainer decision. "Ms. Lee, with all due respect, how old was Mark Zuckerberg when he started Facebook?"

Great shot. That should take her off her pace.

For all of two seconds.

"That's a bit different, Mr. Holden."

"Really? I disagree. The point is he was young. A college dropout—some Ivy League school, I believe."

She shifted position and leaned forward aggressively. "He was also on the forefront of a business no one had previously conceptualized."

True. But...now was the time for a smart answer, but he didn't have one.

"On the other hand," she continued, holding up the folder again, "you're proposing to enter a business almost as old as prostitution. One with a well documented record of failures. A high percentage of failures, if you haven't noticed. What makes you think you can succeed in a competitive marketplace at a time when the economy is in recession? Especially when you're up against real pros with career experience at setting up new restaurants."

He laughed. "Those pros? Usually, they open franchises in successful formula driven chains. I'm not referring to the inexpensive cookie-cutter family menu places like Applebee's or Outback. We're talking about the upscale steak houses that charge sixty bucks for an eight-ounce filet on top of another twenty for a baked potato. Those aren't concept plays at all. They cater to the business clientele. They're totally formula-driven and predictable, specializing in reliability. And you know why?"

He continued, "Say you're a Chicago businessman visiting Seattle for a meeting and you need to take a client out for dinner.

Where do you go? To a place you *know* is going to be good because you've been at the same place in San Francisco or Denver or Fargo. That's the kind of place ninety percent of your pros open.

"But the good restaurants?" he continued. "The ones that demand a six-month waiting list, the ones like The French Laundry? They're built around an excellent chef, good service, and a mystique that means you can serve a food critic canned cat food over rice, swirl a glaze over it and still come away with a rave review. And that's the kind of place I'm planning to build. Orcas will be a restaurant everyone will want to experience. And when they do, they'll be so blown away, they'll want to keep coming back because it is *the* place. It will be timeless instead of just another fad."

Lee laughed in his face. A muted laugh, but a laugh nonetheless.

They stared at each other several seconds, deadlocked.

She propped the reading glasses up on her forehead. "Kid, I got to hand it to you, you got chutzpah out the ass."

What the hell was that supposed to mean?

"Thanks, I guess. But do I have the loan?"

She gave another laugh. "One point five? You're either insane or smoking some really good product."

"No, no. That's what I figure I need."

Her face grew dead serious. "Then the answer is, no, your loan won't go."

He was already trying to decide which bank to apply to next when she said, "But I'll tell you what we will do. We'll swing a line of credit for half that amount, and that's only because you just impressed me *and* because you'll be putting up the condo and the municipal bond portfolio as collateral. So if you accept our terms, at least five hundred thousand of those bonds go straight into escrow to stay until the loan is completely repaid plus interest. That's the best I can do. Take it or leave it."

Pros and cons again. Damn it. How could he accept an offer

like that without knowing what his costs of the remodel would be? Or his monthly overhead? On the other hand, since the recent credit meltdown, loans of any type were difficult to come by. There wasn't any guarantee another bank would do better. Looked like a classic "bird in the hand" situation.

"I'll take it."

25

SOUTH LAKE UNION AREA, SEATTLE

Taylor poked him in the ribs, said, "Okay, okay, so this isn't Belltown, but I tell you, this area is going to be equally hot. Maybe even hotter. You watch."

He had his arm around her shoulder as they stood side by side peering through a small observation window in a bare plywood barricade wall on the sidewalk fronting a building under construction. Hard to hear her words over the background din of traffic, cranes, and the warning beeps of trucks backing up. The smell of freshly poured concrete permeated the air. Construction dust coated every surface, including his hands.

In a few months this mass of steel I-beams and bare concrete would be a gleaming twenty-story edifice of black reflecting glass. Five floors of parking, street-level retail, and fifteen floors of living space transitioning from studios on the lowest floor to three bedroom units on the highest. He couldn't imagine the selling price of those upper level condos.

For years Paul Allen's company, Vulcan, had been buying low-rise commercial buildings along Westlake Avenue and south Lake Union. Block by block, teardowns were being replaced with sleek solidly built structures, fulfilling Allen's vision of transforming the drab, seedy area into a trendy, vibrant neighborhood. The strategy was screamingly successful, too. The area was morphing into one of

Seattle's most desirable districts. The mix of costly gasoline, the congested deteriorating freeway system, and the appeal of downtown living made the area doubly attractive for those who worked in the nearby office buildings. As part of Allen's plan, a trolley shuttled people from the east shore of Lake Union into the heart of the downtown retail district. What wasn't to love?

Joel had to admit, the neighborhood was molten. But somehow it didn't possess the soul he envisioned for Orcas. More specifically, this particular space under consideration just wouldn't work. Physically.

He said to Taylor, "But this wasn't designed to be a restaurant. It's more like a dress shop or a Vespa dealership. We'd have to improvise a fix for all the ventilation issues after the fact. That'd be a huge pain in the ass." Admittedly a lame argument because with the build-out unfinished, a good architect could work around it, possibly venting the cook areas directly into the alley. But he felt compelled to point out any shortcomings.

She gave him her you-gotta-be-kidding-me look. "Anything's possible. Get the right people and we could deal with it."

"Sure, if you throw enough money at it. Don't forget, building out an unfinished shell is going to cost a lot more than a simple remodel." Which, with a line of credit half of his estimated minimum, was now a constant worry. Every night since signing for the loan, he tossed and turned in bed for hours, trying to figure out ways to accomplish his dream with a hobbled budget. Each iteration of his plan ended up with the same problem: too large a gap between fantasy and reality. Several times he seriously considered delaying the project until the estate was freed up or just throwing in the towel and settling for something less grand. But he couldn't wrap his mind around either option. Joel's vision didn't include a half-assed job. He'd do it right or not at all. And not at all wasn't acceptable as a significant change for his past way of living life. In the meantime, he and Taylor would keep looking, and would consider every available space Khan came up with.

Taylor turned around and swept both hands out, as if presenting the block across the street. "Look at this! This neighborhood. We can be in on the ground floor of what's sure to be a fantastic block. It's a perfect location with huge potential. This area's going to be the next Belltown. And if you think about it, we could have a better lifestyle by being here. You know, like, you could sell the condo and buy a unit in this building. Think about it. Walk out your door and take an elevator to work. How convenient would that be? That would be fantastic!"

"Try selling cars. You're a natural."

But she had a point. Question was, did she really believe it, or was she just trying to steer him away from his Pampas fixation? No question about it, this would be a great area. In about another five years, maybe seven at the outside. But how much did he want to be a pioneer for building the area's reputation?

His cell started ringing. Took him a second to hear it over the din. He put the phone to his ear without checking caller ID. "Yeah?" He plugged his other ear with a finger.

"Mr. Holden, Latasha Khan."

He glanced at Taylor, but she was looking at the construction site again with her back to him. He stepped toward the street, hoping in vain for more quiet.

"Yes?" He figured this was just another lead on a "great" spot. Problem was, by now they'd exhausted Belltown, so every new space she found was in totally unexciting areas: Greenlake, Ballard, West Seattle. Neighborhoods filled with two-story Craftsman homes with cyclone-fenced yards, sidewalks cracked from overgrown roots, vegetable gardens enclosed in railroad ties, and public grade schools. Sure, you could establish a nice little family restaurant in one of those areas, but that wasn't the Orcas concept—it wouldn't look right to park a gleaming Maserati outside of Orcas with an Ace Hardware next door.

Besides, he definitely wanted to stay away from the south Seattle regions Ortega's crew controlled.

No, Orcas had to be downtown.

"The Pampas property is available again," Khan said excitedly.

"What?" Had he heard right? "Say again."

"The Pampas. The restaurant you originally showed interest in? The group that leased the space? Their financing fell through. It is available if you're still interested. The owners even indicate they'll consider a modest adjustment to thirty-six per square foot if you sign within forty-eight hours. Shall I tell them you are interested?"

26

PAMPAS RESTAURANT

"Sixty thousand! That's a joke, right?"

Sweating, Joel sat in a banquette next to Rick Prince of Red Caynon Construction, The Man when it came to restaurant remodels. During his due diligence, Joel had talked with several other restaurateurs and Prince always came up as the top contractor on their recommended list. The consistent caveat being, "He's expensive, but stands by his work. And it's very high quality." The company had a compelling portfolio of glossy 8 x 10 color photographs of prior jobs, all of which looked like they could be featured in *Architectural Digest*.

Prince shrugged. "I'm sure you can find someone who'll do it cheaper. But with the soffits and lighting you chose, and really need to have, I'm cutting this bid close as is."

Jesus, sixty grand just for the ceiling. And they hadn't yet started discussing the floors, walls, bathrooms, etc. On top of it, other quotes had blown him away too. Like reupholstering these fucking orange banquettes. For that, and the new furniture, he was using Rene Mason, an upscale decorator specializing in commercial interiors. Like Rich, she boasted an impressive portfolio of winners.

And he hadn't even started looking for some of the basic necessities such as linens, glassware, and flatware.

Yeah, sure, he could shake Prince's hand and say, "Sorry, I'll get someone else," but in an attempt to jumpstart a buzz within the restaurant community and food critics, he'd already leaked word to the *Puget Sound Business Journal* that he'd be using Prince Construction. The story was appearing tomorrow. Piss off that reporter and it'd be really hard to recoup.

A drop of sweat slithered down the side of his chest. He studied the ceiling. Shit! This industrial-chic look sucked. It needed to be replaced with good indirect lighting if this place was to have the feel and atmosphere it needed. Not only would it look terrific, but soffits would soften noise, making the dining experience better for the customers while not bothering the homeowners above. He hated restaurants in which the noise was so loud that he had to either strain to hear the person directly across the table or lip read. No, he couldn't cut costs by not installing a new ceiling. Any savings would have to come from scrimping on something else.

"No, no... we need to do it. The cost's a little shocking, is all."

Prince shrugged again, pulled out the plans for the bathroom remodels.

Chris holds the pen above the signature line, knowing that soon as the contract is inked, he'll be in debt for $250,000. Not much for some people, but it's huge for him. Especially considering the balance he still owes on his student loans.

But they need a home of their own, not another rented apartment. Joel is at that age when he needs to grow up in a neighborhood where he can ride a bike, have a back yard to play in, and maybe walk to grade school.

Besides, once he's out of training, he'll start making money. Investing in a home at this stage of his career has to be a good move.

But Jesus, $250,000. A quarter of a million. The sum is staggering to him.

He thinks of Joel, now two month old, and signs the contract.

A half hour later Joel walked Prince to the front door, unlocked it to let him out. "One final thing."

Prince raises an eyebrow. "Yeah?"

"There's a five thousand dollar bonus for you for every week ahead of schedule you complete the project."

The idea came to him a few minutes ago. To do things right, he and Taylor would have to hire their staff weeks before the doors opened to the public. Considering the expense of a full payroll, supplies, and other fixed overhead, this training period would easily exceed five grand a week. Plus, each week ahead of schedule was one week closer to bringing in money. It'd be worth it.

"Thanks for the offer, but keep in mind what I told you: shit happens. All it takes is for the faucets to not show up and the bathrooms don't get finished. The bathrooms don't get finished, you can't open for business. Everything links to everything else in a project like this and there are some things I can't control. See what I mean?"

"Got it. But while you're waiting for the faucets, there're other things you can be doing. Right?"

"Sure. Up to a point. But you can't paint unless the drywall's up. You can't drywall until you've passed inspections. On and on. Everything has to be in an order."

"But you'll try?"

Prince smiled, put a hand on Joel's shoulder. "For five grand a week, you bet I will."

Back at the banquette, Joel reviewed the budget. And cringed. Worse yet, they were just getting started. Well, couldn't be helped. There was always the unexpected...

Just then Taylor came through the front door. "Hey there."

"Hi."

She threw the deadbolt, started his way. "Oh man, you won't believe what they're asking for wine glasses. I was floored."

He believed all right. He just didn't want to hear it.

27

The phone rang with the distinctive tone that signaled the call originated from the doorman's desk instead of his outside line. Joel answered it.

"Mr. Holden, there's a Mr. Rabb here to see you. He says you're expecting him. Should I have him to come up?"

"Yes, please. Thanks, Marshall." He hung up but remained facing the kitchen window for a few seconds, not wanting to deal with Taylor's reaction. It wouldn't be pleasant.

"Who was that?" she called from the living room.

Here it comes. "That was the doorman. Luther's on his way up."

They hadn't discussed Luther's involvement in Orcas since their initial argument. What was there to say? She didn't like him. He did. She didn't want him working with them. He did. Hiring Luther would be one of those decisions he'd have to make in spite of her misgivings. He hated doing that, preferring instead for them to agree on all important issues like this. But he knew total agreement on everything was never realistic in any relationship, no matter how good it might be. However, it was probably moot because he doubted Luther would leave the sweet deal he had going at Chez to move here.

She exhaled audibly and slowly. No words. Just that simple sound that made her reaction to the news excruciating clear: disapproval, disappointment, and resignation in knowing Luther's visit signaled a decision that had been made without her input. Fact was, Luther hadn't been asked yet. Not officially. But even if

Luther declined, Joel had to give him the right of first refusal. In truth, he and Taylor had interviewed no one better for the job thus far. But they—or at least he—hadn't looked into an alternative all that hard. They had been too swamped with other things.

He said to her, "Hey, I know we've been through this, what, a hundred times already, but we need someone with his talents. He's really good with people."

Silence.

Which was her way of making a point.

Exasperated, he threw up his arms, walked to the front door, opened it to wait for the elevator to arrive.

What were they getting so wrapped around the axle for? They didn't know if Luther was even interested. How idiotic was that? Besides, Taylor's intentions were good. All she really wanted was to see Orcas succeed. He loved her because of that. He decided that if Luther opted out, he'd do something special for her, like take her out to dinner tonight.

A moment later Luther stepped into the hall and began looking at door numbers. He wore a beautifully tailored navy pinstripe suit, navy silk mock tee, and what had to be deer leather Ferragamo loafers. The man was always perfectly groomed, whether in business or rapper attire, which were his two preferences. His hair was close-cropped to match an equally cropped beard. His look was topped off with stylish glasses. Mister GQ.

Joel called, "Looking good, Bro."

They did the ghetto shake—smooth, fluid, ending in a vertical fist bump, not the white-bread knuckle-bump thing.

Inside, Luther glanced around. "Whoa dude, nice place."

"Come on in the front room. Taylor's here. Want a beer?"

Luther was already sliding off his suit coat, draping it over the back of a chair. "Better not. Have a long drive back to Portland once we done."

"If you want, stay in the guest room tonight. We can all go out to dinner later."

Luther waved away the offer. "Thanks, but I need to get back. Hey, girl," he said, casting a smile at Taylor.

"Luther," she replied in a neutral tone.

Joel decided if Luther wasn't going to have a beer, he wouldn't either, but offered Taylor one.

She declined, probably for the same reason.

The front room held a small couch with a coffee table and two chairs in front of it. Taylor sat on the couch, legs tucked under her. Luther folded himself into one of the chairs facing her, Joel taking the other one, saying, "Thanks for coming up, it's a lot of driving for just a conversation." One hundred and fifty miles each way.

Luther shifted in the chair, getting comfortable. "Dude, this thing's more than idle conversation. The thing you mentioned on the phone, about getting this new place started, intrigues me. Tell me about it."

Joel sucked a deep breath and consciously tried to temper his enthusiasm, wanting to describe their plans objectively so Taylor couldn't claim he'd pushed hard selling the job.

"This could be a real showstopper, man. We can build a place people talk about." He went on to explain the overall plans followed by the more specific remodeling of the Pampas space already underway.

Taylor seemed more interested in the view of downtown—which Joel knew was not the case at all—but was listening intently in spite of her blasé demeanor.

He finished up describing their plans by offering Luther the job as Orcas' maitre d', the idea being he'd be the first person hired so that he would help select the best staff possible. Taylor was clearly upset with the conversation. Nothing blatant enough for Luther to pick up on, just that silent communication between couples. To make matters worse, Luther was interested enough to ask questions.

The conversation lasted another hour before Luther wound down, seemingly satisfied with what he'd heard. He pushed out of his chair. "Your offer's really interesting, dude. Mind if I think it over a day or so before making a decision?"

Joel stood too. "Sure, but if possible, I'd appreciate a decision within the week. That enough time?"

"Probably only need a day. I'll call tomorrow." Luther shrugged on his suit coat and shot the cuffs as Taylor made a silent beeline for the bedroom.

Luther called after her, "Night, girl."

She answered by shutting the bedroom door. Not a slam exactly, but hard enough for Joel to recognize a statement.

As he reached for the front door knob, Luther stopped him and in a lowered voice said, "I know Taylor knew what we had going in Portland. 'Cause she made it diamond clear she didn't approve. More than once. I understand how you feel about her. What I'm saying is, we going be doing the same thing here, right?"

Joel glanced down the hall to make sure the bedroom door was closed. It was. Still, he kept his voice low, said, "Glad you brought it up because I intended to discuss this before you made up your mind. In case it affects your decision. Things are going to be different here. No selling. You choose to use, that's cool. But no dealing. Not even as a gift. Understand?"

Luther recoiled. "You serious?"

"Nothing personal, Luther. Understand a couple things. Most of all, I'm putting a lot into this. Not just money, but every ounce of myself. No way I'm gonna risk losing it. Understand?"

Luther shot his sleeves again and readjusted his coat. "Cool. But you also need to understand I have certain, ah, income requirements. What I make at the Chez doesn't cut it, dude. We both know that."

"I do. I appreciate that." Joel ran a quick calculation in his head. Sure, he could make it without Luther, but the guy had skills Orcas needed. Enough so, it would be worth offering him more salary. "How about I raise your salary five percent and put you in charge of the tip pool?" Meaning Luther would be free to skim a higher amount to supplement his needs. Not enough to draw attention from the other staff sharing the pool, but enough to help. "When we become profitable, you get another five percent bump."

Luther smoothed the lay of his lapels. "Gives me something to think about on the drive back. You'll get my answer tomorrow."

Joel opened the door for Luther. "Safe trip."

They did the hand thing again.

Taylor was waiting in the kitchen when he walked in to pop a celebration beer.

"What was that all about?" She was still radiating disapproval.

He thought maybe she'd gone in the bedroom to change clothes before going out for dinner, but she wore the same hip huggers and a short halter.

"Just getting some ground rules established, is all. No drugs."

"Really?" She sounded encouraged.

He turned a serious face to her. "Taylor, you think I'd actually be stupid enough to risk our dream by committing a felony?"

She reached past him to open the fridge door. "I certainly hope not." She handed him a beer. "Sincerely hope you're not that stupid."

28

ORCAS RESTAURANT

Joel looked at the thirty-two-year old man sitting across the banquette from him. Impeccable resume, having worked as line cook in several top kitchens up and down the West Coast. Which might signal a problem. Too many places. Meaning he moved around more than he should have. Meaning he either had a drug or behavioral problem. Maybe both, if they were causally related. That, plus the pronounced early signs of aging hinted, more specifically, to a meth problem. Maybe coke. But Joel guessed from the look of his ravaged face, it was likely meth.

This applicant was a perfect candidate for Luther's scrutiny. Luther would size this guy up in ten minutes or less.

"One more thing you should know, Bradford. We have a zero tolerance policy for smoking anywhere inside or in front of the restaurant. You smoke, you take it out to the alley." He didn't see a pack in Bradford's breast pocket, but so what?

The interviewee flashed a smile, giving a full view of gum disease. Nice.

"No problem."

"And one more thing. We have a zero tolerance for drugs anywhere in or outside Orcas during work hours. What employees do on their off time, away from here, is their business. What they do on my dime is my business." He locked eyes with the cook and asked, "That a problem?"

Bradford hesitated enough to verify Joel's suspicion.

"No, no problem."

"Any questions?"

The guy smiled. "When do I start?"

Joel sighed and glanced at Luther, said, "We're not through with the interview yet. Once we finish that, we talk as a team. Is this your contact phone number?" He held up the application form.

Bradford's smile faded. "We?"

Joel nodded. "We're sort of a family here. Taylor—she handles the bar—Luther, and me." He leaned out the end of the banquette, yelled, "Yo, Luther, you ready?"

Luther sat at table in the distant corner of the dining room, a place as far removed from the remodel noise and commotion as possible. He glanced up from his paperwork, nodded. "Send him over."

That's when Joel noticed Rick Prince waiting for a word with him. He handed the job applicant his forms to give to Luther and signaled Prince to occupy the seat the line cook just vacated.

Prince slid an 8 x 10 manila envelope across the table to him while sitting down. This banquette, the only one with a clear view down the full length of the restaurant to the front door, had become Joel's official office, his desk, conference room, and the first place anyone looked for him.

Prince said, "Second payment's due."

The contract stipulated three payments: a third before starting work, a third at the halfway point, the final third after satisfactory completion of the punch list—the list of small things overlooked or not done to Joel's satisfaction.

"No problem." He opened the envelope, pulled out a sheaf of papers. The top page was the overview summary with the amount due. The remaining pages were copies of the accounting and receipts. His eye went straight to the bottom line.

Shocked, he did a double take.

Jesus, had they mixed up accounts? This wasn't his. He glanced back at Rick. "Whoa, here," he said, handing it back to him. "Wrong account."

Prince pushed the papers back to him. "No, this is yours. Double-checked it myself while I was waiting, just to be sure."

A sick feeling seeped through his gut. *Something's wrong here.*

"But the contract says payments in thirds. This is more like half."

A knowing smile crept into Prince's face. "The *agreement*, not *contract*, was for the initial estimate. It didn't include any change orders. I have copies of those, if you want. You signed 'em."

Okay, sure, there were several minor changes, but nothing that was any big deal. Little modifications here, a few more there. Couldn't add up to *this* much.

"Right. A few minor changes. But this..." He held up the sheaf. Way out of line.

"Mr. Holden," Prince said, obviously losing patience. "I'm not here to argue with you. You think I'm cheating you, get a lawyer or accountant to go over it in detail. But until this account is paid up, work stops. Right now."

"But—"

"Check it out." He took the papers from Joel, pulled one from the sheaf and slapped it on the table. "Here. This is a good example. Wall sconces. You changed from the original ones to what's up there now. Those puppies cost three times what the originals would've been. You changed it. Do they look good? Yep. No question, they do. Do they cost more? Yep. No question, they do. Did you order that change? Yep. No question you signed off on it."

Then Prince pulled out another page. "Oh, here's another good example. Lavatory fixtures. The original bid was for some functional chrome Deltas. You ended up with fancy German ones in brushed nickel. Again, each one cost three times what the Deltas would've. Shall I go on to another example?"

"Okay, okay, I get it." *Shit!* But, he reminded himself, they were all very real upgrades—vital for Orcas's image of classy good taste.

"Image is important, son." Dad leans over, grasps Joel's necktie in one hand, the Windsor knot in the other. A slight tug this way, a pull that way and Dad lets go. "There. Your tie's straight."

"Dad, I don't—"

"How do you think my patients would view me if I wore jeans and a sweatshirt to the office? Would that give the right impression of professional competence?"

Joel doesn't like wearing a suit, much less a freshly laundered white shirt. They're restrictive, binding, unnatural. What's more, he doesn't like being in a church, no matter what the occasion. Feels creepy. Everybody looking out the corner of their eyes, talking in lowered voices, acting friendly when they didn't really give a shit or are looking for an opportunity to evangelize. A bunch of fucking hypocrites is what they are.

Besides, he doesn't even know the people getting married. Some daughter of someone Dad knows from the hospital. Who gives a rat's ass?

And now Dad's haranguing him with another lecture on how to be presentable. Shit!

Chris says, "I'll go check on Janice, then we should be ready to leave."

Good, he has enough time to sneak a toke or two off the roach hidden under his bed. If he has to go to church, might as well go loaded. Should help pass the time.

Prince was going on. "...to say nothing of the change from laminate to granite counters."

Aw shit. The more Prince explained the sum, the more he accepted the amount. Each improvement, by itself, only amounted to only a couple thousand bucks. But, start piling one on top of the other and they add up quickly. Apparently, more than he'd appreciated.

Well, that wasn't quite true, now was it? Overrunning the budget was the reason for visiting Ms. Lee yesterday. To plead for an increased line of credit. She laughed before turning him down. Chris never would've allowed this to happen. Then again, living differently was what this was all about.

He said to Prince, "Hold on. Let me get my check book," which was right there next to him, inside the cool laptop bag on the new leather upholstery. He wrote the check, tore it from the book, handed it to Prince.

Luther slid into the same spot Prince had occupied and leaned forward, the applicant still across the room, waiting at Luther's table.

In a lowered voice Luther said, "Dude's a fucking loser."

"What are you thinking, meth?"

"No shit, Tonto."

A veil of disappointment descended over him. How could finding good responsible restaurant workers be so difficult?

"Okay, send him back over and I'll tell him no."

"Naw," Luther waved away the suggestion. "I'll be bad cop this time. Looks like you got your hands full."

Joel watched Luther slide out of the banquette before turning back to the computer to pull up the spreadsheet. At this burn rate, they'd barely open for business before he was broke. Time to look at the numbers again and search for any way to squeeze a few more bucks from someplace else.

29

Joel unlocked the front door to Orcas and slipped inside, then made sure the deadbolt was securely locked again. A couple of times, when they forgot to do so, people brazenly walked in off the street even though the restaurant was obviously under renovation and had brown paper shrouding the street windows. Mostly neighbors, curious to see their progress. Which was a by-product of Taylor having mailed every resident in a five-block radius an announcement of the planned opening. And, of course, there had been a few street people looking for handouts. Amazing.

The air still smelled of sawdust, spackle, and fresh paint even though the sawhorses, ladders, and paint tarps were removed two days ago when the structural changes had been completed. Tomorrow morning a janitorial crew would give the place a thorough final cleaning.

All the street-facing windows remained taped over, leaving the bar area in deep shadows when the overhead lights weren't on. At the far wall, featuring the harbor view, all the Venetian blinds had been raised to allow in as much light as possible. A mixed blessing, those windows: they provided a fantastic view but at the cost of collecting a ton of solar heat. Which meant the A/C was required to run 24/7 to keep the heat from becoming insufferable. Which turned out to be another expense he'd failed to budget for. He had considered—but nixed—the idea of keeping the front door open to improve natural ventilation, but doing so bred other problems he didn't want to deal with.

Taylor was busy behind the bar. He scanned the room but didn't see Luther.

"Hey!" He called out to Taylor, while holding up a cold six-pack of beer. "Celebration time."

"Bring it over here," called Luther.

He looked again and this time saw him crouched next to the banquette by the windows, the glare and angle of the setting sun making him almost impossible to see.

Grinning, Taylor stepped from behind the bar, drying her hands on a towel. As always, she looked stunning, even in jeans and a tank top. They walked to the banquette where Luther was kneeling, fixing something. The other employees had long since gone home.

She slid into the banquette first, he and Luther taking opposite sides, the seating generous, not at all crowded. He plunked the six-pack in the center of the table, then handed both a beer. "It's official."

"What?" Luther twisted off his bottle cap and tossed it on the table. The cap spun a couple time before spiraling to a stop, top up.

Joel pulled a paper from his inside coat pocket and passed it to Taylor. "This is for the display case in the kitchen," he said. That's where all the licenses were posted: food permits, liquor license, business license. "As of today, in the eyes of the State of Washington and King County, we're officially Orcas."

"Cool!"

Joel uncapped a bottle for himself and slipped back into thinking about the name, Orcas. Wasn't one-hundred-percent sold on it, but even with all the head scratching, none of them could come up with something more suitable. Because the menu featured local seafood and produce, it seemed appropriate that the name should contain a Northwest flair. Orcas Island—named after the Orca whale—was in the nearby San Juan chain and the symbol of the killer whale was frequently incorporated into Northwest Indian art. So, what could be more Northwest? Then again, Orcus—he subsequently learned—was the name of the Roman god of death and the underworld. Not that he was superstitious, but...since his—what? transformation?—he'd become less sure that beliefs such as karma, reincarnation, or afterlives didn't exist. He'd always discounted what he couldn't explain by rational, scientific thought and physical laws. If reincarnation were real, how could one explain population growth? At any one time shouldn't the world contain the same number of beings as a decade ago? And if God is good, how could there be so much suffering and life be so difficult for 99.9% of living beings?

He let his gaze sweep over the renovated interior.

"Aw man, look at this." He swept his hand in a horizontal arc, to turn their attention to the newly renovated interior. Beautifully transformed from an ugly loser restaurant into a show-stopper. "It really came together."

They all raised their beers in a toast. "To Orcas."

He asked Luther, "How's the training going?"

They all interviewed cooks and wait staff, but Luther was tasked with the actual hiring paperwork along with checking green cards on three of them. Last thing he wanted was to be busted for employing illegal aliens.

"They'll be ready by mid next week." Meaning by then the cooks would know the menu and station assignments and the wait staff would be fully coached on the Orcas culture.

"Perfect."

Slumping back against the cushion, Joel basked in a warm sense of pride and accomplishment at having guided a huge project to completion in an unbelievably short time—something the old drug-dealing Joel could never have done. He'd successfully navigated a minefield of hassles and permits to reach this stage while keeping Rick Prince's crew on schedule. To top it off, Orcas now offered an outstanding menu. Not so many options to make it impossible for the kitchen to handle, but offering a satisfying variety from a realistic number of recipes. As time went by, dishes would be added and others removed as they constantly honed their menu to adjust to the customers' tastes.

They'd had their strokes of luck, too. Two weeks ago an upscale Bellevue restaurant declared bankruptcy, allowing him to purchase their flatware and glasses before the repo guys could get their hands on them. All high quality stuff that saved several thousand bucks.

Which brought up the money issue again.

Fuck it. Don't dwell on that tonight. Tonight is only the positive.

He'd lined up excellent suppliers for seafood, produce, and meat while Taylor had negotiated some great prices from two wine distributors who specialized in local vineyards. Same with the liquor supplier.

How could he—Chris—have trivialized the job of chief chef? Especially one who owned the restaurant. Like all prejudices, his had been born from a total lack of appreciation for the required skills. We judge most harshly the things we know least, he decided. A good lesson, one he vowed to not repeat but knew he undoubtedly would.

Okay, but how did Joel's desire to be a chef originate? He certainly had no role model, and Chris believed the majority of career choices come from those whom we most admire.

"Let me show you how to do it," Dad says.

Joel climbs up to stand on a kitchen chair so he can watch Dad remove the metal toasted cheese sandwich mold from a kitchen drawer. To Joel it looks like a big clam shell with handles. Dad places it on the counter, coats the two inside halves with butter.

"You can do it without butter, but it sure makes every bite taste better if you use it," Dad explains. He sets two pieces of bread on the counter, then slices a thick slab of golden cheddar cheese. "And then here's the real trick. Coat the inside of the sandwich with mustard. Dijon, preferably." With a knife, he spreads the thick layer of mustard over the bread.

"Be sure to put the cheese only in the center so it won't leak out the

sides." He shows Joel how this is done.

"Okay, now we close the mold." He folds the two sides together and locks it in place, squeezing off the corners of bread, forming a disk-shaped sandwich. "Be sure to get these off," he adds, removing the corners and tossing them in the garbage.

He turns a stove burner on high, then begins to heat the mold. "One minute on each side should do it. Just enough to toast the bread and melt the cheese."

Finished, he holds the mold over a plate and opens it. Out falls a perfectly round toasted cheese sandwich that looks to Joel like a 1950's flying saucer.

"Let it cool to the touch before you bite into it or the hot cheese will stick to the inside of your mouth and burn like crazy."

When it's cool enough to hold, Joel picks it up and takes a bite, savoring the combination of cheddar and mustard. It's wonderful, the best toasted cheese sandwich in the world, maybe even the universe. More than that, he actually saw how it was made and is fascinated at the process. It's food magic, something he can now do.

It crosses his mind to add bacon bits or even a strip or two of bacon. Yeah, that might really make it better.

Or even fool around with another kind of mustard.

He could create his own style of sandwich! The Joelwich.

At the time he didn't appreciate that his whole life had just changed by seeding an ambition.

With Luther and Taylor now chatting, his mind wandered back to those moments on the mountain trail...the chest pain...his new life was the chance he'd dreamed of having and he was really doing things differently. Reed was wrong: he wasn't being held hostage to his old personality. Orcas proved that. Never in a million years would the old Chris have undertaken such a radical and risky project. And, for the sake of argument, if Chris had started a restaurant, it would have begun as a small café or bakery as a buy-out from an established owner.

Which raised an interesting point: whose life was this? Chris's or Joel's? And if he were a mixture of both men's personalities, was he really living differently? If, in fact, it was a hybrid...

Huh! Stalemate.

Damn, he wanted to know how this worked, how he awoke in Joel's body. Chris's life had been consumed with understanding how the world around him worked. Not politically but scientifically. This basic curiosity was what channeled him into a scientific career instead of literature or art. He was most at ease when able to understand the underlying mechanism of a phenomenon. But this new life was a mystery he couldn't begin to understand. It was the first time he was forced to accept something on faith alone.

Still bothering him, the sword hanging over his head, was the fear his life would just as easily slip away. Chris unconsciously counted on living until he reached the actuarial limit of his generation, at which point, he'd begin walking on thin ice. It had given him confidence that his life wouldn't end tomorrow. In contrast, Joel was too young to begin dwelling on his own mortality. But now, knowing that he'd died at fifty-five, he worried incessantly that tomorrow would never come, that this was only his spirit, a vesper of thought still on that mountain trail, and his new "life" was nothing more than his last thought. Was that what we took into eternity? Our last living thought?

Taylor stretched and yawned. "Aw jeez, this beer's making me sleepy. Time for me to head home. I can hit it again tomorrow morning." Then to Joel, "You coming?"

30

10:03 PM

Taylor said, "Joel?"

Oh man, not that tone of voice. He knew it too well. In particular, anytime she turned one word into a question. Because it usually indicated she intended to talk about something weighty. Or sensitive. Or both. Sometimes she was cuing up for an argument, although she'd never admit that. That's the way her tone sounded now.

They were bent over their respective bathroom sinks brushing teeth, rinsing faces, doing all those get-ready-for-bed things. For some unstated reason and without any negotiations, the left sink, counter space, and two bathroom drawers had become hers since her first day here. He guessed it was a natural extension of the way things had been in Portland. Just like her preference for sleeping on the right side of the bed.

In fact, their relationship had eased back into the same limbo that characterized life in Portland, only this time with a bit of role reversal. Now, he was the one wanting more commitment while she preferred to "wait and see."

"See what?" he'd asked.

"See what happens to us," she'd replied.

Why?

She claimed his different persona made her cautious. It

worried her. "It makes me less sure of us," she'd said.

He didn't get it, but what could he do?

He rinsed his mouth and face, stood and toweled off. "What?"

She carefully folded her face towel, set it down, turned to him, the preciseness of each movement just one more sign—not a good one either—of where this conversation was headed.

She wore her usual bedtime clothes; oversized white tank-top undershirt and panties, a combo he found uniquely sexy, to her dismay.

She said, "Let's go in the other room, okay?"

Aw Christ, what now? He was tired. The last thing he wanted was a long involved discussion. But, he reminded himself, listening to your partner during times like this was important to maintaining a strong relationship. Relationships took effort.

In the bedroom, by the window, two reading chairs faced each other, sharing a common ottoman. The curtains were drawn, blocking off the city view as well as an unobstructed view directly into their bedroom from the buildings across the street. She climbed into her usual chair, feet tucked under her, knees in hand. He dropped into his chair, legs out, feet on the ottoman, wondering what this was about.

She asked, "How are the finances?"

Suppressing a yawn, he massaged the bridge of his nose in an attempt to fend off a subtle but nagging headache. "So far, so good."

She cocked her head in that questioning manner of hers. "Really? Even with the remodel overruns? We never actually discussed the costs in any detail, but from just a mental count, they seem pretty huge."

He continued to squeeze the bridge of his nose. Her tone was irritating. Not because of her concern—which was well-intended—because, after all, she *was* looking out for him and Orcas—but because the timing sucked. He wasn't intentionally trying to hide the finances from her. He just hadn't discussed them because he knew damned well how she'd react. She'd start nagging about how he let such costs overruns happen and he didn't want to have to even try to explain.

Chris's life had been dominated by depression-era fiscal values and dictums, an attitude inherited from his grandparents. Buy only what you can afford. No mortgage should exceed 28% of your income. Salt away a portion of every paycheck for retirement regardless of whether you have a company pension. Plan for the future. Yada yada yada. All bullshit. With this second chance at life he was damned well going to operate outside of that box if the payoff seemed worth it. Especially since he didn't know if this life would end tomorrow. Besides, fulfilling Joel's dream was worth every ounce of risk. And, he had to admit, it was a total mind-buzz to see Orcas come together so beautifully. This was something Taylor would never understand.

He said, "How come I'm getting a strong déjà vu about now?"

"Please, just answer the question."

Aw shit, just get this over with and get to bed.

Joel said, "The answer's the same as last time." *And the time before that.* "When I budgeted, I factored in a ten percent overrun for exactly this kind of contingency. We're still in our comfort zone. Why do you ask?" He hated lying to her, but he couldn't see any other option.

She began running her fingers over the chair fabric, smoothing out the grain. "It's just that this seems to be getting so expensive...so much more than I ever dreamed it'd cost. It makes me very nervous. I worry, is all."

Leaning over, reaching across the ottoman, he took her hand. "That's sweet of you, but even if everything goes down the drain, all you've lost is your time."

She jerked her hand away. "That's a terrible thing to say."

"What?" He mentally replayed his last words, looking for what might be so awful. And couldn't find it. "All I said was—"

"Don't!" She held up both hands. "I don't want to hear it."

"Hear what?"

"Hear how innocent your comment was. If you gave it more than one self-serving miniscule thought, you'd realize what you were *really* saying is that if things go bad, *you* would be the only one who loses anything significant: money. In other words, I have no investment in this other than my time, and that my time really isn't worth a penny. Isn't that what you said? Isn't that what you meant?"

Aw man, totally fucked.

At this point nothing he could say would change where this was headed. Something had been building inside her for the past few days and just now it was coming to a head, like it or not.

What's bothering her?

He sat back, trying to figure that out.

She continued, "What you seem to forget is that money is power. You're the one putting up all the money for Orcas. Well, fine. That's wonderful. But that also gives you all the power. It makes Luther and me subservient."

She held up a hand, cutting him off. "I know what you're going to say, something along the lines of, 'I never said that.' Not in so many words, you didn't. But that's the point. You don't have to say it. It's an unstated understanding between all of us: you have the power. And if you've never considered that before now, you're more naïve than I thought."

He hadn't intended to have a drink tonight, but suddenly he wanted one. "I'm getting a beer. Want one?"

No, make that scotch.

She followed him down the hall to the kitchen. "As long as you got me all worked up and pissed, yes."

He turned to her. "Got *you* pissed? As I remember, I was happily brushing my teeth when this started. *You* brought it up. So far my total contribution to this entire conversation is what, maybe three words?"

He pulled down two tumblers and a bottle of Balvenie, did a double take at the label and replaced it for a big bottle of Johnnie Walker Red. No reason to waste the good stuff on an argument.

Hands on her hips, feet apart, she drilled him with her best dose of Taylor Eye.

"And another thing," she said. "When did you suddenly develop this taste for scotch? Especially single malts? Jesus, talk about pretentious! That's not the Joel I used to know."

You're right, it's Chris's taste.

But he couldn't very well tell her that. He handed her a drink, held up his glass to toast. When she didn't clink glasses, he shrugged, took a sip, headed back to the bedroom, the slap-slap-slap of her bare feet on his heels.

He dropped back into his chair as she resumed her modified lotus in the other.

After a few beats he asked, "So what's this all about? I think things got derailed somewhere along the line. What's bothering you?"

She appeared calmer now, perhaps a tad apologetic. Almost, but not quite.

"I don't know," she said, finger-stirring her ice cubes. "You've changed so much since your dad died."

He inspected his ice, intrigued at how the scotch smoothed the cubes so quickly. "Thought we've been through this. I thought you said the big change was that I'm more mature, was all. Why is that a problem?"

"No. Well, yes. That. But part of it freaks me. The way you talk, the way you think. Your touch. This restaurant thing. The old you never could have accomplished what you've done."

True. For diametrically different reasons, neither Chris nor Joel singularly would've been able to pull it off. Chris didn't have the balls to take on the high risk. Joel didn't have the initiative to push through to completion. This new combination produced a more capable person. He loved this new "him," but Taylor obviously had reservations.

He sipped, said, "Well then, is my new-found maturity as a good thing or a bad thing?"

"Joel, you're not listening. Maturity is one thing. What I'm talking about is entirely different." She studied him again, those brown eyes moving over his face to his eyes, his nose, back again.

"Basically, I'm the same person," he said. *At least physically.* "The difference is that Dad's death forced me to see life differently. That's all you're sensing."

"Oh, come on, sweetie, that's a load of crap. We both know you've changed. We've talked about it. You're more mature, more organized, more businesslike. Overnight. I don't know if those words capture what I'm trying to express but it makes me very nervous and edgy because you may no longer be the person I fell in love with. Which brings me back to the conversation we just had but didn't finish."

He wanted to ask what was more appealing about the other Joel, the dreamer who couldn't get things done. Instead asked, "What part was that?"

"The part about me having nothing to lose if Orcas goes bust. What about *my* dreams? What about all the time we sat together talking about how *we'd* put something together like this? Now it's almost a reality. Maybe I haven't put any money into this, but emotionally I'm just as invested as you. Maybe even more."

He couldn't see how that was possible.

"And Luther?" he asked, curious. Since the afternoon of the job offer, Luther's participation had been a taboo subject. Eventually they'd have to acknowledge the two-ton elephant in their lives. Never mind that Luther had worked hard to do an excellent job for them so far. His continued presence in Orcas remained a point of contention between them.

"You know damned well what I think about him. Do you really want to discuss this now?" She made it sound like a direct challenge.

He weighted his answer a beat. "We probably should, just to clear the air."

"Fine." She upended the drink, draining it in one final gulp.

"Want another?" he asked.

"No." She thumped the glass on the table a little too hard. "After this I'm going to try to sleep. Huh! Fat chance."

"Continue with what you were saying," he said.

She leaned over and began inspecting her toenails. "Luther is an opportunist. His dreams and future aren't invested in Orcas like ours are. He only sees an opportunity for himself."

"For what?"

She stopped with the toes and shot him her stupid-question-look. "For whatever comes along. An opportunity to make a few bucks."

She stood, moved to the side of the bed and yanked back the covers. "A good con artist doesn't always plan the next play. He just observes whatever's going on around him until some sixth sense recognizes an opportunity. Then he's on it, more out of shark-like instinct than analysis. He takes advantage of the situation. That's Luther."

"You see us as victims in this?"

She slid between the sheets, pulled the cover up to her shoulders and turned off her bedside lamp. She lay still for a moment.

"No. Not yet I don't. All I'm saying is what he wants is very different from what you or I want. Never lose sight of that. Never. You coming to bed or what?" She turned on her side, back toward him.

"In a few minutes. I want to think about things. Things you said. I'll try not to wake you if you're asleep when I come to bed." He started toward the hall and the living room.

"I wanted this to be a good conversation," she called after him. "Not like it turned out."

He stopped walking but didn't turn around.

She added, "Guess what I really wanted to say is don't get cocky. You've done amazingly well so far. Just don't do anything to screw it up."

"And that's where you see things headed?"

"I didn't say that. All I know is you've changed and it's a little scary at times. We're doing great. Please don't ruin it. I love you. Goodnight."

"Call for Dr Holden, line one," issues from the overhead speaker.

Chris is in the hall in front of an exam room, about to pull up his next patient's chart from the wall holder.

An ill-formed premonition hits. It's about Dad. And it's not good.

He hurries back to the communal room where the residents and attendings write chart notes between seeing patients. They're in the Internal Medicine Clinic at the county hospital where care to "indigent patients" is provided. This is his first year of residency.

He picks up the phone and punches the blinking light. "This is Dr. Holden."

"We need you here in the Emergency room STAT."

"Why, what is it?" But he knows. Dad.

He rushes through the double doors with the large red sign reading AUTHORIZED PERSONEL ONLY, pauses a moment until he sees someone wave him over to one of the trauma rooms. Inside he sees his father on a gurney with scrub-clad personnel clustered around, a defibrillator on a stainless steel cart next to a senior resident who is administering closed heart massage. The resident sweats from the hard work and stress of a resuscitation. That and the debris from opened packages scattered around the room tell Chris this has been going on a long time.

The doctor leading the resuscitation announces, "Give it another try."

A resident places the defibrillator paddles on Dad's chest already gooey with electrolytic gel, yells, "Clear away."

The doc squeezing an ambu bag to force air into Dad's lungs raises both hands, away from any contact with the body.

The one with the paddles calls, "Here goes," and thumbs the red trigger.

Dad's shoulders jerk as a jolt of electric current surges through his muscles.

All eyes lock onto the cardiac monitor. The screen resolves from shock artifact to a flat green line streaking across its surface.

"Nothing," someone calls. Another doctor opens Dad's eyelids. "No change. Pupils fully dilated, non-reactive."

They resume resuscitation efforts.

A voice to his right says, "You Chris Holden?"

Chris turns to face the doctor leading the team.

"Yes?"

"This your father?"

"Yes."

"We've been at it fifteen minutes now. I'm sorry, but I'm going to call it." Then, without waiting for an answer, he tells the group, "Okay, that's it. Official time of death is two fifteen."

31

ORCAS RESTAURANT, SEATTLE

Joel made a quick detour through the kitchen to spot-check the quality and supply of hors d'oeuvres. On the counter nearest the door sat two fully loaded trays ready to go. Shrimp, smoked salmon, Penn Cove mussels, a lovely variety of cheeses, other assorted goodies. The air was dense with humidity and scented with spices and fresh fish.

This must be heaven.

Over the clatter of kitchen noises he called to a young girl—a young girl? Jesus, she's my age—in black pants, white ruffled tuxedo shirt and cummerbund, "The station over by the bar needs replenishing." He decided to wear a spotless starched chef's blouse, white apron, black slacks, just to let his guests know exactly who he was.

She called back, "I'm on it, Mr. Holden."

Mr. Holden. Being addressed so formally by staff would require some getting used to, especially if they were older than he was. "You're doing great, Kara. Keep it up."

She was perfect. Tall, slender, with classic good looks, a classy attitude, and an innate sense for five-star customer service. Exactly the image he wanted associated with the Orcas brand. Every employee had been carefully selected and trained to build that image.

He couldn't believe his luck in hiring such great staff. To a person, they equaled, if not bettered, her caliber. Which on average, miraculously trumped the Chez Pierre crew.

Ah, man, if this place didn't become a huge success, nothing would.

He literally had everything he owned, and then some, riding on it.

Then he was out the kitchen door, heading for the bar to check on the wine supply when a hand grabbed his arm. "Mr. Holden?"

"That would be me," he said, turning to the voice.

A black man about fifty held out his hand. "Nate Douglas, president of the homeowners association in the building." Douglas was the same six feet in height but considerably heftier than Joel's 180 pounds. Thinning salt and pepper hair matched a neatly trimmed beard. But his squinty brown eyes were intense. And he appeared to think over every word twice, both coming and going.

A bit embarrassed, Joel pumped Douglas's hand. "Sorry we haven't met before tonight, Mr. Douglas. Entirely my fault. I apologize. I've been so busy getting this up and running I just had a hard time arranging it. I know you met with my assistant manager, Luther Rabb, a couple times." He'd intended to meet with Douglas personally to talk about building politics, but because of constant scheduling conflicts, it never worked out. So he'd sent Luther to meet with him instead. Afterward, Luther had debriefed him.

It turned out Khan's description of the reason for Pampas's demise had been dead on. So it wasn't too surprising that the association was monitoring Orcas's opening with a pretty enormous chip on its shoulder. Douglas had made it clear to Luther they'd be have Orcas under a microscope and would begin a campaign of complaints to the city the first time noise spiraled out of control.

"Yes. We had two reassuring discussions." Douglas pointedly glanced around as if assessing things, gave a slight nod. "Nice place. Much different, nicer ambience than your predecessor's."

"We've certainly done everything in our power to change the image. Let me assure you we'll be good neighbors and a credit to the building."

"We'll see," Douglas said with an ominous tone.

A combination of the man's soft voice and the white noise of conversation in the packed area made it difficult to hear Douglas's words. The ceiling soffit certainly helped baffle noise but did little to help a private conversation with wall-to-wall smiling people spewing small talk and laughter.

"I guarantee you'll be pleased." He noticed Douglas holding an empty wine glass. "May I get you another, sir?" Nothing like a little schmooze and booze to calm the waters.

Douglas glanced at his glass as if it were an afterthought. "Well, since you offered." He handed it over.

"Follow me." Joel led him around a cluster of customers to the bar where Taylor and two other women were frantically stocking trays with glasses of chardonnay and cabernet for the guests. Joel parked Douglas at the end, placed his empty glass on a tray to be bussed to the dishwashers, slipped behind the bar, grabbed a clean glass, and inspected it to make sure it was spotless.

"Sticking with chardonnay or may I interest you in the cab?"

"I'll stick with the white. Reds give me headaches."

Joel handed him an overly generous pour. "Enjoy."

He was about to head off to check with Taylor when Douglas said, "I'm glad to know you're not planning on live music."

Luther had warned of this hot button, a major cause of complaints. Starting at ten PM each night Pampas had featured a local rap group that, not surprisingly, became a huge gang magnet. Problems quickly escalated from there.

"No, sir. Just excellent food and service. Consider this an invitation for you and a guest to join us one of these evenings soon, compliments of the house." The guy struck him as the type to cash in that one immediately. Probably order the most expensive items too, figuring to take advantage before Orcas went belly up. What the hell, it would be a small price to pay for a good relationship with the association board.

"I would be delighted. I'll bring my wife."

"Excellent. And I hope that if any issue arises with your neighbors you'll talk with me about it personally so I can resolve the issue before hard feelings develop."

Douglas frowned. "Speaking of issues, you aware of the late night music issue?"

"I am, but just to make sure we're talking about the same thing I'll summarize it: the cleanup crew cranked up the sound system while they worked. Is that what you're referring to?"

Douglas nodded vigorously. "It was intolerable. They had absolutely no concern for the poor homeowner directly overhead trying to sleep." He pointed at the ceiling. "That, Mr. Holden," he said, still jabbing the finger upward, "is nothing but a slab of reinforced concrete. It's a perfect sound transducer. We complained multiple times to the manager—in person, I might add—but they never did a damned thing to stop it. Well, let me tell you, it finally did stop. Do you get my meaning?" Eyeing Joel, he downed a gulp of wine.

"I understand. And you have my guarantee you'll not have that problem with us. Did you notice we installed a false ceiling to baffle sound?"

Douglas glanced up with a flash of embarrassment. "Ah, yes...I guess I did. I just want to make sure there's no confusion on this point. If the noise starts again, we will respond accordingly. Count on it. We'll make damned sure you don't survive your first year of business. Am I clear?" Douglas seemed to be getting steamed up from his own rhetoric.

Joel leaned on the bar, closer to Douglas's ear, not just to be heard, but to keep it private. "Mr. Douglas, I want us all to live and work in harmony. I don't need any more problems than running my restaurant and to have your homeowner enjoy Orcas. Hey," he added with a laugh, "I need their business."

Douglas nodded, patted Joel's shoulder. "I certainly hope so." He turned to wander back into the crowd.

Joel sidestepped past another bartender to Taylor. She was furiously washing a wine glass, held it up for a quick inspection before inverting it on a drainage pad next to the sink. Then she started on another glass. Like a machine: Smooth, efficient, no wasted effort, her skill honed to professional standards.

He asked, "How's the wine holding out?"

"Aw jeez, it's going to be close. I had no idea we'd get this kind of response. Hey, you notice Nancy Benson's in the crowd?"

"She's here?" he said, unable to mask his excitement. Okay, he reminded himself, she's not here for a real meal, so she can't rate the actual menu, but being here means Orcas had pinged her radar, which meant they stood a good chance she'd mention it in her column tomorrow or the next day, which also meant that one of these days she'd return for a real test. A rave review from her could catapult a restaurant into delirious popularity.

"She came by the bar and asked for a double Knob Creek instead of wine. I told her I'd have to charge for it since we were only serving wine."

His gut sank. "You didn't!" No, Taylor wouldn't...would she? "Did you?"

She poked his ribs. "Just fucking with you, sweetie. Of course I gave it to her. A triple, in fact."

He gave her a quick kiss on the side of the head. "That's why you're so wonderful."

She picked up another glass. "We can talk about my raise when we get home. Right now, I need to get back to work. So do you."

He felt a tap on his shoulder and turned. Reed Allison was leaning on the bar with Betty Ann, waiting their turn to talk with him.

"Hi, Mr. Allison, Mrs. Allison."

Reed extended his hand but Betty Ann remained sullen, as if still unable to get past what "he'd done to his father." Neither Allison held a glass.

"May I get you guys something to drink?"

Reed smiled. "That would be nice."

"Single malt for you." Then, to Betty Ann, "And you?"

"I'll just have a glass of water."

He handed Reed scotch and Betty Ann a Perrier with a slice of lime.

"Very nice," Reed said appreciatively.

Joel leaned on the bar to hear over the din. "Thanks for coming."

"Chris would be proud of you, putting all this together."

He felt warmth ascend his face. "Thank you. I wish he'd have lived long enough to see this."

"If he'd lived longer, this probably never would have happened." Reed held up a hand. "I don't mean that as anything more than fact. Please don't take it as judgmental."

"I didn't. But it is true. His death gave me this opportunity."

"Looks like you have your hands full. I'll let you get back to work. Thanks for inviting us. We wouldn't have missed this for the world." Reed raised his glass to toast Joel.

Inappropriate time to ask, he knew, but couldn't resist. "Any word yet?"

"On the estate? No. They asked for, and were granted, a continuance. But I'm very hopeful we can resolve this issue soon. It is unfortunate the market has done so poorly. I'm sorry your portfolio has lost so much value."

"Nothing's a loss until I sell. It's only a paper loss at the moment."

"Well." Reed raised his glass. "Like I said, I'll let you get back to work."

He was heading toward the kitchen when a hand grabbed his shoulder. "Yo, Holden."

He turned toward the voice and was face to face with Armando Delgado. Fuck! What was he doing here?

A second later he recovered and smiled. "Hello, Agent

Delgado."

"Was wondering if you were the same Joel Holden. You know the one I mean? The scumbag who died in the avalanche? So I had to come find out for myself. And guess what? It's you."

If Delgado knew, what about Ortega? Joel's heart was pounding, his forehead sweating. He swallowed hard. Think! "What can I get you? Wine, a drink?"

"How about an explanation. We had a date. You stood me up."

Joel glanced to where he'd last seen Reed, but he wasn't there. Say something.

"You succeeded in nailing Ortega. Wasn't that what it was all about?"

Delgado shook his head. "You missing the point, bro. I gave you a break, saved your fucking life. Fucking trusted you. An' what do you do? You fucked me like a little bitch. That what you think I am, bro? Your little bitch?"

Try to explain? Delgado wouldn't understand. He said, "Look, man, I'm sorry, I really truly am. I didn't plan it. The avalanche… just happened. What was I supposed to do?"

"Testify. That's what the fuck you were supposed to do."

"What can I do to make it up to you? I mean it. Sincerely."

"Watch yourself, bro. 'Cause you know I'm watching you." Delgado turned, walked off.

Joel watched Delgado meld into the thinning crowd and then disappear from sight. He stood in stunned silence with a chunk of ice freezing the pit of his stomach. A moment later, he turned and headed back into the kitchen to check on things, a queasy feeling gnawing at the lining of his gut.

32

ORCAS RESTAURANT, LATER

With a sigh, Joel slumped against the front door and threw the deadbolt, officially ending their first night of business. And man, what a humongous cost! He didn't have the final figure but whatever it would be, the money had been well spent. Considering all the compliments, body language, and number of people that turned out, the Orcas début party was a huge success. Warm, heady pride and self-satisfaction glowed deep in his chest. One more step had just been checked off in the process of achieving Joel's dream.

At the bar Taylor and crew were cleaning up. Someone jacked their iPod into the sound system and some rapper began telling them about street life. Joel turned it down a little bit more to keep from pissing off the upstairs neighbors, yet loud enough to help the exhausted crew unwind.

He grabbed a longneck from the cooler, called out, "Hey guys, take a quick break and come with me a minute. Oh, and grab a drink. We're going to have a toast." His policy—which he intended to fully enforce—was no drinking alcohol before or during work, a rule especially aimed at the line cooks who had tended to sop up everything they could get their hands on during a shift. This opening night celebration was to be their one exception.

While uncapping the beer, he led the group to the center of

the main dining room and called out to the kitchen staff. The entire crew assembled in a crude circle around him. To a person, they all looked fried. Bowties off, sleeves rolled up, sweat-soaked t-shirts clung to chests. Joel raised his hands to quiet the crowd and the conversations stopped.

"Hey, guys, you did it! With all your hard work, in spite of all the crap the city threw at us, we opened on schedule. I want every one of you to know just how much I appreciate the effort every one of you put into this. Not only that, you should know how proud I am to have you as part of the Orcas family. Tonight we launched Seattle's coolest, most desirable restaurant. We'll keep that status because of you guys. You're the greatest!"

His words were greeted by eager applause.

He raised his beer in a toast. "Here's to each one of you."

The group joined the toast, clinking wine glasses or beer bottles, then broke into clots of separate conversations. For five minutes they stood chatting before the first of them drifted off to finish straightening up their stations. The rest quickly followed.

He walked over to Luther and put his hand on his shoulder. "Wanted to give you special thanks for helping pick such a great crew. Nice job."

Luther beamed. "Dude, they *are* good, aren't they."

They stood for a moment admiring the interior until Luther said, "Need to finish a few things," and walked away.

Joel set his half-finished Bud on a table, grabbed the vacuum cleaner someone had pulled out of the cleaning closet and started on the dining room floor, thinking what a wonderful opportunity this was. The fulfillment of a fantasy, a dream come true. Even if the process by which he became Joel remained a total mystery, it was overridden by the joy he felt.

Ironically, Reed was right: if Chris hadn't died, Joel never could've received the line of credit to start Orcas. Sure, maybe after years of building a master chef's reputation—assuming he could crawl out from underneath another chef's shadow—he might've be able to scrape together enough investors to start a restaurant. But how many years would that take? And what were the odds?

Very small indeed.

And what about Chris?

Well, Chris was a winner in this too. How many fifty-five-year-old men got the opportunity to live life again? Then again, if anyone had had this opportunity, no one would ever believe it actually happened.

He laughed at that thought.

Interesting conundrum. For all he knew, this very thing might be happening every day but who would know? Anyone who claimed to be living again in another body would be immediately labeled as stark-raving nuts. So, what did that mean about the belief in reincarnation? He'd have to think about that. He paused to look at Michael, one of the waiters. What about him? Was he some old geezer brought back to live a dream? Doubtful.

He shook his head and marveled at the craziness of this new life. He'd stopped questioning the why and how it happened for simply enjoying every day. Such a different life than Chris's.

Flat on his back, wide awake, he steals another glance at the glowing numbers on the clock radio, watching the slow increment to midnight, then on toward 1:00 am, and ruminates about Janice. What to do? Crunch time.

For a year and a half they've been "seeing each other." An occasional movie or dinner out, but most nights here at home so he can include Joel. It's hard to line up a sitter on weekends, and the nanny who cares for Joel weekdays isn't available on nights and weekends. Her hours are long enough as it is.

What a bind. Janice hasn't handed him an ultimatum, but essentially that's what happened last night. The message came across clear enough: either marry me or I'm out of here.

Although she never hinted at a time-line, the implication is clear: a decision within days.

Changes

As with everything, marrying Janice poses pros and cons. The pros are he'd have a wife and Joel would have a mother. The con was more complex: he doesn't love her.

The trouble is that too many things obscure what "love" might feel like. Mostly she's convenient. Harsh as that might sound, it's true. She's there when he has time off, offering companionship and sex. The only fear worse than marrying Janice is the fear of starting all over again. All the dinner parties in which the host says, "Oh by the way, there's this wonderful woman we're dying for you to meet. She'll be coming tonight too. We think the two of you..."

So there it is: Janice vs. starting over. And Janice knows this is her trump card. The fact that she's playing it grates on him. But what other option is there? Besides, would being married to her be all that bad? Don't they have good times?

He glances at the clock again: it's after 2:00 and tomorrow is a busy day. Shit.

Taylor was still working behind the bar while nursing a beer when he flicked off the main overheads to shut down the place down for the night.

"You have a few minutes to sit and relax?" she asked.

They both had to be back in Orcas in six hours to start the ball rolling again. But starting a new restaurant is always initially a huge investment of time and effort. Once Orcas had been up and running for six months, many of his responsibilities could be delegated. With a sigh of relief, he dropped into the chair next to her.

"Oh, man," he said, "what an evening. You did great."

She asked, "Want me to get you a beer?"

He leaned back, massaging both temples, releasing some of the tension that had gone unnoticed until now. "Sounds wonderful."

She set the longneck on the table in front of him. "Is it what you wanted?"

He looked at the bottle. "Yeah, thanks."

"No, you idiot, I was talking about this," she said with a nod at the dining room. "Orcas."

Laughing, he glanced around, taking in the beautiful interior yet again. After working here so intently day after day, he'd lost sight of what had been created. Now, seeing the interior with momentary objectivity, he gasped at the incredible beauty. Tastefully elegant understated simplicity.

He went to the light switches and turned them back down to the soft levels used during the serving hours.

"Oh my God, Taylor. It's beautiful."

She came up behind him, wrapped her arms around him. "It is. Just beautiful."

He turned and hugged her. "Unbelievable. We actually did it. We created this."

Hard as it was for him to believe, the reality began to sink in: they had.

Could life get any better?

Doubted it.

He flicked off the lights. "Let's go home."

Walking south along First Avenue, he asked, "Why don't we make it official and get married?" They weren't the words of proposal he'd imagined—if this generation "proposed." And now that they were out of his mouth, they sounded really lame. But it was what he wanted.

She stopped to look at him a beat. "Ask me again in six months." She resumed walking.

"Oh," was all he said. *How disappointing.*

She stopped, gave his hand a little tug. "You want a reason?"

"Wouldn't you if your proposal was just turned down?"

The street, deserted this early in the morning, glistened from an earlier shower. A metro bus approached from the south, the interior brightly lit except for a curtain behind the driver to block windshield glare.

She resumed a slow walk. "Too many things are going too well

214

right now. It makes it hard for either of us to think straight. Getting married would be just one more thing to worry about. Besides, I'm superstitious. I don't want to do anything to break this bubble. Let's see how things are in six months. Okay?"

Six months. A lot could happen in half a year.

Was he losing her?

Suddenly the earlier glow of success was replaced by the chill in his gut as he remembered Delgado's surprise visit. For the first time since vanishing, he was very frightened.

33

FOUR MONTHS LATER

Joel told the wine distributor, "Hey, keep it down, will you." They stood on the sidewalk just outside Orcas' open front door, the delivery truck idling in the passenger loading zone; a dolly with the handle wrapped in duct tape was stacked with wine cases.

But only half the number of bottles in Taylor's order.

The guy, a bald overweight Italian, spat on the street. "What's wrong? You don't want your crew knowing you ain't paying bills?"

Joel cast a nervous glance over his shoulder at the open door. Thank God no one was watching. Particularly Taylor. "Jesus, come on, man, you know I'm good for it."

"I do? Really?" The Italian tapped a Marlboro from a pack, pulled out a lighter. "Who do I work for?"

"What?"

"Do I work for you?" He lit up.

Trick question. He looked for the angle. Where was this going?

The driver exhaled in his face. "Answer's no, I work for my boss. And he says starting next delivery, everything—and I mean every last bottle—is COD. Understand what that means, this COD?"

"Of course I know what it means, but you're killing me here. How am I supposed to manage with only half an order?"

The driver hiked a shoulder with a think-I-give-a-shit flip of his hand. "How are we supposed to run a business if our accounts don't pay up? Huh? Settle your account and you'll get the rest of this order." Patting the dolly. "Until we get the cash, this is it. So, you want it or not? As it is, I'm running late already."

Joel sat in the banquettes staring at the wine invoice. There were other huge financial difficulties too. Nothing as disastrous as the wine and liquor part of the business, but if not dealt with immediately, the debt would drive Orcas into bankruptcy. He'd seen this sequence of events drag down two other places he worked before Chez Pierre. The spiral starts with getting behind on a few payments. Soon as that happens, suppliers start delivering second-rate produce *if* they deliver anything at all. Or the restaurant becomes the last stop on the delivery route, meaning the truck unloads maybe five minutes before the day's opening, giving the chef zero time to check the quality of product. Which usually means the chef ends up with the day's worst tomatoes, seafood, or whatever, leaving him no option other than to serve shitty food. There are thousands of little ways suppliers can screw you over if you didn't keep your account current. Or if your checks started bouncing. Orcas's death spiral had just started. Jesus, he couldn't believe it!

Two months ago Reed finally put an end to Janice's nuisance suit. Burned two-hundred grand of the estate's assets to do it, but the flip side was it freed up the portfolio for Joel.

Couldn't have come at a worse time. With the bond market tanking, his collateral fell below the balance owed the bank on his line of credit, technically putting him in default. The banker, Ms. Lee, had called with the news: either pay down the loan or she— meaning the bank—would become the majority owner of Orcas. Well, fuck that. He paid off the loan. But that left him with zero income from the estate. Meaning his only income was what Orcas generated and that, at the moment, wasn't enough to stay afloat.

So he'd quietly spoken to a real estate agent about selling the condo. And to his horror, learned that the present market would mean taking a loss. Fuck that too.

Okay, sure, Orcas was doing okay, building a steady loyal customer base, but not enough to quite cover monthly expenses. The figures showed it becoming reasonably profitable in, say, six months. But now, with the death spiral starting....

Even the thought of what lay ahead ripped his gut out.

Shit! He was going to lose everything. The condo, the restaurant, every speck of asset.

His gaze wandered the dining room. Everything appeared normal: Taylor readying the bar for the first customers, Luther double-checking reservations while waiters smoothed wrinkles from tablecloths or straightened a place setting here and there. In the background water flowed down a six-foot etched-glass scene of three killer whales in front of snow-capped mountains, the sound of the water a soothing balm for his raw nerves. The waterfall was a custom piece of statement art, one more add-on that had completely trashed what remained of a budget. Beautiful, stunning, creating a subtle ambience of understated elegance that was, in itself, art. Damn! If he hadn't gone nuts and insisted on extravagances like that, he'd be on budget right now.

There had to be a way out of this financial mess. And soon. Next week would be too late. The wine delivery—or lack of it— drove home that realization.

Just yesterday he'd scoured the books for ways to minimize overhead or increase profits. But nothing came to him. Not unless he abandoned his vision of excellence. Cheaping-out on ingredients or service would send Orcas into the morass of mediocrity. That would be intolerable. And the moment that slide began and word leaked to competitors and foodies, Orcas' initial status would be lost forever.

Okay, so he paid his crew top dollar. Every cent came back in attitude and effort. They were the most dedicated, ass-busting group he'd ever had the pleasure of working with. And it showed in any number of objective measures. Tips, for example. Generous. Night after night, consistently at twenty percent.

But if he did begin to scrimp on ingredients, would customers *really* notice the difference?

Maybe, maybe not. Point was he couldn't risk finding out.

And Taylor...she ran one of the best bars in the city, stocking only premium liquors. Their wine list, though far from the most extensive, was slated to grow each year as they laid down more than they consumed, building for the next year. It took ten years to develop a really killer cellar.

Of course, there was always the boogieman of restaurants: the stealers. Employees who slipped friends free meals and drinks, took home a bottle of cabernet or scotch, shaved a few extra bucks off the tip pool when no one was watching.

He, Luther, and Taylor had been keeping an eye out for that. And he knew all the tricks not taught in cooking school. The little scams he'd learned during OJT. And he'd been coached by masters. No fucking way was the staff robbing him. Just no way. And Luther was in charge of the tip pool.

Luther...

That thought had crept into his mind so many times now it was becoming a mantra.

"How'd you get enough money to buy it?" Dad asks, referring to the shiny new bicycle.

Joel says, "I earned it."

"We've gone around on this twice. I'm asking how *you earned it."*

Joel doesn't want to lie but sees no way not to. He's sure as hell isn't going to admit where the money came from. "You know..." he said with a shrug, "mowing lawns. Washing a few cars." True. He did. But not enough to account for the bundle he dropped on the bike.

Dad eyes him with suspicion. "You sure about that?"

"Yes."

"Would you lie to me about this?"

And there it was: a crossroads. He's never really lied to Dad about anything before. At least nothing this big. Makes him feel low-down rotten, but what choice did he have?

"Seriously, I earned it."

Dad gives him a look of heart-slicing disappointment. What's worse—admit what he was doing or skirt the issue? And if you really think about the question, he isn't lying. He did earn the money. Just not the way...

His father shakes his head, turns and walks away.

Who does a dealer really hurt? No one. If your customers didn't get product from you, they'd get it from the guy down the street. Right? So what the fuck difference does it make? Besides, if it kept Joel's dream alive, it'd be worth it. Right?

Absolutely.

Besides, he wouldn't do it forever. Just long enough to make it through this difficult period. Once that happened, he'd shut down the drugs. Consider it a "bridge loan," sort of.

He glanced around. No one else around except for Luther.

"Luther, got a second?"

Luther slid into the booth across from him and leaned forward. "What up?"

Joel picked up a corner of the folded white tablecloth. If he pulled the corner as he slid out of the banquette, the linen would spread across the table and be ready. He started bending it back and forth, into a small triangle.

Do I really want to do this?

Luther waited.

Joel sucked a deep breath, took another glance around.

"This is totally off the record, okay?"

Luther nodded. "Most def."

"Our customers, they like the ones at the Chez?"

For a moment Luther remained blank, not quite getting it. Then he lowered his head a bit and leaned closer. "You mean, they open for business? Like Portland?"

"Exactly."

"I suspect so. No reason to think differently."

"You have a supplier?" Five to one Luther did, but he needed to ask, just to be sure. Now that he'd made up his mind, he wanted to start cash flow soon as possible.

Luther gave an almost imperceptible nod.

"No one else on staff can know. Especially Taylor. We cool?"

A faint smile crossed Luther's lips. "No reason for anyone to know. Give you my word."

"Got it together enough to start tonight?"

Luther checked his watch, thought about it. "Might be a few minutes late for happy hour, but yeah, count on it." He nodded to punctuate the sentence.

Joel pulled the check book out, thinking Luther could stop by the bank and cash it. "Most I can start with is five large." Small enough withdrawal to not attract attention if someone ever audited the ledger. "We can bootstrap up from there."

There were other considerations too. The most important was personally keeping a distance on this. Give Luther one-hundred percent of the exposure. Not just to protect Orcas, but to protect himself too. There was no fucking way he'd ever risk word getting out to Ortega's crew that he was alive and well in Seattle. Much less, profitable and dealing in the same city.

"You handle everything. You'll be discreet."

"Dude!"

Just to make the point absolutely clear, Joel said, "Taylor must never know."

34

THE NEXT NIGHT

Joel was helping to tidy up the kitchen for the evening when Luther came rolling in like an NBA point guard, all twinkly eye smile and loose-limbed in his perfectly tailored tuxedo. He nodded, "Yo," to two of the line cooks while making his way toward Joel.

With a chin jut toward the back door, Luther said, "Need to talk with you outside."

Dog tired, Joel wanted nothing more than to finish cleaning up so he could go home and hit the sack. Taylor had left a half hour ago, saying she'd wait up to share a drink.

"Now?" he asked, hoping Luther would get the point.

"Now," Luther replied, insistently.

A knot formed in his gut. Luther's tone didn't seem to match his appearance, meaning something must be wrong. "Outside?"

Luther scratched the angle of his jaw, glanced around. "Right. It's personal."

The dread in Joel's gut worsened. "Outside-outside, or outside in there?"

"Outside-outside." He gave another nod at the back door.

It was hot and steamy in the kitchen and Joel had his chef's blouse unbuttoned all the way down to his smeared white apron, an appearance he permitted only after the last customer had been served. Even then, no one was allowed in sight of the dining room looking like this. He started buttoning up in spite of being only in the alley. The night air would be refreshing, but his gut continued sending bad vibes to his brain. "Personal" could mean a lot of things, but here at work it usually meant trouble.

He followed Luther to the back door.

The building foundation had been sunk into a hill that angled from First Avenue to the west, down to the harbor, making the alley exit one level lower than restaurant entrance. The building's two garage levels also exited onto an alley. He and Luther marched single file down grease-stained concrete steps to the steel fire door that the crew propped open with a sand-filled coffee can during business hours. A constant complaint of the homeowner association was that doing so produced a huge security issue by allowing anyone access to the back stairwell. Probably true. But the residents weren't the ones hauling all the bags of garbage to the dumpsters every few hours. Besides, the doors to the residential floors remained locked, so anyone without a key who gained access to this stairwell couldn't go anywhere anyway. Still, as a precaution, every night before he left, Joel personally checked the door and stairwell before locking up.

A chilly breeze blew across his hot face, bringing the familiar rankness of piss, fry grease, rotting garbage, and car exhaust from the Alaskan Way Viaduct on the other side of the Jersey Barriers. City smells. Rap from the nightclub a block south echoed along the brick walls and asphalt alley, momentarily louder each time their back door opened.

Luther pulled a pack of cigarillos from his tux and held it out to him as a string of cars whooshed past on the viaduct.

Joel was about to decline when whimsy changed his mind and he accepted one. Luther offered him a red lighter, then lit his own. Luther sucked a long drag and then let the smoke curl from his lips into his nose.

"Jesus, you inhale these puppies?" Joel asked.

"Dude," he glanced down at the one in his hand, "they're not strong. Not like cigar strong. No one in their right mind actually smokes a 'gar."

Joel puffed his, enjoying the harsh taste. After another puff he couldn't stand to wait any longer. "Well?"

Luther beamed. "Dude, we moved it. Every fucking ounce."

Took a second to register.

"The whole stash? In two nights?"

Luther's grin grew wider. "Fuck yes."

"No problems?" He hadn't heard of any, but had to ask. Just to be sure. He didn't know any details either. Like how Luther spread the word that product was for sale or how transactions were carried out. He didn't want to know. His main, and only, concern was for Luther to keep a low profile and cater only to moneyed customers. The ones who, in return, couldn't afford to have a mug shot on file at the West Precinct. A little recreational cocaine now and then, maybe a taste of hash. No meth. No smack. Meth really *was* death. Worse, it attracted the dregs of druggies. And smack? Well, junkies couldn't afford to dine in an upscale establishment like Orcas to begin with, so why even consider it?

"No problems," Luther confirmed.

Joel blew a long, slow breath. Part relief, part excitement for things going so well. Unbelievably easy. Maybe too easy. And that thought triggered a bout of gut-edginess.

"How much we clear?"

"More than we thought," he said, saying the words in rapper-rhythm accompanied by hand claps. "Shit moved so well, I stepped on it and upped the price about halfway through. We're selling only primo shit, dude. Not cut shit, pure shit."

Joel exhaled another long breath. Unbelievable.

For a moment they stood watching the viaduct, the cars humming past. He forgot the cigarillo between his fingers, his mind tallying the profits, estimating how much they'd have to move before Orcas was bailed out and on its own.

Luther said, "My opinion? Roll every penny into the re-up.

Keep doing this until we get a good feel for the limit of inventory needed to keep up. Once we know that, we level out at that amount and start pulling down some *serious* coin."

Joel nodded, running more figures in his head. "Two nights. Jesus, we moved all that in two nights. Unbelievable."

Luther grinned. "Dude, consider it seed money well spent. We rolling now. But I know we most definitely underestimated our potential. We can double this. Easy."

Joel shook his head, uncomfortable with escalating too quickly. "I don't know." A basic equation about risk and reward kept bubbling into his consciousness. On the other hand, the sooner they started pulling in the money, the better. The risk of losing Orcas was intolerable, so the sooner he stood on stable economic footing...

The heat of the burning cigarillo between his fingers caught his attention. Took another puff but this time it tasted like shit, so threw it away.

Luther bent down, picked up an empty beer bottle, walked it over to a blue recycle bin and dropped it in. Turning, he slipped, caught himself. "Fucking grease. Dude, you gotta have someone pressure wash this or at the very least pour some TSP over it. They're dripping grease all over the place each time they haul out trash."

"I'll make a note."

Luther brushed dirt off his hands. "Then we agree? Roll these profits into a bigger stash?"

"You think Taylor caught on?"

Luther flashed a hurt expression. "Dude! What kind of doofus you take me for?"

"I know you're slick, but don't ever underestimate Taylor. She's slicker."

"Understand I'm not saying anything negative about her. Alls I'm just saying is she's busy behind the bar. She can't be watching everything I do."

One of the things Chris had tried to teach Joel was to never underestimate an opponent. Doing so would surely court disaster. "I'm just saying, don't underestimate her."

"So what you think? We roll our entire nut back in this time? Hell, that's my vote."

Eyes closed, Joel massaged the bridge of his nose.

Why am I hesitating?

"Yeah. Do it."

Changes

35

In the heat, humidity, and kitchen clatter, Joel checked the flat screen that listed all the pending orders from the dining room. Nothing new and the list was rapidly shrinking. Good, this lull probably indicated the end of a fairly sizable dinner rush. He allowed himself a moment of pride. How many orders had he knocked off tonight? One-thirty? One-forty?

Every night about this time he played the same head game, testing his brain's subconscious counter. A reality test of sorts that also measured just how engrossed he'd been. Overestimate the number and it was probably a slow night. Underestimate and you'd been busy as hell.

He typed a command on the keyboard then checked the screen. One hundred fifty-three.

The pride bubbling through his chest ratcheted up a notch. He'd been low. Which meant a good solid night. Better yet, there had been no glitches. No orders bounced back with complaints, which was another thing to be proud of.

The last big order, a table of eight, covered a spectrum of entrees from filet mignon to seared sashimi-grade ahi. Some with sauces, some without. He'd read the order to the line cooks without making assignments, each one nodding and starting in knowing exactly what to do and what the others would do. A solid endorsement of their abilities. Better yet, their teamwork flowed so smoothly that the entire order rolled off the line at the same time. Leaving him only to inspect each dish, wipe a drop of sauce off this, add an extra garnish or a swirl on that, before sliding the plates onto the stainless steel serving counter for the wait staff to pick up.

He washed his hands, buttoned his chef's blouse, exchanged his smeared and stained apron for a freshly laundered one, and was just about to begin an inspection trip through the dining room when Taylor came flying through the doorway saying, "I just called the cops."

"Something wrong at the bar?" he asked, starting out toward the bar.

Grabbing his arm, she tugged him back into the kitchen. "Stay out of it."

"Out of what?" Ignoring her warning, he pushed through the swinging doors into the dining room.

She followed, saying. "A couple guys came in, started giving Luther shit. They took him outside."

Several of the remaining diners turned to watch him flash by.

He detoured to the front door as she clutched his arm again. "Please, Joel, don't get involved."

He jerked free, kept moving. No one was going to give his maitre d' shit.

Out on the sidewalk, on hands and knees, Luther rocked back and forth, dazed, face bleeding, passers-by giving him a wide berth in spite of the tuxedo he wore. Anyone witnessing what had happened was probably long gone or just didn't want to become involved.

He squatted down, put a hand on Luther's shoulder. "You okay?" He immediately realized what a dumbass question it was.

Luther leaned on him to stand up, then was upright on shaky legs. For three or four seconds he swayed too far over. Joel caught him. Luther straightened up and with one hand holding Joel's arm, used the other to gingerly probe his face. His left eye was swelling shut with a cut above the brow. Bleeding from his nose too, but not as badly as would be guessed from the blood on his white shirt.

"You good enough to go inside?" he asked Luther.

Luther nodded and staggered toward the door, Joel helping him stay upright. The entrance was now packed with gawking Orcas staff. Without a word, the group parted, letting them pass on their way to the kitchen.

Joel followed Luther into the kitchen as all eyes in the dining room watched. Customers and staff, everyone wanted to know what the hell happened but were smart enough not to ask. At least not now.

He led Luther to a stool and instructed him to sit while he collected a damp cloth. He tilted Luther's head back and told him to press the cloth against his nose to help control the bleeding. With another rag he dabbed at the wound over his eye, cleaning away the blood to better inspect it.

"I should take you to the ER, see if this needs stitches."

Luther waved away the suggestion. "Just butterfly it. I'll be fine."

Taylor pushed through the doors, followed by a uniformed police officer. The kitchen staff suddenly became engrossed in their assigned jobs.

The officer approached Luther. "Want to tell me what happened?"

"Veuve Clicquot cork, is all."

The officer said, "Say what?"

Taylor explained. "Restaurant humor. He was opening a champagne bottle. The cork popped up and hit him."

Bullshit. Obviously Luther had been beaten by someone.

The cop drilled her a hard look, said, "Expecting a laugh?" before quickly taking stock of the people standing around watching. "Any of you want to tell me what happened?"

Luther said, "I'll be okay. It was a misunderstanding. You shouldn't have been called. I apologize."

The cop hitched up his belt, shifted his weight. "That a fact?"

"Yes."

The cop eyed Taylor again. "You?"

229

"Sorry, officer."

Soon as the cop left the kitchen, Joel asked Luther. "Can you make it down the stairs?" Meaning, to the alley.

Joel stepped past the door into the alley to find a guy in baggy pants and wool shirt sorting through Orcas' dumpster.

"What the fuck you think you doing?" he called to him.

The smells of urine and grimy body odor from the food scavenger competed with the stench of garbage even from this distance. The only problem Joel had with the man was that he'd strewn garbage all around the dumpster and now Joel would have to pick it up. He wasn't in the mood. Immediately, he felt a pang of guilt for yelling at the man. Most of his anger, he realized, was from having no idea what just happened with Luther. Clearly things were going on at Orcas that he, Joel, knew nothing about. That was a problem.

The street guy turned his head to Joel, said, "Fuck you," and upended the dregs of a beer bottle into his mouth before throwing it against the wall, shattering it. He smirked before shuffling off down the alley, most likely heading for the nightclub's dumpster.

With the bum out of earshot, he turned to Luther. "Okay, tell me what the hell just happened in there?"

"Here." Luther offered him a cigarillo. He stood steadier now, working his neck to loosen it up.

Joel didn't really want one but accepted it to be friendly.

After a couple puffs, he asked Luther. "Well?"

Luther turned toward the viaduct. "Dealers."

"Dealers? The hell's that supposed to mean?"

Luther glanced at him without making eye contact. "Where I get our shit, dude. What you think it means?"

Took a second to compute, then another second to ignite a bolt of rage. "Fuck! You brought drug dealers into Orcas?" Suddenly he was more concerned about repercussions on the Orcas image than Luther's injuries. How could Luther be so stupid? Then he immediately regretted that thought. He and Luther were in this together. This was his problem now too.

"Aw, man, Luther, I'm sorry," he said, resting a hand on Luther's shoulder.

Head back, Luther started squeezing his nose shut again, the lit cigarillo in his other hand. "Naw, it's cool. But just so you know, I didn't invite them, they showed up."

"Yeah? Why?"

Luther shook his head best he could while holding his nose. "Fuck if I know."

That didn't make sense. "C'mon, man. They come in, drag you outside and whip your ass and you don't know why? Don't insult me."

Luther looked away. "They're suspicious."

Jesus, Luther is lying.

"Of?"

Luther half-shrugged. "That maybe I'm a CI. For the narcs."

An informant? No way. Unless…

The empty feeling in the pit of his stomach roared back. "Are you?" The words slipped out before he had a chance to think about them.

"It was supposed to be a warning or something. They came to see where I work. Or something like that."

Where he worked? Shit! All he needed was druggies hanging in the bar. Another gut-chilling thought struck. *Who the hell else knows we're dealing? Has Luther mistakenly sold to an undercover narc? Were they building a case against them?*

Suddenly the air was sucked from his lungs. Seeds of panic sprouted under his heart and tingling shot out his limbs. He was sweating in spite of the chilly night air.

What if the cops had something on Luther and were manipulating him? Would Luther be smart enough to realize it? And if so, what did that mean for Orcas?

"Jesus, Luther. *Are* you working for the cops?"

Luther hesitated a beat too long. "No."

Something about his answer—subtle body language, the hesitation, intonation—something—told Joel he had just lied. "C'mon, man. This doesn't make any sense. What's going on?"

Luther let go of his nose, dabbed at the nostrils with his finger. The bleeding had stopped again. He took a drag on the cigarillo. "Beats the shit out of me."

"Yeah? Well someone just did. Why?"

Luther's tone turned dead cold. "Dude, I just told you, I don't know. Let it be."

A sick acidity burned Joel's gut as he realized he could no longer trust Luther. "Why you lying to me? I thought we could be straight up with each other."

Luther flicked his smoke at the dumpster. "Don't worry. It's under control."

Joel's hands balled into fists. "What the fuck's that supposed to mean?"

Luther turned and walked back into the building and started up the steps.

"Luther!"

Luther didn't even bother to pause.

36

After Luther disappeared up the stairs, Joel stood in the stink of rotting garbage and spilled grease, listening to the rhythmic whoosh of passing cars on the viaduct, trying to reason through things, but the anxiety eating at him was making concerted mental traction too difficult. He flicked his cigarillo toward the same dumpster as Luther had. It caromed off the side, showering sparks to the asphalt, and died.

Shit! Having drug dealers drag your maitre d' out the front door to stomp his ass wasn't the image he envisioned for Orcas. Worse, Luther wasn't able to give him a good excuse for it. Not that there could be one.

Take that back. Luther had coughed up an excuse, but the story sucked. Didn't make sense.

So what now?

"There you are."

He jumped.

Taylor stood just inside the doorway, the fluorescent stairwell light turning her skin pasty and sickly. She was frowning.

"I was just about to come back up."

She stepped out next to him. "Luther went home."

What a relief. "Probably a good idea. He needs to ice that eye and take some ibuprofen."

"He's a goddamned mess," she added matter-of-factly. "Shirt bloody, coat ripped. What happened?"

He started to turn toward the door to leave when she put a

hand on him. "Wait. You know we're not done here. I asked you a question. What the hell happened in there?"

Great. She wanted the same answers as he did, but he didn't have any. Make some shit up? No, that never worked. Repeat what Luther said? That'd sound worse. He opted for, "I don't know. Truthfully."

Her frown deepened. "Why not? It's your job to know."

"Because he didn't tell me."

Arms crossed, she widened her stance slightly, as if readying for a confrontation. Which, by the look on her face, he knew was intended. "He didn't tell you or you didn't ask?"

He turned toward the dumpsters rather than continue eye contact. Maybe it would send her a message: he was tired and didn't want to have this discussion now. He suspected she already knew that.

"Taylor, I asked. He hemmed and hawed and gave me some bullshit story about how they wanted to send a message."

"What—"

"I don't know," he said, interrupting, a clear tone of irritation in his voice. He turned to face her. "He wouldn't tell me. Or at least, what he said didn't make a goddamned bit of sense. Some rambling words about whoever beat him up suspected he's a CI for the narcs."

She started rubbing the back of her neck, then shook her head in disgust. "I told you before and I'm telling you, he's nothing but trouble."

Before she could say it, he added, "Yeah, so you said a long time ago. But look at the good things he's accomplished for us."

Her head snapped around, eyes glaring.

More cars whooshed past on the viaduct.

She locked eyes with him. "What're you going to do about it?"

"You tell me. I'm open to suggestion."

Out came a sarcastic grunt. "Fire him."

"For?"

She flashed a you-gotta-be-kidding look. "For unsanitary personal hygiene, for drinking at work, for porking the pooch." She threw up her arms in a gesture of frustration. "Christ, I don't know and I don't really care. Make something up. Just get rid of him."

"Well, that's helpful."

"It's your restaurant. Deal with it."

"Think it's that easy? He's Local 21. All the staff are. Remember? Power to the people and all that shit."

She cracked the knuckles of her right hand. "Aw, jeez, that's right, I forgot."

But she was right. He also had a bad feeling about Luther and what he might bring down on them. Especially after tonight's episode.

Thinking about it now, he tried to recall what he knew of Luther's past and it was surprisingly sparse, especially considering all the time they'd spent together. What he did know, he'd heard one night after work at Chez Pierre when the two of them had gone out drinking and the conversation drifted to their pasts. Luther had grown up in Los Angeles, the younger of two brothers—the son of a single mom who worked in a strip mall shop doing nails. At thirteen, his brother was shot to death by a Mexican banger, but Joel couldn't remember hearing the whole story beyond that. Or maybe he had but the fatigue and alcohol of the moment hadn't logged it into memory.

"When's his performance evaluation due?" Taylor asked.

"I don't know. I haven't had time to even think about such things." They'd been too swamped to care about instigating the niceties of HR bureaucracy. But she was right. He should be more professional about managing Orcas. Without the proper paperwork, he was screwed if he had to discipline a union member.

"Time to start." She ran her fingers through her hair. "Fucking unions. They make it impossible to fire someone."

But he was off in his own thoughts again.

She asked, "You coming?"

"I'll be up in a moment. I need to think."

"You bet you do. And clearly." She started back up the stairs.

Alone again, he thought about Luther.

What exactly was making me so nervous about him?

It hit. Pretty simple, too, now tumbling to it. Orcas was now supposed to be free of drug dealing. Initially, to get over the financial hump, he'd okayed a limited amount of dealing, but, as soon as they made enough money to get over the financial hard times, Joel had told Luther to stop dealing. But selling drugs was in Luther's DNA. That had to be it—he was still dealing. Why else would something like this happen?

And another thing: Luther knew nothing about *his* past, his Ortega problems, or the reasons he'd left Seattle for Portland. Far as Luther knew, Joel had never sold drugs until Luther broke him in on the Chez Pierre action. Meaning, that when he went to Luther looking for the temporary cash infusion, he hadn't bothered to check out who controlled drugs in this area. What if Ortega controlled this neighborhood now? The more he thought about it, the worse it got.

"Shit," he muttered.

How could I be so stupid?

He glanced around the deserted alley. Looking for...?

Taylor was right. There were two things he had to do immediately: find out if Luther was still dealing and get rid of him. Quickly, too. Before things really got out of hand.

37

A WEEK LATER

Joel glanced at the grill station. At the moment Chavez had nothing cooking and no orders had been placed in the past few minutes. Over the cacophony of rap, dishwasher hum, and clatter of plates being scraped and stacked, he called to his sous chef, "Hey, Chavez, take over for a few minutes, will you?"

"You bet, boss." Chavez—the bald spot on the back of his head glistening with sweat—never turned from scraping down the grill.

Joel balled up his dirty apron and shot a fade-away jumper five feet from the overflowing hamper. Swish.

Someone—maybe one of the line cooks—yelled, "Two points!"

He wrapped on a fresh apron, tugged the strings around to the front, tied a bow, unrolled, buttoned, and smoothed both sleeves.

Okay, ready.

He made a quick stop in the fridge to eyeball supplies and double check that the meat and seafood deliveries were scheduled for the morning. They were. He made a mental note to show up early to be damned certain the quantities were what had been ordered.

Not that it'd been a recent problem. In fact, just the opposite. Business was great and the financial disaster fading from memory. Amazing how things turned around the moment Orcas had the cash to keep suppliers current.

Drug money saved Orcas. Or, to put it another way, Luther saved Orcas.

But he could never explain that to Taylor.

And this realization left a potpourri of emotions: on one hand, he felt sleazy for now looking for reasons to fire Luther. On the other hand, if Luther had been honest with him and explained what was going on, they would've found a way to work things out. But that hadn't happened. He'd lied—not an act of commission, but an act of omission. Apparently, Luther had gotten Orcas involved in things Joel knew nothing about. Placing Orcas at risk to be shut down was an intolerable act of deceit. Then again, hadn't he been the one to suggest running drugs to enhance cash flow? Yes, but only temporarily. Who knew what Luther was now doing?

And now Taylor kept harping on him, saying, "Get rid of him. He's trouble waiting to happen."

He believed her. Taylor had the canniest ability of anyone he knew to sniff out scams and cons almost from the moment she sized someone up. How she developed that skill was a mystery to him. There were probably Wharton graduates who'd get taken in by cons that she would recognize from the pitch's opening line. He suspected she could read body language, eye flickers, and intonations as well as any seasoned CIA interrogator.

But when he'd asked what she was so uneasy about, what she suspected Luther of doing, she couldn't say. Mostly she relied on intuition, a sixth sense that was impossible to put into words. He had never known her sixth sense to fail. So, he had to believe her.

He walked through the dining room into the bar, looking for Luther. He wasn't at his station, wasn't in the dining area, wasn't at the bar. And he wasn't in the kitchen ten seconds ago when he left. He stopped at the bar and motioned Taylor over.

"Luther around?"

She seemed surprised. "He's not in the kitchen?" Her voice implied that that's where he should be.

"No. I just came from there."

They simultaneously turned toward the front window. Luther wasn't out on the sidewalk either.

"Thanks," Joel said, heading back to the kitchen. Taylor's tone made him even more curious to find out what he was up to.

He wasn't sure why the need to be sneaky, but he silently descended the stairs to the back entrance, moving swiftly, his right hand sliding along the greasy railing, being careful to not slip on a step. At the bottom stair he waited a beat before silently stepping into the alley.

Luther, either sensing his presence or hearing the door open, spun around. The light from the doorway caught his wide, frightened eyes.

38

"The fuck you doing, dude," Luther said, "sneaking up on me like that?"

Another person darted from Luther into the shadows of the neighboring apartment building. The only functional light in the alley was directly behind Orcas, making it hard to see the person standing there.

"I've been looking for you," Joel answered, craning his neck for a better view of the other person, but all he could make out was a general shape. Still, for whatever reason, he came away with the impression it was a male. He made a mental note to demand that the building property management replace the burned-out bulbs back here since the city was in no rush to repair alley streetlights.

"For?"

To check up on you. "To bum a smoke."

"Dude, that's some serious bullshit you shoveling." Luther glanced side to side, then back to him.

"Seriously."

Luther moved closer to the doorway, further obstructing Joel's view of the alley. "Why now? You don't smoke, 'less I offer you one."

He'd never seen Luther so nervous, which only heightened his suspicion. "So, offer."

Three cars sped by on the viaduct in rapid succession.

Luther fumbled a pack from his tuxedo jacket, jerked his wrist, extending two cigarillos to Joel. Joel took one, Luther pulled out the other.

Luther flamed his lighter but held it lower than usual so Joel would have to lean down.

Joel bent to light up, but soon as he heard footsteps, he straightened up to see the person Luther was shielding jog down the alley.

A second later he thought, *Delgado!* But wasn't sure exactly why. He hadn't gotten that good of a look at the silhouette.

Stunned, he stood frozen, watching the DEA agent hustle across the street and on into the alley behind the nightclub.

What the hell were he and Luther doing out here?

Then he flashed on Luther's mumbled statement when he got the crap pounded out of him a week or so ago, the bit about being an informant. Could that be true?

He took the lighter from Luther, lit up, asked, "Who were you talking to?"

Luther glanced over his shoulder. Delgado was gone now, swallowed in the shadows of the alley behind the nightclub. "Fucking panhandler, dude. I laid some change on him was all. Why?"

"Why lie to me, Luther?"

Luther looked at the viaduct. "Dude. Sometimes the less you know, the better. Trust me." Luther flicked his unsmoked cigarillo at the nearest dumpster, turned and headed upstairs to Orcas.

39

LATER THAT NIGHT

Joel knocked on the lobby's glass door to catch the doorman's attention rather than riffle through his keys. The front door remained locked at this time of night. Homeowners either used their common-area key or had the doorman buzz them through. God forbid the lazy bastard should leave his comfortable oversized station to make the short trip across the lobby to let in a homeowner. He squinted at Joel for a moment, then nodded. A buzz, then the metallic snap of the lock.

As he passed the desk, Joel asked, "Quiet night?"

"So far." An open copy of the *Seattle Times* lay on the desk next to a Michael Connelly novel.

"Let's hope it stays that way."

"Got that right, Mr. Holden. Good night." The doorman returned to reading.

Joel stopped in the alcove to check his mailbox. Nothing but junk mail. He continued on to the elevators.

He dumped the mail in the recycle bin for his floor, circled back and entered the condo. "I'm home."

Taylor padded barefoot from the bedroom, wearing a blue terrycloth robe cinched tightly around her waist and a seriously pissed expression on her face.

Uh-oh. What now?

Initially, he'd figured on skipping a drink tonight. Now, after a glimpse of her scowl, he reconsidered. *What is it this time?*

"Want a drink?" he asked and decided on scotch instead of beer.

"No, we need to talk." She followed him into the kitchen.

"What's up?" He loaded a glass with ice cubes.

"Do you have any idea what Luther is doing?"

Fuck! She knows.

Hold on. Maybe not.

What would happen next depended on exactly what she was referring to. So he decided to not answer. He sloshed an unmeasured amount of scotch into the glass, glanced at it, figured it looked about right, held it up to her. "Want a sip?"

"Joel! Just answer the damned question."

No, this wasn't good at all. He made a toasting motion with the glass before taking a sip. "I would, but the question is ambiguous. What are you referring to? Specifically."

She crossed her arms, eying him. "You don't know?"

Drink in hand, he headed for the bedroom, figuring better to keep moving than make eye contact, because if he did, she'd sure as hell nail him.

"Like I just said, what are you referring to?"

"He's dealing, Joel. You know that, don't you?"

"Dealing what?" He entered the walk-in closet, pulled off his shirt, dumped it in the clothes hamper.

"Damn it. You know how much it pisses me off when you play this dumbshit routine. It doesn't serve you well. But you already know that. Drugs. *That's* what I'm talking about. Are you aware that Luther is selling drugs at Orcas?"

He brushed past her on the way to the bathroom.

"I guess."

She followed. "You *guess*. What? That he's dealing drugs?"

He set the drink on the counter, started the hot water in the sink, bent over to rinse his face.

She waited for a response.

He said nothing.

"Goddamn it, Joel, now you're really fucking with me, and you know how much I hate that. Discussion: take two. This time try giving me a straight answer. First: do you know that Luther Rabb, the maitre d' you insisted on hiring against my advice, is selling illegal drugs at Orcas? Yes or no?"

Well, shit, that was pretty specific. No way to dodge an answer.

Rather than discuss it, he rinsed his face and toweled dry. He was too damned tired and upset to deal with an argument now.

She continued to stand there glaring at him like an angry vulture.

A few seconds of heavy silence was followed by, "I assume that by not answering you admit you know about it."

Still trying to think of a way out of the confrontation, he gulped a mouthful of scotch and concentrated on the alcohol burn working its way down the back of his throat. What to do?

Say yes, I admit complicity. Say no, I admit I don't know what the hell's going on in my own restaurant. Either way is disastrous.

Try explaining that the drug dealing was supposed to be a temporary fix for a shortfall in finances but that Luther just kept going would only piss her off more for not being included in the original decision. Especially after she confronted him about the start-up expenses and he'd lied to her. He saw no easy way out of the conversation and no excuses that would fly.

He flashed on that awful day in the Cascades, the conversation about wishing to live life over, of all the things he'd do differently. One of the things—one he never mentioned to Reed—was to take ownership for his decisions, no matter what the consequences. Shirking responsibility had been one of Joel's weak points.

Well, here's a perfect opportunity. Time to step up.

He exhaled in resignation, looked directly in her eyes. "Yeah, I know he's been dealing."

She flinched as if slapped on the face. "You do?"

He sighed and half-sat on the edge of the counter and downed another slug of scotch. Time to fess up.

"We were having financial problems. I needed more cash. I figured he could move a tiny bit of recreational coke." He held his thumb and index finger a half inch apart to trivialize the amount. "Sell it to a few select customers. It's not like we're,"—now making finger quotes—"*dealers*. It was only to take care of our good customers. That's all. It was to be temporary. A source of income. It worked. End of story."

"You're saying it's not like you're *dealers*. Did I hear that right?"

She stared at him. Hard.

He held her stare. "What do you want me to say?"

"What I *didn't* want to hear is what I just heard. That's the lamest goddamn reason for dealing drugs I've ever heard. I kid you not."

He took another slug of scotch. "What's done is done. Let's move on."

He chugged the rest of the drink and headed back to the kitchen, keenly aware of her bare feet padding along directly behind him, feeling her eyes drill into his spine.

More ice, more scotch. And, he knew, more argument.

"We're not done, *dammit*. Just what the hell were you thinking? What?"

He flicked off the kitchen lights and started back to the bedroom. This conversation wasn't going to just go away. He had to tell her. She would either deal with it, or...or not. But he had to come clean.

That last part made him cringe. This could be disastrous to their relationship. Would she leave and return to Portland? He hoped their relationship was stronger than that, that they could work things out.

In the bedroom now, he settled into the reading chair and tried to calm his fears. "Look, I needed the money. Orcas needed the money. We were late with our suppliers. It was a temporary fix for a bad problem. We're above water now, so I stopped it. I talked to Luther and made it official."

She threw her arms out. "And that justifies what you did?" she said with an irritatingly incredulous tone. She was right, of course, but still, he didn't want to be reminded what a crazy-stupid decision it'd been.

"He's being discreet," he said, scrambling for some shred of argument to lessen the humiliation. "Only selling to customers who…"

"Who what?"

She dropped into the other chair and leaned forward, eye to eye. "Those who, because of their exalted professional positions, also must be discreet? Was that what you're trying say?"

He set the drink on the small table and wiped his face. "That's part of it, yes."

"Reality check, Joel, so listen up. Luther is fucking insane. And he is *not* being discreet. He's selling to any warm body with enough cash to buy. You're just damned lucky he hasn't sold to an undercover narc. But then you don't know for sure he hasn't already made that mistake, do you!"

He flashed on Delgado in the alley. And the bottom dropped out of his gut. Is that what was going on? Was the horse already out of the barn? But that wasn't something to tell Taylor now, so he groped for a fallback position.

"He's being careful. Besides, he gets caught, there's nothing to link it to you or me. *He'll* be the one who takes the hit."

She gave a dismissive snort and said, "You actually believe that? You think he's stupid enough to get caught holding the bag?"

Since she put it that way…

He gulped another slug of scotch, thankful to begin to feel the effects of the alcohol, especially on an empty stomach. He massaged the bridge of his nose, still scrambling for an excuse. "Let's talk about this after we've had some sleep. I'm dog tired."

She stabbed a finger at him. "No, dammit! We talk about it now. Right now there's nothing more important. Certainly not sleep. Besides, you promised me you were out of this shit when you left Portland. I believed you. What am I supposed to do now that I catch you lying to me? Huh?"

That really hurt. He didn't see it as lying. More like it'd been a temporary change in policy, one easily reverted after the financial crisis was fixed. At the time he said it he had no intention of using any drug stronger than alcohol. Still didn't. "I didn't lie. *I'm* not using and I'm sure as hell not the one selling. I'm clean."

Aw Jesus. The stupidity of his last words was embarrassing. And he certainly wasn't living up to his own expectations by taking ownership for actions. To the contrary. In typical Joel fashion, he was trying to wiggle out of the consequences. He despised himself for it.

She cocked her head, studying him, as if gauging his sincerity. "You know Carter's moving the shit too, don't you?" All the harshness was gone from her tone now, as if she sensed his vulnerability and felt sorrow for him.

Carter, the kid who bussed dishes in the bar area.

"Shit...no, I had no idea."

His entire operation, he realized, had slipped from his control. And to be honest, he had subliminally known this would happen. Eventually. Luther always did what Luther wanted. Luther would've started moving drugs with or without Joel's permission. And now that he thought about it, he probably already had a business going before Joel brought it up. The more he thought about it, maybe this explained the ease with which he'd liquidated the first stash. This realization made him sick to his stomach. What a fool.

She said, "You better damned well believe it. And frankly, I find it insulting that Luther thinks he can pull this crap off right under my nose and I'm too stupid to notice."

He started to reach for the drink but caught himself. More

alcohol wasn't going to help him now. Ignoring the issue wouldn't do much good either. If he were really going to do things differently this time, he needed to stand up and deal with the consequences of his decisions like Chris, to do what was necessary to correct his mistakes.

"What are you going to do about it?" Taylor had her arms crossed again, that determined look etched in her face.

He headed for the walk-in closet to finish undressing, knowing what had to be done. Luther had to go regardless of the reason. He would deal with the union later.

"I'll talk to him later today, before we open." He checked his watch. It was almost 3:30 in the morning. "He's gone. I swear to you he won't work another day at Orcas."

Taylor came over, put a hand on his shoulder. "I don't want to be a bitch, sweetie. But I know how much you want Orcas to succeed. I just hate to see you do anything to lose it."

He wrapped his arms around her and hugged. "I'll take care of it."

Changes

40

Joel wasn't always the first one to arrive at Orcas each day. Often the sous chef came in ahead of him because he had the responsibility for procuring fresh produce and seafood. Even so, Luther usually arrived ahead of the majority of staff. Joel planned to talk with him the moment he stepped in the door, before everyone else was there. He dreaded the task.

The morning sky was signature overcast Seattle weather when he stepped from under the condominium's awning: drizzle so light that he felt like a wuss for opening the umbrella. But if he didn't he'd be drenched by the time he arrived at Orcas. He walked, rehearsing lines, anticipating Luther's objections, planning appropriate rebuttals. Luther wouldn't roll easily on this. Not with so much tax-free money at stake. His lifestyle depended on substantial cash flow. In particular, his wardrobe. But for Joel it all came down to risk management. There was simply too much downside to continue selling drugs. Best to cut it off before Orcas got nailed and he stood the possibility of losing everything, including Taylor.

Chris always believed in several rules: greed kills, being one. One of Reed Allison's favorite sayings about the stock market was bulls make money, bears make money, but pigs eventually are slaughtered. He and Luther had pulled good money out of the drug thing. Enough to keep Orcas afloat. Now was the time to back off before their luck turned sour. Chris also believed in facing truth head on. Truth was, he—Joel—really hadn't lived differently this time around. He still defaulted to the easy way out. Selling drugs being the prime example. Well, that had to change.

He stopped at a window in the Army Navy Surplus Store to gaze at a display featuring a female mannequin modeling matching camo bra and panties. Nice touch, the Vietnam era M-16 in her right hand; a 50-caliber machine gun at her feet fed with a belt of bullets snaking out of an olive drab ammo box. Probably a real eye-catcher for any white supremacist. The camo undies, that is. Those skinheads probably already owned the weapons. More modern ones, even.

He realized he was doing everything possible to delay dealing with Luther. Time to get on with what he had to do. He continued on toward Orcas.

When Joel pushed through the front door, Luther was already in the booth closest to the bar area, a ledger and a cup of black coffee on the table in front of him. He glanced up just as Joel dropped his umbrella into a large green ceramic pot next to the door. It contained four big green and white golf umbrellas the valets used to cover customers to their cars.

"Ain't that weather a bitch?" Luther said. "Don't know why it doesn't just rain and get it over with. This drizzle shit makes me crazy."

Joel didn't see any other employee nearby. "We need to talk. Out back, preferably."

Luther frowned and pushed out of the booth. "What up?" He had on his vintage gangsta look—a prized vintage red Ben Gordon Swingman jersey and baggy pants, the redundant cuffs frayed from constantly being tread on with outrageously expensive sneaks.

"Wait till we're outside." A knot had already cinched Joel's gut tight, anticipating the flak he knew was coming.

Luther headed to the back of the kitchen. "Be right there, dude, gots to grab my coat. A nigger could catch cold out there."

His words surprised Joel. Luther never referred to himself or other blacks as niggers.

Outside now, the steel fire door propped open with a sand-filled coffee can ashtray. Shoulder to shoulder they faced the alley with just enough room in the tiny alcove to avoid the drizzle. Large green and blue dumpsters lined their side of a row of Jersey Barriers across the alley. Three seagulls waited patiently for another gull to tear open the corner of a black Hefty bag pooching out from under the lid of one bin. It appeared to be taking some effort.

Luther pulled a pack of cigarillos from his breast pocket, flicked his wrist, popping one halfway out. He offered it to Joel.

"No thanks." His stomach knotted tighter.

Luther caught the end between his lips, withdrawing it from the pack. He lit up with one smooth slick motion. Typical Luther.

"Dude?"

During the walk here he'd grappled with an opening line. Now, face to face with Luther, none of them seem to fit, so he said, "Taylor knows."

Luther took a leisurely drag, unfazed, "Knows what?"

He resented the tactic but he immediately saw the symmetry. He'd done same thing with Taylor last night. Didn't work then either.

"Knows what you're doing. She says Carter's involved. That wasn't part of the deal."

Luther shrugged. "Carter's smart. Slick as a lubricated Trojan. Dude's not a problem. What's yours?"

The answer took him off pace a moment. "What's my problem?" Jesus, he couldn't believe it. "You and I had an agreement. No one else involved. Remember?"

He hated the way that came out. Whining like a little playground pissant, immediately ceding any semblance of power. Fuck!

Luther shrugged again. "Saw an opportunity to expand our

business. I took it. Executive decision." Like, no big deal.

Joel struggled to not totally go postal. Luther's indifference, his complete lack of respect, was humiliating. True business partners didn't demean each other like this. But, he realized, there was more at stake here than simple pride. This was a struggle for control.

Why even hesitate? Just fire him.

Joel leaned into Luther, their noses almost touching. "That right? Listen up. Go fuck your executive decision. I already told you—no more selling drugs at Orcas. If you're still doing it, it stops this minute."

Luther didn't back away or move. He just drilled Joel with a steady dose of dead-eye. "Who the fuck are you, telling me what I can or can't do?"

"Newsflash, Luther, I'm your boss. I'm the one who pays you. You're an employee. We clear on this?"

Luther turned away far enough to casually drag from the cigarillo, then let the smoke curl out from his mouth while inhaling it back through his nostrils, the whole time never breaking eye contact.

Control the situation. Don't let him dominate you like this.

An almost imperceptible change in Luther's eyes said, "Well?"

Too many emotions—including self-loathing—swirled through his mind, blocking out any answer.

Stop being a pussy! Isn't this the same way you handled Janice? By getting trompled?

A moment later, Luther turned, flicked the cigarillo onto black glistening asphalt and watched the ember roll into a puddle to die with a weak *pssttt*. Hands in his coat pockets, shoulders hunched against the chill, he said, "All these weeks,"—he pulled out a cellular phone—"I been recording every word, every one of our discussions. Documented everything we did. You so much as *think* of turning off our business, everything goes straight to Delgado."

What the fuck? That's crazy.

"That's nuts. You'd be incriminating yourself."

Luther laughed. "Think so?"

Joel didn't answer.

"That thing out here last night? You got good eyes, Dude. That *was* Delgado, all right. We got ourselves a business agreement. I feed him information about people. He makes sure I'm protected. I'm what's called a confidential informant. See?"

Luther laughed.

Joel realized his face had to be showing the shock his mind was recoiling from.

Luther said, "Ever wonder why we never got busted in Portland? Had the same thing going there, Dude. You just never tumbled to it."

Jesus Christ, say something. Fire his ass.

Luther continued, "I know you love this place. I'd hate to think how you'd feel to lose it. Not only that, but I don't think a bitch like you's gonna do well in lockup. You way too soft, boy."

Luther turned to leave.

Prime example, Joel. Your chance to do the things you didn't do right the first time. Make a tough decision. Unless, of course, you really enjoy being walked over. Step up, do this right.

"You're fired, Luther. You're fucking fired."

Luther grinned. "No, I'm not." He slipped through the partially opened door.

41

LATER THAT DAY

Joel tried to inspect the seafood delivery, but the neurons between his eyes and his consciousness seemed short-circuited, effectively blocking any ability to concentrate. He saw glistening pink slabs of salmon on the counter, but what he was supposed to do with them? The fish vendor cleared his throat, a subtle way to jar Joel from mental paralysis.

This supplier had served him well in the past. Why should it be any different this time?

Joel mumbled, "They're fine," and signed the receipt on the clipboard, handed it back, and blankly started at delivery man weaving his way out through the kitchen.

He was an emotional train wreck, with every ounce of his mind consumed by a toxic mixture of anger, fear, and loathing as he replayed his confrontation with Luther. How could he get rolled over so easily? Shit!

He knew that if he didn't immediately gain control over the situation, he'd lose Orcas.

Lose that, you lose everything. Taylor included.

Worse yet, Luther knew this too.

Fantasizing over what he should've done and said wasn't going to help him now. Fact was, he failed. Why?

Well, for one he didn't have Luther's street smarts or

confidence. And confidence was everything in this type of situation.

That was Chris talking to Luther. No doubt about it. I should've been different. But I wasn't. Was Reed really right? Am I nothing but the same man in a younger body?

I've got to do something! This is exactly what happened with Janice. But this time I can't hire a private detective to build a case. I simply need to get rid of him. Today.

How?

"Boss?"

Joel looked up at the sous chef next to him.

What? Oh yeah, he's waiting for something. Yes, the salmon.

With a dismissive wave, he said, "They're fine. Sorry, got distracted for a moment."

He realized Taylor was off to his left, giving him the weird eye.

Jesus, when did she come in?

"Oh, hi," he muttered.

"I need to see you out at the bar for a minute. I have some questions," she said, loud enough for anyone listening to hear, so he pretty much knew what her question would be.

She reached the empty bar area, turned, crossed her arms, locked eyes with him. "Well? What happened?"

Here it was, the moment he'd been regretting since climbing the stairs from the alley: telling her what happened. He glanced around. No one in earshot, but still…

"Aw Jesus, can we talk about this later? Like maybe tonight when we're at home?" Preferably never. Speaking of which, where the hell was Luther? Now that he thought about it, he hadn't noticed him since their discussion. Then again, he hadn't been noticing much of anything other than his own ruminations.

She leaned forward, getting close, lowering her voice but keeping the emphasis unmistakably strong. "No. I need to know right now whether or not he'll be pulling his shit tonight. Or, better yet, I need to know he's gone for good."

He didn't see the relevance.

"What difference does that make?"

She looked as if that was one of the stupidest questions of all time.

"Makes a big difference, Joel."

She never called him by his first name.

She continued, "If he's planning on business as usual, I'm out of here. Right now. And that, by the way, is non-negotiable. Hey, *you* want to be a willing accomplice, go right ahead, be my guest. But count me out."

He thought about that. Businesswise, Tuesdays were usually the slowest night of the week. Need be, he could squeak by without her. But that's not what he wanted. He wanted her here. Not just for the way she handled the bar, but because her presence gave him extra strength. All he needed was maybe twenty-four hours. By then he'd have worked out a plan for dealing with Luther. Maybe bounce some ideas off her later, when they were home alone, when things were quiet, maybe with a drink, and brainstorm. She'd be good for him on this and help him.

"Well?"

He didn't answer.

She studied him a moment. "It went that badly, huh? What'd he do, tell you to fuck off?"

How the hell did she know? Was she psychic or just so damned street-smart she could predict Luther's response precisely? Or did she suspect he'd been an ineffectual little pussy?

"Something along those lines," he admitted.

She inhaled audibly and finger-combed her hair. "What exactly did he say?"

He gave her a bullet point recap, but embellished his action a bit to make it sound stronger.

When he finished, she shook her head. "What a total asshole." She looked around. "Speaking of which, where is he?"

"I don't know. I haven't seen him since." He shrugged. "Maybe we'll get lucky and he won't show up when we open."

She checked her watch. "Only a half hour 'til the front door opens. It'll be interesting to see if he doesn't show. He should be here by now." Sighing, she finger-combed her hair again. "Okay, so you lost round one. What's your plan for round two?"

What a relief. She sounded more like an ally than a critic. He wanted to hug her for not deserting him.

"I haven't worked one out yet. Figured I'd wait to see what happens tonight. If he leaves, we're okay. If not, we can discuss it at home."

She made the wrong-answer buzzer sound. "Discuss it? You kidding me? Come on, Joel, there's nothing to discuss. Your maitre d' is selling drugs on the premises with the full knowledge of your staff. You allow this to continue, I'm out of here." She started untying her apron.

"You know I don't like ultimatums."

She glanced up, threw the apron on the bar. "Tough shit. You just got one." She put her hands on her hips and stared back at him. "Luther or me. Your decision. Right now."

"Hey, I'm open to suggestions. What's your great solution?"

"Jesus Christ, Joel. You want to beat this asshole, you got to think like him. Be preemptive. Drop the dime on *him* before he cuts you off at the knees. Because he will, you know. Either you stop him now or he's going to leave your dead body on the street. Either way, it's not a pretty picture. That DEA agent who drops by now and then," she snapped her fingers, "what's his name..."

"Armando Delgado."

"Yeah, Delgado. Call him up. Tell him Luther's dealing. Tell him you just found out about it."

The gut knot was back, even tighter now. Things weren't quite that simple. She had no idea about his history with Delgado, much less Luther's claim of being Delgado's snitch. Why hadn't he been totally truthful with her from the beginning?

257

"It's more complicated than that," he said. "Luther claims to work for Delgado. His informant. Says Delgado knows he's dealing and gives him immunity in return. It gets worse. He's recorded our conversations."

Shit, I'm whining again.

She shot him an incredulous look. "You know all this for a fact? Especially that part about the recordings?"

Well, now that she mentioned it...

"Not exactly, but—"

"No, of course you don't. And I bet you even money Luther pulled that one out of his ass right out there in the alley."

Good point. Only problem was, he didn't know for sure.

Taylor sensed it. "He's a con-man, Joel. He reads people and reacts accordingly. He survives by turning any situation to his advantage on the spur of the moment. He'd win an Academy Award if they had a Con Artist Improv category. And okay, so what if he has a few recordings? Claim they're bullshit. You think he can prove any different? Any twelve-year-old with a computer and a couple sound bites can make up just anything they want. Same way any ten-year-old with Photoshop can produce an I-swear-to-God-it's-real picture of Marlene Dietrich blowing Richard Simmons. What's to say that anything he claims is evidence isn't just manufactured from your everyday conversations here at work?"

He laughed.

"Think that's funny?" She was drilling him with her hard-ass look again. "I'm drop-dead serious here. Hey, I'll call Delgado myself if you won't," she said, pulling the phone from under the bar. "Even if he *is* giving Luther a free pass, he's probably not going to love the idea of an informer's identity being blown. *He's* the one who has something to lose with this, not us."

Maybe she had a point. Maybe he could work something out with Delgado. Joel grabbed the phone from her. "No, I'll do it."

Changes

42

A male voice answered the phone with, "Drug Enforcement Agency, Agent Milford speaking."

Joel swallowed hard and wiped his sweating palms across his thigh. "I'd like to speak to Agent Delgado, please."

Taylor was leaning on the bar listening and watching intensely, making him feel like this was some weird practical exam he'd be graded on. He turned away to avoid her hard eyes, his stomach still knotted tight.

"Just a moment, I'll connect you."

He heard a click, some dead line, another click, then, "This is Special Agent Delgado. I'm either on another line or away from the phone. Leave a message and I'll get back to you soon as possible."

Joel's gut sank. He'd amped up his courage to speak with him and now he couldn't. He should be relieved but wasn't. By now, he just wanted this nightmare over no matter what the consequences. Now what, leave a message?

"Agent Delgado, this is Joel Holden at Orcas. I need to talk to you, right away. It's very important. Call me at the restaurant soon as you get this." He hung up wondering when Delgado might pick it up. And once he did, would he call? They didn't have the greatest history of cooperation and collaboration.

"Call back and have them page him," Taylor said.

He nodded, picked up the paper napkin with the number scrawled across it, and dialed again. It started ringing.

Another employee hustled through the front door, making

Joel aware of the minutes flying by, bringing this evening's opening closer and closer. A thousand little tasks still needed to be done, like briefing the staff. But Taylor was right. Right now nothing was more important than straightening out the Luther situation.

He shook his free hand to stop his fingers from tingling. His heart was beating like a rabid bat out of hell and his lungs couldn't seem to get enough air.

"Drug Enforcement Agency, Agent Milford speaking."

"I just called for Agent Delgado, but he didn't answer. This is *extremely* urgent. Find him. I need to talk to him. Now."

"Hold on, I'll see if he's here."

The connection went dead for ten endless seconds before the agent returned and said, "He's out of the office. If you give me your name and number, I'll try to reach him."

Joel recited his phone number.

Milford said, "Be advised he may not be reachable. And if he is, he may not be able to return your call anytime soon. If this is a real emergency, I advise you to speak with another agent. I can put you through to someone. It's your call."

His anxiety ratcheted up another notch.

"Tell you what. Try Delgado first. If you reach him, ask if he can call me immediately. If he can't call back immediately or if you can't reach him, ask whoever's available to call right now." He was past the emotional tipping point and wanted this over. And now that he thought about it, it didn't really matter if he negotiated with Delgado or someone else as long as he gained the offensive against Luther.

"Will do."

"Joel, look." Taylor was pointing toward the front door.

Luther was inside now, limping along the front windows, jerking down the shades in quick movements.

Joel started toward him, still royally pissed at their encounter in the alley. "What the hell you doing, Luther? We open in half an hour. You know that."

Luther spun around, eyes wide with fright. "The back door locked?"

"Christ, I don't know." From the look on Luther's face, Joel wasn't sure whether to be alarmed or angry. A second later his gut iced over with fear. "Why?"

Front shades drawn, Luther limped toward him, gesturing toward the back. "Lock it. Now!" He was still in street clothes instead of his tuxedo.

Joel didn't move. "I asked you a question. What's going on?"

Luther told Taylor. "Go lock the fucking door, girl. The one to the alley too, if it's open."

Taylor took off running, muttering, "Oh shit, oh shit, I knew it..."

Leaning on the bar, Luther grabbed one of the drink hoses and shot a glass full of Coke, foam sloshing over the top. He gulped it down, looked at the glass, threw it across the room. "Motherfucker!" His hands were shaking, his forehead slick with sweat.

Any anger Joel felt a moment ago morphed into raw fear.

"Jesus, what's wrong?"

Luther jerked a chrome-plated revolver from under his Chicago Bull's shirt, glanced at it before slamming it on the counter. He poured another glass of Coke, downed half in a gulp. "Dude, we gots us a huge fucking problem."

"We?"

Luther was trying to pace, but was having difficulty keeping weight on his right ankle. He stopped, leaned forward, holding onto the bar with both hands..

"Those beaners who came around the other night?"

A nauseating déjà vu flooded Joel's gut. He knew what was coming. "The ones who took you outside?"

Luther pushed back up and tried walking again. "Yeah, them."

"What about them?"

Luther turned, took a couple steps the opposite direction,

stopped again. "Fuck." He bent down to massage his ankle again.

"Luther! What about them?"

Joel heard the panic in his own voice.

Luther said, "They're our source, right?"

Joel's déjà vu of impending disaster worsened.

"I don't know. Why?"

"I went there for a re-up, but they're on to me. They fucking knew."

"Knew what?"

"About me and Delgado." Luther shook his head. "I can't figure how, we were so careful, but they *knew*."

Joel looked from the revolver to Luther, then back again.

"What the hell happened?"

Luther started shaking his head. "Was him or me, dude. Had to cap him. The other got away."

The bottom of Joel stomach did a flip, threatening to vomit. He knew what was coming. "They're coming here?"

"Hell yes. Probably the same fuckers as the other week."

Joel's eyes wandered over Orcas' interior, so beautiful, so elegant. It could be ruined in a matter of seconds. Fear morphed to anger.

"They're coming here? Jesus Christ, you dumb shit, why'd you have to come back here?"

"Dude, think about it." Luther picked up the revolver, flipped open the chamber, pulled a handful of slugs from his cargo pants, started exchanging spent shells for live ones. "They looking for me, right? They're coming here whether I'm here or not. You want them barging in on you while customers are in here or you want fair warning? You want to open up, business as usual? Fine. Do it. Let those motherfuckers walk in and blow your ass away. But I suggest you close for the night. Well?"

Joel didn't answer.

43

"Back door's closed and locked," Taylor said, face red, breathing hard, looking like she'd run the stairs up from the alley. "Now will someone please tell me what the hell's going on?"

Joel summarized Luther's story for her.

She shot Luther a look of astonishment. "Those fools know you came here?"

"Fuck if I know," Luther shot back. "What I *do* know is they looking for me. They'll come around sooner or later. I mean tonight most def."

"The same one's who took him outside the other night," Joel added, his mind going crazy, trying to figure out how to deal with the impending disaster.

The phone rang. He glanced at it. The back line. Not the line for reservations and such. "Back line," he muttered and ignored it.

"Wait, might be Delgado." Taylor said.

"Oh, shit, I forgot." He picked it up. "Hello."

A male voice asked, "Joel Holden?"

"Yes," he said, trying to remember what the DEA agent's voice sounded like.

"Delgado. You called, said something about urgent?"

"Right. Hold on a sec, will you?" His mind seemed suddenly clear, as several ideas tumbled into place forming the rough edges of a plan. Palming the phone he told Taylor, "Close the place. Now. Shut it down fast as you can. I want everybody out the door ASAP. Including you. Everybody."

She started to say something but he cut her off with, "No argument. Just do it."

Luther was on a knee, pant leg rolled up, sock pushed down, massaging an ugly swollen ankle.

For a brief moment Taylor appeared either taken aback or surprised but then got it together and nodded and hurried toward the back, her movement all business.

Phone back to his ear, he told Delgado, "I need to talk to you in person, soon as possible. Can you meet me right now?"

"Come on, Holden, I'm a busy man. I prioritize things. You want to talk, okay fine, but give me an idea what it's about."

Luther was now bending over the ice dispenser, scooping cubes into a white bar towel on the drain board. Joel could hear urgent, hurried voices from the back of the restaurant, then a door slam. How much should he tell Delgado with Luther right here listening? Did it make any difference? This was too important to worry about what the fuck Luther thought. The future of Orcas— his future—was on the line. Besides, what could Luther do about it? At the moment, Luther didn't hold much bargaining power.

He said, "I just found out there's been some drug dealing going on here at Orcas with my maitre d'. I want you to speak to you about it. I want it stopped."

"The fuck you think I am, bro? Head of HR? You got a problem with one of your employees, deal with it." Delgado didn't sound at all surprised or interested.

"Get's more complicated. It's in your best interests to speak with me."

"You got a short fucking memory, bro. Last time I wanted to speak with you, you stiffed me. Now you want me to drop everything, come running over? Fat fucking chance. What's so urgent?"

Suddenly a series of offhanded comments and events over the past weeks crystallized. Luther wasn't lying: he *was* supplying Delgado information. And when the time came, Luther would probably testify for Delgado. And, like Luther claimed, he probably did play the same game in Portland. Which would explain why he was so quick to leave his sweet deal at Chez Pierre to come here. Only this time, whoever Luther was about to rat out found out about it first. So the question was: to what lengths would Delgado go to protect an informant? That, he realized, was the angle he needed to exploit.

"Here's the deal. I know Luther's your CI. Right now things have turned to shit. Whoever he was ratting out just tried to kill him, but he got them first. Now they're coming here for him."

"Fuck!" Delgado paused a moment before asking, "Rabb's there now?"

"Yes." He could hear traffic in the background of Delgado's voice and visualized him standing on the street somewhere.

"Was he part of the shit storm an hour ago?"

Joel didn't know for sure, but suspected so. "Yes."

"Fuck me, bro, you *are* in trouble." Delgado paused a beat. "Here's what you do, you shut that place down. Now. Clear everybody out except you and Rabb. Understand what I just told you?"

"I'm all over it. We're doing that now."

"Good. Lock the doors, turn off the lights. It'll be a couple hours before I can get there, but you wait for me, understand? Don't let anyone in. No one. When I get there I'll call this number so you know it's me outside. Any questions or we cool?"

Yeah, much cooler that a few minutes ago. Taylor had been right about calling Delgado. Involving him might just solve two problems—dealing with the assholes out for Luther's ass and getting rid of Luther. She'd also been right about Luther being trouble. Was a damned shame he hadn't listened to her.

Joel said, "We'll be waiting. All night if need be. And when you call, use this line, not the restaurant listing. I don't answer, try again. I could be taking a leak or something."

Luther was sitting on the floor pressing the ice pack against his swollen ankle, flashing him a look of disgust. "You think Delgado's gonna to change a damned thing? Think that's gonna to solve our problem?"

Luther's voice contained a strange edge that Joel couldn't identify. It did, however, amp up the terrible anxiety filling his chest. He shot a nervous glance at the bar, looking for the gun. Still where Luther put it after reloading.

Taylor had the employees rounded up now, herding them out the front door, most throwing silent questioning glances at Joel and Luther as they passed the bar. Whatever Taylor told them was being taken very seriously, because they were moving quickly without a word, their faces etched with worry. With the last of them out onto the sidewalk, she closed the door and threw the two deadbolts.

She turned to him and crossed her arms and asked, "You sure you want me to leave?"

"Yes."

"Why?"

"Because things might turn ugly. That happens, I don't want you here. It won't be safe. I'll handle it."

She looked from him to Luther and back again. "You sure?"

Hell no.

"We'll be fine. Delgado will be here soon as he can. I'm sure he'll be able to work everything out. I don't know how long it'll take, but I'll meet you back at the condo after this is all over. Don't wait up."

"Yeah, right, like I could sleep." She came over and hugged him tightly. "Be careful."

On her way to the door she drilled Luther a hateful look.

Luther muttered, "Bitch."

Then she was at the open doorway, saying, "I'll lock it from the outside, but double-check to make sure it's secure," then was out on the sidewalk.

As soon as the lock snapped shut he missed her. He hustled to the window, pressed both hands against the pane and watched her hurry down the sidewalk. She was moving quickly away from him in her confident, purposeful stride. A strong premonition hit: he'd never see her again. Ever.

Don't let her go. Go after her! Just walk away and let Luther deal with his own problems and sort out any damage to Orcas later. Orcas was, after all, only a material thing. Material things could be fixed.

It sounded so easy...just walk out the door. Leave Luther to deal with his own problems.

That's what Joel would do. You always took the easy way out. Never faced up to your responsibilities.

This time he had to make Joel live life differently, do things against his instinct. Wasn't that what this was all about?

Besides, he couldn't allow Orcas to be trashed by drug dealers. He had to stay and protect his dream the best way he could. Besides, the dealer's issue was with Luther, not him. They might not even know who he was.

"You didn't answer my question," Luther said.

Joel hurried to the back of the kitchen. "What was that? Did I call Delgado? For fucking sure, I did. And if you don't agree with it, give me a better suggestion on how to bail your ass out of this mess. I'm all ears."

On the wall just to the left of the back door was a switch panel for the entire restaurant's lighting. One by one, he flipped them all off.

With the interior now dark, he made his way to the front. Enough street light angled through the front and back windows to allow anyone on the sidewalk to see in if they tried to look. Not good. Especially with him and Luther out here by the bar.

He told Luther, "They could see us from the sidewalk. We need to move back out of view. It's more comfortable there anyway." He grabbed the portable phone from the charger under the bar to take with him.

Limping, Luther followed.

Joel started lowering the large sections of Venetian blinds that covered the back windows, angling the slats tightly together to choke off light from that direction. The pewter overcast sky was growing darker, becoming more menacing as the sun—somewhere above the clouds—dropped behind the Olympic Mountains. The rain had stopped, but streets remained gloomy and chilly. Soon as the sun set it'd become even darker in here. Good.

Luther said, "The way I figure is you must've called Delgado before I got here. What were you planning to talk to him about?"

Joel's patience was turning raw. "Fuck you, Luther. Think about what went down between us. I tell you to stop dealing and you tell me to go fuck myself. Wrong answer. This shit is going to stop. I'm not going to waste Orcas on a few grams of fucking blow. And as far as you being Delgado's bitch, that's over. At least in this city and here at Orcas. But knowing you, you can start back up in Portland or San Francisco. Easy. So, life is good, huh?"

Fucking Luther.

Luther slid into one of the banquettes around the corner and out of the line of sight from the front window, gun firmly in hand. Joel watched him set the weapon on the table directly in front of him, within easy reach.

He chose a different booth than Luther's, one that if he leaned right, gave an unobstructed view all the way to the front window. For when Delgado showed up.

"Dude, why you want to fuck me up like this? You have any idea what you've done? To both of us?"

The aggressive edge to Luther's voice was gone now, replaced by what? Disappointment? Resignation? Shit, what did he expect?

Joel asked, "You hear anything I just said?"

Luther leaned forward, elbows on the table, and buried his face in his hands. He stayed like this several seconds before saying, "You think you know what's happening, but you don't have a clue. You just totally fucked us. I'm a dead man now. You too."

Luther raised his head and stared at his hands. They were trembling. Barely noticeable, but the tremor was there just the same. For the first time in their friendship, Luther seemed deflated, stripped of his irritating self-confidence. And something else in that look was extremely disconcerting.

Made him wonder...what *had* he done by calling Delgado? Could he really trust the man? Especially given their history. Was that what Luther was talking about? But what other option did he have? And could he trust Luther? Taylor was right, they needed help. The DEA seemed like his best option. After all, they were law enforcement, right?

Doubt seeped into his consciousness...

He shifted his stare from the front door to Luther, asked, "What the fuck you talking about? Delgado's on your side. You shot a drug dealer, man. Just explain what happened. He'll figure a way out of this for us."

Luther gave a cynical laugh and shook his head. "Don't even try to understand. You have no idea the way things are. You live in a world of contrasts, black and white. That ain't real, Dude."

He started to say something else but stopped.

"What is it I don't understand? Jesus, Luther, you're in quicksand here. The more you struggle, the more it's going to suck you down. Cut your losses. Get your ass out before it gets worse. Because, believe me, it always does."

Luther slid from the banquette, stood, testing the weight on the bad ankle. "Gots to take a leak," he said. He limped toward the front where the restrooms were, across from the bar area.

Joel called after him, "Hey, man, tell me. What don't I understand?"

A nebulous floating sensation blossomed in the pit of Joel's stomach. Something was going very wrong and he had no idea what it was. Worse was that just when he was getting it together, he wasn't.

Man, this is totally fucked.

The floating sensation intensified, morphing into panic. Suddenly he knew he'd screwed up again but didn't know how. He yelled, "Come on, man! Tell me."

"Gots to piss first, dude."

Joel checked the time.

Shit, call Delgado and tell him to forget it? Or wait until he heard what Luther had to say?

The gun. Where was the gun?

Shit, it wasn't on the table anymore.

BOOM

He heard glass shards tinkling onto the floor in front.

BAM-BAM

Joel leaned right to see down the hall toward the front. The door was blown away and a stocky gang-banger stepped through the aluminum frame, pistol grip shotgun in hand, right out of Arnold Schwarzenegger in *The Terminator*. Luther lay spread-eagle on the floor, struggling to lift his revolver. The ganger casually pumped another round into the chamber, aimed point blank at Luther's head.

BOOM

Joel scrambled out of the booth, shoving the table out of the way, making loud scraping noises.

The gangbanger glanced up and zeroed in on Joel, automatically racking another shell into the chamber. He raised the shotgun and aimed.

44

Joel hit the floor a half second before *BOOM.*

The Venetian blinds to his right blew out through the back window.

Then he was up, scrambling for the back door, convinced he couldn't possibly move fast enough, certain the banger was racking another shell.

Fuck, I can't hear.

BOOM

Wood exploded off the door jamb to his right.

He flew through the kitchen, slammed his hip into the horizontal push bar, throwing the back door open. He paused a half second on the landing, unsure which direction to take. Down to the alley or parking garage or up to residential floors 2 to 8? If the killer planned this attack at all, he'd have someone waiting in the alley in case Luther made it out the back.

Go up, not down.

He started running, taking two stairs at a time, fumbling the fat set of keys from his pocket. Hit the second floor and kept going. On his way to three, he was able to sort out the common-area key. Gasping, he made the third floor, slid the key into the lock, heard the slap of shoes on the steps below.

He turned the key. It didn't move. *Wrong way.*

Rotated the key in the opposite direction and felt the latch click open.

Then he was through the doorway and into the hall. He spun

around, threw his shoulder against the door to slam it, but the hydraulic mechanism resisted as the footsteps raced closer.

He pushed harder, leaning into it.

The steps grew louder.

Finally, the door seated and the latch clicked into place.

He ran to the elevator, punched UP, punched the button again, the whole time keeping his eyes on the fire door, bouncing from foot to foot.

C'mon dammit, get here.

There was another stairwell at the other end of the hall but where did that go? He'd never used it before.

Pounding started on the door he'd just come through. Chances were the shooter didn't have a key, but would the lock withstand a shotgun blast? Maybe. It was a metal fire door.

Come on, come on!

The cage arrived empty. He stepped in, pressed the button marked ROOF.

The door slid shut and the elevator started up.

Half the roof was covered with decking that held groupings of teak lawn chairs, tables, potted plants and a beautiful three-sixty degree view of city and the harbor. The remainder of tarred roof—blocked off by pots—was riddled with ventilation ducts and housing for mechanical equipment and shrouded in dense shadows.

Hide.

He ran along the side of the roof looking for a good hiding place, his heart hammering his chest, his breaths in ragged gasps. He saw a small space over by the parapet along the east edge, where several shadows overlapped. Perfect. He crouched down behind an air duct, making himself as small as possible.

Delgado. He here yet?

Five feet away was the broad parapet. If he leaned his chest on it and edged his head out, he could probably look straight down to First Avenue and the passenger loading zone at the curb. That's where Delgado would park. Easy enough. Unless you feared heights.

Kneeling, he sucked in a deep breath, inched his chest onto the cold sheet metal and slowly edged far enough out to peer straight down onto the street. Then opened his eyes.

And was immediately overcome with dizziness.

Without thinking, he recoiled, landing butt first on the safety of the tar roof.

He closed his eyes and tried to talk himself back to feeling normal. He needed to look down, but couldn't bring himself to open his eyes again. Fucking heights. He could hike mountain trails, but put him on top of a building like this, a high bridge, or a balcony...

He tried again, breathing deeply and slowly, forcing his lids into slits. Okay, two Seattle Police cars were double-parked in front of Orcas, blue flashers blazing, clots of lookee-loos thickening along the sidewalk. Meaning that the banger with the shotgun was probably long gone by now. Well, maybe not. If clever, he could simply hang back in the crowd with his weapon down a leg of his baggy pants, watching what happened.

He scanned the crowd more closely. Okay, two guys looked like they could be bangers. And they were hanging in the periphery. But so what? At this distance he couldn't make out their faces well enough to spot the killer.

He slid back down onto the security of the tar roof and sucked a couple deep breaths. Then he wedged into the shadows near the corner where there was a good view of the elevator door.

Think! What now?

Sure, the killer could come up here, but probably wouldn't chance it with cops all over the place. Most likely, he'd get the hell out of the building and try again. Assuming, of course, he knew who Joel was. And what were the chances of that?

Well, that depended on a lot of things...

Orcas had been dark, the guy coming in from the light, and as far as he knew they'd never seen each other before. Unless of course they knew he was the owner of the restaurant. No way to know for certain.

Meaning he was still in danger.

He dug the cell from his pocket, dialed the condo.

Taylor picked up immediately. "Joel?"

"Hey, sweetie, you okay?" he asked, trying to sound upbeat, cherishing the simple pleasure of hearing her voice.

"Where are you?" She sounded frantic. "I can see all sorts of cop cars down near you."

He summarized what happened.

"Joel, you need protection and legal help. Call Reed. See what he says."

"Soon as I hang up. I just want to know you're okay."

"Jesus, that's sweet, but hang up and get help. Now. Please."

"Okay. But hey, listen…"

"What?"

"I love you."

He'd never said that before with so much feeling. Had never felt the need. But it now seemed very important to tell her.

She gave a little sob. "I love you too. I do. Now please, hang up and get some help. And for God's sake be careful."

He called Reed's cell next, but Reed didn't pick up, so he sent a numeric page to call back. Before stuffing the phone back in his pocket, he switched from ring to vibrate, thinking it was the little things that can trip you up.

Jesus, it was getting cold. He wasn't dressed for outside, especially up on a damned roof where the wind from the harbor carried a real bite. He hugged both knees and glanced around for a better place to hide that would also give him some shelter. Maybe one of the other ventilation ducts would be warmer.

Just as he was about to move the cellular started vibrating. He flipped it open, expecting Reed. "Reed?"

"Joel, what's up?"

Yeah, Reed. He quickly briefed him on what had happened.

When he finished, Reed said, "Holy cow, give me a minute to think about this." Then, "I know a good criminal lawyer. I need a few minutes to track him down. Call you right back. In the meantime, this DEA agent you talked to, you say he intends to meet you there?"

"Yeah, here at Orcas. But the guy with the shotgun showed up first."

"Right. So call him. Find out where he is. He should be able to provide you with sufficient protection until we can sort this mess out."

That made sense. In fact, he should've thought of that before calling Reed.

"I will, soon as I hang up."

"Wait one second. A word of advice. Don't give any statements or talk to anyone from any branch of law enforcement until we have a lawyer sitting right next to you. Understand?"

"Yes."

"Keep your cell on and stay hidden. I'll get you some help. I just can't guarantee how long it'll take at this time of night."

45

Delgado picked up the call almost immediately. Soon as Joel identified himself, Delgado asked, "Where the fuck are you?"

His tone—definitely pissed off—caught Joel by surprise. "I'm where I said I'd be. Where are you?"

"The fuck you are. I'm outside your place right now. It's a damned zoo. So I know you're not here. The fuck you trying to pull on me, Holden?"

Great! Delgado was downstairs. Joel gave a sigh of relief. He *would* see Taylor again. "The guys I mentioned? They came after Luther. I barely got out the back without getting blown away."

He turned around to the parapet, knelt, leaned on it, inched his head over the edge. The queasy feeling flooded back so hard he couldn't stretch far enough to see straight down. He backed up, dizzy, again thinking it was great news that Delgado was down there.

"Then you know your homie got his ass blown away? Oh, excuse me. We assume it's him. The bro don't have 'nough face to make a visual."

He could hear several voices in the background of Delgado's phone and a siren he could also hear in his free ear. For a moment he couldn't respond, his mind still paralyzed from the scene of Luther on the floor, the banger raising the gun for the kill shot.

"It's him, Luther. I saw it. A banger blasted through the door, stepped in and shot him point blank. I went out the back door but he came after me."

"You witnessed it, the execution?"

"Yes. But I'm hiding. Fucker chased me into the stairwell. If I didn't have keys...." He didn't want to think about it.

"Relax, Holden, we'll get you safe. First tell me—and this is important—you see the shooter? Clean enough to identify him, you get the chance?"

"Hell, yes. It was dark, but there was enough street light to see his face. Believe me, I'll never forget it."

"Outstanding. That's huge. Hold on."

The background noise became muffled—Joel suspected Delgado's hand was over the microphone. A few seconds passed before Delgado came back on with, "You say he shot at you?"

"Hell, yes. Check out the back window and the door to the kitchen, you don't believe me."

"Okay, okay...you all right? He didn't hit you, did he?" Delgado sounded concerned.

"No." Jesus, he'd been lucky. That one blast into the door jamb...

"Outstanding. Where the fuck are you?"

"Up on the roof."

"The roof! You shitting me?"

"No."

Delgado laughed. "Here? In this building?"

"Yes."

"Anyone with you?"

"No."

"Okay, okay, tell you what. How about I escort you down? That feel all right with you?"

Another wave of relief hit. "Yeah."

"Okay, so how do I get up there?"

He had to think about that. The building didn't have a doorman, meaning people either had to unlock the front door with a key or security fob or have another homeowner buzz them in. Orcas had its own street entrance and didn't connect with the residential area except through the back stairs.

"It's a secure building. You need...no wait, there's another way." It was simple. "Can you get inside the restaurant?" he said, thinking maybe the cops wouldn't let anyone in since it was a crime scene.

"No reason I can't. Cops know me."

"Okay, here's what you do. Go through the kitchen to the back door. It opens into a stairwell. Unless you can find someone with a security fob, the elevator won't work, so you're gonna have to hike up eight floors. I'll wait by the door. Just bang on it when you get here and I'll open it."

"Got it. Be there soon as I can."

He was shivering now, the cold seeping deeper into his body, but he took comfort in knowing it wouldn't last much longer. More confident now, he walked to the stairwell door to wait and make sure not to miss Delgado's knock in case the wind muffled it. For a moment he considered opening the door and waiting in the stairwell or even starting down to save Delgado the entire hike. But shit, who was to say the killer wasn't just on the other side of the door, waiting. No, he should stay here. Wouldn't be too much longer. Would it?

The wind picked up, becoming more cutting and cold. He moved behind the wall to shield himself as much as possible and still be able to hear the door, hunkered down on his haunches and hugged his knees to preserve what little warmth remained. His chest started aching from the cold.

He thought of Luther and tried to reconstruct what probably happened. The killer was outside the window when he saw Luther approach the front. He waited until Luther was close enough to be shredded by flying glass before firing the first round. Most likely Luther was holding his gun as it happened. Maybe he even saw the guy and anticipated it. Whatever, after the first blast, Luther squeezed off two rounds but probably wasn't even aiming, but that was all. Joel witnessed what happened next. The only good thing was that Luther died mercifully fast.

Man, it was cold. He shivered.

What's taking Delgado so long?

The ache in his chest intensified.

The moment Delgado arrived he'd get into the stairwell or the elevator, out of this cold and start soaking up some warmth. Or at least stop freezing. They could talk anywhere, just as long as he got out of this wind.

He glanced back to his first hiding place, where he could lean out over that parapet and look south and see his building four blocks away. He visualized the warm comfortable apartment with Taylor waiting for him. Well, it wouldn't be too long before he could be there with her. First thing he'd do was take a long hot shower. Hot as he could tolerate. Just stand under the stream, adsorbing the water's blissful warmth deep into his bones.

Delgado and the cops would want a statement. Would he need it tonight? How long would that take? Would the cops talk to him in Orcas or over at the West Precinct? Either way, he'd stick to Reed's advice and not say one word without a lawyer present. Especially since he didn't know for sure what the hell was going on between Delgado and Luther, or how much Delgado knew about his involvement in their side business.

Which brought up another thing. Had Reed lined up a lawyer? Aw, man, whoever it was, it'd take time to explain about the drugs and Luther. Meaning even more delay. But at least he survived. Being cold a little longer was worth it if it meant saving Orcas and his life.

Damn! What a mess.

He thought about that day in the mountain when it all started, thinking how much better he'd do things if given a second chance. Well, it didn't work out so great this time around, did it? He couldn't believe the series of fuck-ups he made. Blowing the budget on Orcas, which put him into debt. Then sliding back into the easy money dealing drugs. Both those tendencies were Joel's. Both contrary to Chris's way of doing things. How could he have let this happen?

Now that he thought about it, he saw an ironic symmetry to this situation. Delgado had been the one to put the squeeze on him five years ago. Now Delgado was saving his ass. Weird how things turn out.

Okay, so starting right now, he really would do things differently. He'd give Delgado whatever information he had, set the record straight, make things right with Taylor, and settle down to run Orcas. He really *would* change his life.

Ironic. Chris had been right about so many things. He never realized that until this moment.

He heard someone bang on the door. Christ, how long had that been going on? Delgado at last!

He threw open the door. Delgado stood there grinning, Luther's killer shoulder to shoulder with him, shotgun pumped and aimed at Joel.

Delgado stepped onto the deck as Joel backed away from the entrance.

Delgado asked, "Whassup, bro?"

Then Delgado and the killer were on the roof, the heavy door swinging shut behind them...

46

Joel backed up another step.

This can't be the same guy. This isn't happening.

Sure as hell looked like him though. Big, tough-looking Mexican pushing six feet, two hundred twenty pounds, holding the shotgun like it weighed no more than an ounce, gang tats over his neck and exposed forearms.

Delgado glanced around. "Fucking freezing up here, bro."

Joel said, "I don't understand," and glanced around, looking for a place to run and hide, a heavy feeling of doom clogging his gut. He took another step back, keeping as much separation between them as possible, thinking this was some kind of sick joke Delgado was playing, some sort of payback.

"Don't know the exact words, but the Bible mentions something about vengeance is for the Lord," Delgado said. "You believe that shit?"

Delgado's tone was hard, measured. What had Luther said? Something about getting involved in things he didn't understand? Well, nothing made sense now.

He backed into a deck chair and tripped, but caught himself before toppling over. "Jesus, Delgado, we can work this out."

Delgado shook his head. "Myself, I think it's a crock of shit, that part of the Bible. Personally? I love vengeance. Gives me a fucking hard-on. Like right now. My dick's exploding just anticipating it. Want to see my dick, Holden?"

"Help me out here. What do you want from me?"

"Just told you, bro. Vengeance."

"Jesus, for what? Because I skipped out on you five years ago?"

"You think of a better reason?"

Delgado nodded at the Mexican.

A sickening feeling exploded in Joel's gut. His new life was about to end.

He thought of Taylor, remembered how good it felt to tell her he loved her. Why hadn't he done that more often? He wanted to tell her now and reached into his pocket for the cell.

The Mexican leveled the barrel dead center at his chest.

There was nothing to do. No place to run.

He was totally fucked. Unless…

He remembered pictures of people jumping from the Twin Towers, taking their own lives rather than being burned alive. But he couldn't do it. There was still the possibility this was some sick joke.

"What do you want from me?" he asked Delgado.

"Fuck, you're dumber than I gave you credit for, bro. You a witness. Can't let a witness live. So," he said with a shrug, "you die."

"Witness what? I didn't see a thing."

Delgado shook his head. "Not what you said a few minutes ago. Shit, who knows who you phoned since I talked to you. A lawyer? Bet you called a lawyer. Hey, Holden, you call a lawyer?"

"I didn't see a thing. I was too scared. Scared shitless. On the phone just now? I told you what I thought you wanted to hear so you'd help me."

"Expect me to believe that? Know what? Luther talked too much. So…" he shrugged again.

"I don't get it. You're supposed to be DEA."

Delgado grinned. "I am. But that doesn't mean I don't have my own action, just like your bitch Luther. Entrepreneurism. That's the American way, bro."

"But Luther said he worked for you."

Delgado laughed. "Most definitely. Did a good job too. Problem was, he learned too much. About us, how we run things around here."

"About you?" What was he saying? "You two are——"

"Fuck, you even dumber than I thought. Ortega? Shit, he was my competition, bro. And I was counting on you to help me shut him down. Didn't happen like I wanted."

"But see, it worked out without me. You got him anyway."

"So what? Doesn't change a thing with you and me. And Luther? Fuck, Luther was nothing but a snitch. Been a snitch all his life. Things never change. So when you two wanted to open up shop, he came to me, made a deal. But see, you can never trust a snitch. They always looking for an angle. Bitch tried to shake me down, tried to fuck me like I was his bitch. Couple of my crew were supposed to take him out, but he got lucky, capped one. Now you involved."

Joel caught movement, realized he hadn't been watching the Mexican. He turned just as the killer's finger was tightening on the trigger.

BOOM

The force blew Joel back off his feet. He landed on the tar roof, his chest a mass of terrible crushing pain. He pressed both hand to his chest.

Shit, it hurts!

Then tried opening his eyes, but the bright sun made him squint. He heard WHOMP WHOMP WHOMP. A helicopter? Sun? But he felt so cold.

He moved his head and saw the lake still on his right. Saw the two hikers. *Wait, no, they're not hikers.* He saw them more clearly now with their dark olive Forest Service rangers jackets. That's what they were. They were bent over, pulling something from the snow. A body?

"Good, you're still with me. Hang in there, Chris."

Reed Allison was kneeling at his side.

Reed said, "Hear the chopper? That's for you, Chris. They're going to take us to a hospital and get you help. Just hang on."

God, what beauty.

Spectacular.

He couldn't take his gaze away from the deep blue lake, the green pines, the azure sky. In his fifty-five years of life, he'd never seen anything so beautiful. It brought a feeling of calm, of contentment. This was where he was going to die. He couldn't think of a better place. Right here next to Joel.

47

A big Sikorsky chopper hovered above them. White with the wide orange-red Coast Guard diagonal stripe over its bulbous nose. Dust flew everywhere, getting in Reed Allison's eyes, but he couldn't stop waving both arms like a jumping jack, watching the helicopter settle in overhead.

Then a figure in a DayGlo orange jumpsuit and white helmet was leaning out the open cargo bay, a cable from a hoist hooked to him. He waved at Reed.

In response, Reed did the jumping-jack thing.

The guy dropped from the bay and was suspended in a horseshoe as he slowly descended until his boots hit the rocky dirt. He slipped the harness over his head, came running over. The embroidered name tag on his left breast pocket displayed FILLIPI.

"You the one who called in the emergency? That him?" The chopper crewman yelled over the deafening sound of the helicopter.

"Yes. I think he's having a heart attack."

"Can he move?"

"Barely."

Fillipi said something into his helmet mike that Reed couldn't understand. The horseshoe began racing back up to the chopper. He asked Reed, "How long's he been like this?" while kneeling over Chris.

Reed realized he'd lost complete sense of time. Could be as long as an hour but an hour seemed ridiculous. "Jesus...I really

285

can't say. A half hour maybe?" His best guess.

Fillipi sat on his haunches yelling at Chris, "Hey partner, you in there?" He pinched Chris, only to get a weak movement as his right arm tried to push his hand away.

Then a wire stretcher arrived from the chopper.

"Okay, give me a hand. We want him in there."

Reed kneeled next to Chris, yelled, "Chris, can you hear me? We're going to move you."

Chris became aware of WHOMP WHOMP WHOMP.

This couldn't be what it feels like to be gunned down. There's no pain.

His mind became blurry now, his body so light it didn't seem real. He fought to open his eyes and finally managed to slit his lids far enough to see two men in flight suits kneeling over him.

Where am I?

Then, he recognized the sound: a helicopter. Somewhere—an unknown time ago—Reed yelled something about a chopper. Yelling and shaking him. That memory was rapidly fading now.

Reed saw Chris's eyes open to slits, pupils large and round at first but then constricting to the light. Chris's eyes went one way, then the other, and what little facial expression remained showed confusion.

"Chris, we need to move you to the helicopter."

But Fillipi was already dragging him. "Give me a hand...here!"

Each one taking a shoulder, they pulled him to the basket and lifted him in. Fillipi made sure Chris was strapped securely before flashing a thumbs-up to the crew member leaning out of the bay. Chris started up, the basket rotating slowly as it ascended.

Fillipi yelled. "Plan is to fly him to Harborview. You family?"

"No, just a friend—"

"Got the name of a family member, someone we can contact?"

"There's no one. He's all alone. I'm his lawyer. I have legal power to sign consents, if that's what you're getting at."

Fillipi nodded. "In that case you need to come sign papers and take care of things."

"In that?" He pointed at the chopper.

"Affirmative, sir."

The thought of being hoisted up—what, a hundred feet on a goddamned wire—made him nauseous. "No, that's okay. You have my verbal consent to do anything deemed medically necessary until I get there. I'll be there soon as I can. My car's at the trail head. I have to get it back to the city anyway."

The litter had been replaced with the horseshoe and that was dropping quickly. Fillipi slipped his arms through it and grabbed the cable. "Better hurry, sir. Your friend doesn't look in the best of shape," he said, then signaled another thumbs-up to his crewmate.

Reed watched Fillipi disappear into the chopper. A few seconds later the Sikorsky tilted away from the side of the hill and swooped out over the lake, rippling the icy blue water below before it disappeared behind a peak.

Carrying both rucksacks, Reed started hoofing it down the trail as fast as possible.

Chris looked left, through the wire mesh of the litter and out the side of the chopper, saw the alpine lake and the snow field flowing into it. Then he remembered being on the annual hike and being resuscitated by paramedics, a Philips defibrillator lying next to him. Jesus, how ironic.

How many times has he used one of those in his practice?

He thought about the crushing chest pain, like an elephant stepping on him. How much time had passed since all this started? Not much, he realized, only seconds, a few minutes at most?

Aw shit, an MI.

Jesus, a big bad-ass serious one, too. And this realization brought with it the cold odds of survival. Data he knew only too well. Suddenly, everything that had happened in the past few minutes became clear to him. For the half minute his heart stopped beating, he was dead. Had it not been for the defibrillator, his heart would never have beat again.

Like Lazarus, he'd been returned to the living.

But for how long?

The odds were dismal, odds he didn't want to face. Instead, he wanted to go back to Taylor and Orcas and his dream of making things right with Joel.

But he knew that was impossible now because the entire transformation into Joel's body had been nothing more than what Tom Holmes referred to as a "Life Review." The process of having your life pass before your eyes in the moments preceding death. He never believed in the phenomenon until now.

There would be no more chances because when his heart stopped a few minutes ago, he'd fallen into the statistical bin of an out-of-hospital resuscitation. The odds of surviving even another 24 to 48 hours were dismal. Assuming his heart kept going long enough to even reach an ER. And shit, with his luck....

He was a dead man flying.

A knot of fear congealed in his heart. He *was* going to die and knew it. Now. He didn't want to die. He wanted to live long enough to make it right with Joel.

His fear snowballed into panic and adrenaline from the fear began irritating his frail heart muscle even more.

He felt an irregular heart beat skip past, then another. And he knew the end was drawing near. He'd started into a vicious cycle: the irregular beats increased his fear, which produced more adrenaline, which...

For Christ's sake, calm down, you're killing yourself...

Which only made it worse.

48

REED ALLISON'S OFFICE, NEXT DAY

Reed Allison filled his favorite mug—purple and gold with the University of Washington's block-letter W on one side and the profile of a husky on the other side—with steaming black coffee from the pot in the break room. He checked the amount left in the pot and figured it contained enough coffee for him to slink away without feeling guilty for not brewing another one. And if anyone deserved to be cut some slack today, it was him. After all, this was the morning after The Night from Hell. Long and emotionally draining, without more than one hour of sleep, leaving him dog tired and tasked with the job of executor of his best friend's estate. Let a wide-eyed bushy-tailed junior associate make the damned coffee today.

After the paramedics had loaded Chris onto the chopper, he busted ass down to the trail head where the car waited, then risked a speeding ticket during the ninety-minute drive to the trauma center.

He didn't reach Harborview until something past eight that evening.

Whereupon the ER doctor unsympathetically informed him Chris had been pronounced DOA. "And by the way, you need to make arrangements for someone to pick up the body."

"Tonight?" Reed asked.

"If at all possible. It's busy here."

So, he had telephoned Bonny Watson Funeral Home, spoke to the person on call and made arrangements for Chris to be picked up. He planned to confer with Janice before giving them final permission to cremate the body. Not that her opinion mattered, but it would be a gesture of peace, the final resolution to a rancorous divorce. Chris's wish—clearly spelled out in the will—was to be cremated and his ashes scattered near the site of the avalanche that took Joel's life. Which was illegal, of course, but only if they caught you. Reed knew the trail all too well.

Aw, jeez...Reed eyed the pot again, then the cupboard above the coffee maker. With a resigned sigh, he set his mug on the counter, dumped the sodden grounds into the garbage, scooped some Starbucks into a fresh filter, and thumbed the START button.

He'd always insisted that integrity was doing the right thing when no one was watching. And to him, integrity was a major ingredient for self-respect.

Back at his desk, he attempted to concentrate on a client's will. But dealing with a Last Will and Testament in the immediate wake of his best friend's death was such a downer, he couldn't bear to continue. He set it aside in favor of a divorce.

Equally depressing.

Sipping the strong coffee, he swiveled around to stare out the window and let his thoughts drift back to their conversation yesterday, the part about what it'd be like to live life again knowing what you know now, the ruminations about the changes you'd make the second time around, the character flaws you'd try to fix.

Wasn't the first time Chris had broached the subject. They'd discussed that particular one so many times, it became noxious. He never complained though, just let Chris verbally ruminate because that's what good friends do: be there for each other. And he couldn't count the numerous times Chris had been there for him. Life with Betty Ann hadn't always been a picnic.

Chris never recovered from losing Joel, especially given the circumstances prior to his death—the squeeze Joel was caught in between the DEA and Ortega. Chris didn't know all the details, only that Joel had been jammed for dealing drugs. That Joel would do such a thing had been devastating enough. Chris blamed himself and considered it a sign of having failed as a parent. He'd always wanted to somehow talk to Joel, to hear from him how he'd failed in performing a parent's most important responsibility: forging your offspring's ethics.

Many times he'd wonder if he should tell Chris about his meeting with Joel that Saturday, the day after Delgado put the squeeze on him, the day before the avalanche. Joel came to him for legal advice even though he'd hired a good criminal lawyer, the same one who'd represented him after a prior bust.

"I don't understand. Why put yourself in that position?" Reed asks. "What's the upside?"

They occupy two overstuffed arm chairs in the corner of a Starbucks, away from the other customers. Joel had called, wanting to discuss whether or not to testify to the Grand Jury. So here they were, an hour into the discussion, going round and round about the same point.

"I have to," Joel says.

"Joel, please, I'll give you the money. You can pay Ortega, settle the debt, then get the hell out. It's the safest way."

"Maybe, but I need to do this."

"Why? Please explain why."

Joel sucks a deep breath and wipes his face before looking Reed in the eyes. "I want to prove to Dad I can do the right thing. That's what he's always stood for. That's all he's really wanted from me. Up to now, I've never done that. I've always taken the easy way out. That's why I started selling joints to the other kids in the first place. Hey, I got myself into this, I need to get myself out. I want to show him I'm strong."

Reed shakes his head. "Joel, listen to me. I think it's wonderful you want to do this for your dad. I just don't think testifying against a person

*like Ortega is the best way to do it. You'd be taking a huge risk. One that's
stacked against you. I have to advise you to leave it alone. Please, just let
me give you the money. I'll never tell your dad."*

"No. I need to do this. For my own sake too."

*"Will you at least think about my offer? Give it some careful
consideration? As a favor to me?"*

"I will."

But Joel doesn't look like he means it.

Chris always believed we made our own destiny, that life was a
complex brew of timing, circumstance and the people we met along
the way. That only a small portion—perhaps as little as ten
percent—of life is left to fate or luck. And if you don't like those
two words, how about: powers beyond our control. Chris and
Joel's journeys served as good, yet opposite, examples. Joel
consistently made the easy choices, never owning up to the
consequences. Except on the last day of his life. He knew the
danger of hiking in that valley under those conditions, yet did it
rather than deal with either facing Ortega or Delgado. And lost his
life as a result.

Chris, on the other hand, chose a life of hard work and
dedication to his personal ethics and values. And just like Joel, Chris
knew the risk of taking that last hike. Out of shape, poor heart, a
steep climb, a perfect storm for the end result. So in the final
analysis, both of them made decisions that quite literally changed
their lives.

After the divorce, when Chris rewrote his will, he asked that
his ashes be sprinkled along the same trail, so he could be close to
Joel.

The phone rang.

Reed swiveled around, picked it up. "Yes?"

"A Sergeant Jim Laing of the King County Police on line one
for you."

Reed looked at the phone in his hand. *Must be something to do with the air evac.*

"Did he say what it was about?" he asked just to be sure.

"Yes. It concerns Mr. Joel Holden."

Joel? "Thanks. I'll take it."

He punched the blinking Line 1 button. "Reed Allison here."

"Mr. Allison, Detective Laing, King County Police. I talked with Janice Marks a few minutes ago and she informed me Christopher Holden, her former husband, died last night."

"Unfortunately, that's correct."

"She also informed me that you're the executor and legal surrogate for the Holden estate. Is this correct?"

"Yes it is."

"In that case, I need to inform you that a group of hikers found two bodies in the Rachel Lake region of the Cascades two days ago and reported it to the forest rangers. The bodies were retrieved yesterday. From the looks of it they've been there several years under snow. It's a known avalanche area. They think it's only because of the abnormally warm spring and summer that the snow melted enough to partially expose one of the parkas. This morning dental records were matched to the IDs recovered on the bodies. One is Joel Holden, the other is Matthew Gardner. As I'm sure you're aware, both men were missing and presumed killed in an avalanche five years ago."

A hollow, empty feeling burrowed into Reed's stomach. Chris always held out hope that Joel had somehow survived and was trying to make a name for himself as a chef. He also believed that once Joel became successful, he would contact him. Now even that fantasy was gone.

"Thank you, Detective. Is there anything else?"

"No, sir."

Reed hung up and sat staring out the window, saying goodbye to his friend.

Allen Wyler

ACKNOWLEGEMENTS

Thanks to Darryl Ponicsan for allowing me to bounce ideas off him; also to Ken Coffman and the staff at Stairway Press for publishing this story.

The author and publisher would like to thank our friends Beth Hill (anoveledit.com) for editing services and Pat Shaw (http://blurbcopy.wordpress.com/) for back cover copy.

CPSIA information can be obtained
at www.ICGtesting.com
Printed in the USA
BVHW030121180122
626455BV00019B/171

9 780985 994259